Aleksandr Sergeevich Pushkin, John Buchan Telfer

Russian romance

Aleksandr Sergeevich Pushkin, John Buchan Telfer

Russian romance

ISBN/EAN: 9783743399914

Manufactured in Europe, USA, Canada, Australia, Japa

Cover: Foto ©Andreas Hilbeck / pixelio.de

Manufactured and distributed by brebook publishing software (www.brebook.com)

Aleksandr Sergeevich Pushkin, John Buchan Telfer

Russian romance

BY

ALEXANDER SERGUEVITCH POUSHKIN.

TRANSLATED BY

MRS. J. BUCHAN TELFER

(NÉE MOURAVIEFF).

HENRY S. KING & CO.

65, CORNHILL; & 12, PATERNOSTER ROW, LONDON.

1875.

CONTENTS.

ERRATA.

At page 2, line 9, *for* "*Monssié*" *read* "*Moussié.*"
,, 4, ,, 27, ,, "Gherassimoona" *read* "Gherassimovna."
,, 7, ,, 23, ,, "ovation" *read* "oration."
,, 9, ,, 8 & 10, ,, "Avinoushka" *read* "Arinoushka."
,, 9, ,, 20, ,, "one," *read* "owl."
,, 10, ,, 1, ,, "*krass*" ,, "*kvass.*"
,, 10, ,, 22, ,, "losedst" ,, "lostest."
,, 17, ,, 11, ,, "*tzynooka*," *read* "*tzynovka.*"
,, 17, note. ,, "bass," *read* "bast."
,, 21, line 9, ,, "unseen," ,, "useless."
,, 24, ,, 3, ,, "Cardina," *read* "Carolina."
,, 24, ,, 18, ,, "all tonn," ,, "all pe tonn."
,, 26, ,, 8, ,, "bass," *read* "bast."
,, 27, note. ,, "cosmas," *read* "cosmos."
,, 29, line 5, ,, "Oustynaja," *read* "Oustynya."
,, 31, ,, 15, ,, "*stcky*," *read* "*stchy.*"
,, 40, ,, 4, ,, "to me in a," *read* "to me with a."
,, 49, ,, 22, ,, "Griueff," *read* "Grineff."
,, 50, ,, 6, ,, "notwithstanning," *read* "notwithstanding."
,, 56, ,, 2, ,, "conditions," *read* "condition."
,, 56, ,, 29, ,, "removal," ,, "renewal."
,, 57, ,, 12, ,, "importacce," ,, "importance."
,, 65, ,, 19, ,, "*Yashee !*" ,, "*Yakshee !*"
,, 80, ,, 6, ,, "*kyvot*," *read* "*kyvott.*"
,, 80, ,, 8, ,, "the simple," *read* "this simple."
,, 83, ,, 10, ,, "persons," *read* "person."
,, 84, ,, 20, ,, "*pyalàck*," ,, "*pyatàck.*"
,, 89, note. ,, "Ischoudoff," *read* "Jschoudoff."
,, 104, line 30, ,, "lead," *read* "send."
,, 149, ,, 5, ,, "Roumiantgoff," *read* "Roumiantzoff."
,, 164, ,, 19, ,, "cying," *read* "eyeing."
,, 270, ,, 15, ,, "Naron," ,, "Narva."
,, 273, ,, 23, ,, "*kisby*," ,, "*kisly.*"
,, 274, ,, 5, ,, "Kymitchna," *read* "Ilyinitchna."
,, 275, ,, 8, ,, "Yeograf," *read* "Yevgraf."
,, 277, ,, 11, ,, "exceptions," *read* "exception."
,, 288, ,, 20, ,, "Ragouziusky," *read* "Ragouzinsky."

THE CAPTAIN'S DAUGHTER.

CHAPTER I.

THE SERGEANT OF THE GUARDS.

My father, Andrey Petrovitch* Grineff, who served in his youth under Count Münich,† had retired with the rank of senior major, in the year 17—. He then settled on his property in the government of Simbirsk, where he married Avdotia Vassilievna‡ U——, the daughter of a poor nobleman in the neighbourhood. Nine children were born to my parents. All my brothers and sisters died in their infancy. My name had been entered on the strength of the Semionoffsky regiment, thanks to Prince B——, a major in the Guards, and our near relative. I was checked as being on leave of absence until the completion of my studies. At that time the system of education was not what it is now. At the age of five I was turned over to the care of the groom Savelitch, whose sober character had earned for him the distinction of being constituted my governor. I managed, under his supervision, to learn to read and write in Russian by the

---

* Andrew, the son of Peter.—Tr.
† A distinguished Russian general; born, 1683; died, 1767.—Tr.
‡ Eudoxia, the daughter of Basil.—Tr.

1

time I was twelve years of age, and was also able to discuss in a creditable manner the merits of a sporting dog. At about that period my father, in writing to Moscow for his yearly supply of wines and salad oil, engaged a Frenchman, M. Beaupré, to be my tutor. Savelitch was much put out upon his arrival.

"Thank goodness," muttered he to himself, "the child is washed, combed, and fed. Where is the use of wasting one's money and engaging *Monssié*, just as if one's own people were not sufficient!"

Beaupré had been a hairdresser in his own country, and a soldier in Prussia; he then came to Russia, *pour être Outchitel*,* without quite understanding the meaning of the word. He was a good fellow, but flighty and debauched to a degree. His greatest weakness was admiration of the fair sex, and he frequently met with such rough usage in return for his advances, that he would groan for days together. He was not *inimical* (as he expressed himself) *to the bottle*, that is to say (in plain Russian) he liked an extra drop. But as wine was served at dinner at an allowance of only one glassful to each person, the tutor himself being generally passed over, my Beaupré very soon got accustomed to Russian spirits, and began to like them better than the wines of his own country, as being incomparably preferable for the stomach. He and I got on very well, and although he bound himself by his agreement to teach me *French, German, and all the sciences*, he found it more advantageous to himself to pick up from me, after a fashion, a smattering of Russian, after which lesson, each of us went his way.

* Teacher.—Tr.

We lived hand in glove with each other. I did not wish for another mentor. But fate soon parted us, owing to the following circumstances :—

The laundress Paláshka, a fat pock-marked girl, and the one-eyed dairy-maid Akoulka, had, it appears, agreed to throw themselves at my mother's feet, and whilst accusing themselves of culpability, to complain weepingly of *Monssié*, who would take advantage of their inexperience. My mother did not treat such matters as a joke, and carried the complaint to my father. His way of settling it was summary. He immediately sent for that rascal of a Frenchman. He was informed that *Monssié* was giving me my lesson. My father came into my room. Beaupré was sleeping on my bed the sleep of innocence. I was busy. It should be stated that a map had been ordered for me from Moscow. It had hung on the wall without the slightest use having been made of it, and its size, and the good quality of the paper, had long tempted me. I decided upon making a kite of it, so, taking advantage of Beaupré being asleep, I set to work. My father walked in as I was about to attach a wisp tail to the Cape of Good Hope. Perceiving that these were my studies in geography, my father pulled my ears, then rushing at Beaupré, he awoke him roughly, and assailed him with reproach. In his confusion, Beaupré would have risen, but he could not—the unfortunate Frenchman was dead drunk. My father dragged him off the bed by the collar, pushed him outside the door, and sent him off that same day, to the inexpressible joy of Savelitch. Thus ended my education,

I stayed at home scaring doves and playing at leap
frog with the street boys. After this fashion I reached my
sixteenth year. Then came the turning point of my life.

One autumn afternoon my mother was making jam in
the sitting-room, and I stood by, licking my lips and
watching the boiling preserve. My father was sitting at
the window reading the "Court Calendar," which he
received yearly. This book ever exercised a strong
influence over him; he always read it with particular
attention, and its perusal invariably stirred up his bile.
My mother, who knew all his whims and ways, constantly
tried to hide away this unfortunate book, and then it
would happen that months went by without his ever
seeing the "Court Calendar." But when he did chance
to find it, he would not let it out of his hands for hours.
Thus it was that my father was reading the "Court
Calendar," now and then shrugging his shoulders, and
repeating to himself, "Lieutenant-general ! . . . . he was
a sergeant in my company ! . . . . Knight of the two
Russian orders ! . . . . is it so long ago since we ? . . . ."
At last my father threw the "Calendar" on the sofa
and remained sunk in thought, which forbode no good.

Suddenly, he turned to my mother. "Avdotia Vassilievna, how old is Petrousha ?"*

"He has entered his seventeenth year," answered my
mother. "Petrousha was born the same year in which
aunt Nastasia Gherassimoona lost an eye, and when——"

"Very well," interrupted my father; "it is time he
should enter the service. He has had enough of nurseries
and of pigeon worrying."

* Pet name for Piotr—Peter.—Tr.

The thought of a speedy separation so startled my mother, that she dropped the spoon into the saucepan, and tears coursed down her face. As for me, it would be difficult to describe my joy. My idea of the service was connected with visions of freedom, and the amusements a residence at Petersburg would afford. I already imagined myself an officer in the Guards, which, in my opinion, was the height of human felicity.

My father neither liked altering his plans, nor putting off their execution. The day for my departure was fixed. On the eve of that day he informed me that it was his intention to write to my future chief, and he called for paper and pen.

" Do not forget, Andrey Petrovitch," said my mother, " to remember me to Prince B——, and say that I beg of him to take my Petrousha under his care."

" What nonsense !" cried my father, frowning. " What should I write to Prince B—— for ?"

" Did you not yourself say you were going to write to Petrousha's chief ?"

" Well ! what of that ?"

" Well, Petrousha's chief is Prince B——. Petrousha is, as you know, on the strength of the Simionof regiment."

" On the strength ! What is it to me that he is on the strength ! Petrousha shall not go to Petersburg ! What is he to learn by serving at Petersburg ? To spend money and to get into trouble ? No ! Let him serve in the army ; let him carry his knapsack ; let him smell powder ; let him become a soldier, and not a puppet in the Guards ! Where is his *passport ?* Let me have it."

My mother fetched my passport, which had been put away in a casket, with my little christening shirt, and handed it to my father with a trembling hand. My father read it attentively, laid it before him on the table, and commenced his letter.

I was eaten up with curiosity. Where was I to be sent to, if not to Petersburg? I never took my eyes off my father's pen, which moved slowly enough. At last he concluded, enclosed my passport in his letter, removed his spectacles, and calling me, said: "Here is a letter to Andrey Karlovitch* R——, my old comrade and friend. You are going to Orenburg to serve under him."

Thus all my bright hopes vanished! Instead of the pleasurable life at Petersburg, I was to look forward to a dull monotonous existence in a distant and unknown region. I had thought with so much ecstasy, a few moments before, of entering the service, and now my joy seemed turned into the heaviest sorrow. But there was no help for it! The next day a travelling *kibitka*† was brought to the door; my portmanteau was put into it, also a cellarette containing a tea service, and sundry packages of buns and pies, the last tokens of the indulgences of home. My parents blessed me. My father said: "Good-bye, Piotr. Serve him faithfully, him to whom thou shalt swear allegiance; obey thy superiors; do not court their favour too much; do not be over anxious to serve; but do not either shrink thy duty, and remember the proverb: *Take care of thy coat from the hour that it is new, and of thy honour from the days of*

* Andrew, the son of Charles.—Tr.   † Carriage with a hood.—Tr.

its youth." My mother, in tears, bid me take care of my health, and ordered Savelitch to "look after the child." A small *touloup** of hare skin was put on me, and over it a pelisse of fox fur. I sat in the *kibitka* next to Savelitch, and set out on my journey, crying bitterly.

That same night we reached Simbirsk, where I was to remain twenty-four hours, for Savelitch had been instructed to purchase all sorts of necessaries. I alighted at the inn—Savelitch started early to do his shopping. I got tired of looking out of the window into the dirty alley, so I began to explore the house. On entering the billiard-room I found a tall gentleman of about five-and-thirty years of age, in a dressing gown, wearing a long black moustache, with a cue in his hand, and a pipe in his mouth. He was playing with the marker, who was to empty a glass of *vodka*† at the end of each game he won, but who was obliged to crawl on all fours under the billiard-table whenever he happened to lose. I stayed and watched their play. As it progressed, the crawling on all fours became more frequent, until at last the marker remained under the table altogether. The gentleman pronounced over him a few vigorous expressions, a sort of funeral ovation, and invited me to have a game. I declined, not knowing how to play. This evidently appeared strange to him. He looked on me as it were with compassion; nevertheless, we continued to converse. I learned that his name was Ivan Ivanovitch‡ Zourine, that he was a captain in the —— hussars, that he was

---

* A short coat lined with fur.—Tr.
† A glass of spirits.—Tr.　　　‡ John, the son of John.—Tr.

sent to Simbirsk to recruit, and that he was staying in
the same inn. Zourine invited me to dine with him,
soldier fashion, taking what I could get. I willingly
consented. We sat down. Zourine drank a great deal,
and pressed me to do the same, saying that I must
accustom myself to the ways of the service; he entertained me with military anecdotes, which caused me
almost to split my sides with laughter, and we rose from
the table fast friends. He then offered to teach me to
play at billiards. "It is quite indispensable," he said,
"to us brother-soldiers. For instance. When on the
march, halts are made at little villages; how is one to
kill time? One cannot possibly be always kicking the
Jews about. One is obliged, in self-defence, to enter the
inn and have a game at billiards; and to do so, one must
know how to play!" I was quite convinced, and commenced my course of instruction with great ardour.
Zourine loudly encouraged me, wondered at the rapid
progress I made, and, after several lessons, proposed that
we should play for money, at half copeck stakes; not for
the sake of gain, but simply so as not to be playing without an object, which, he said, was the worst possible plan.
I again consented, and Zourine called for punch, and
pressed me to taste some, repeating that I must get used
to the customs of the service; and what was the service
without punch! I obeyed. Our game went on. The
oftener I supped my glass, the merrier I became. The
balls were continually flying off the table; I was getting
excited; abused the marker, who was scoring heaven
knows how; I was doubling the stakes over and over

again—in a word, I behaved like a boy loosened from all control. Thus, time passed imperceptibly. Zourine looked at the clock, laid down his cue, and informed me that I owed him one hundred roubles. I was a little taken aback. Savelitch kept my money. I began to offer some excuse. Zourine interrupted me: "Pray do not mention it. I can wait your convenience, and in the meanwhile let us go to Avinoushka's."

What more am I to say? I ended the day as giddily as I had begun it. We supped at Avinoushka's. Zourine kept filling my glass, repeating that I must get used to the service. On leaving the table, I could scarcely stand; at midnight Zourine took me back to the inn.

Savelitch met us at the threshold. He started at the undeniable evidence of my zeal for the service.

"What has happened to thee, sir?" said he, in a sorrowful voice. "Where hast thou managed to get such a skinful? Dear me! never has such a misfortune happened."

"Hold thy tongue, old one!" answered I, stammering, "thou art surely drunk; go to sleep——and put me to bed."

The next day I awoke with a headache, vaguely recalling the events of the previous evening. My reflections were interrupted by Savelitch, who came to me with a cup of tea. "Thou art making an early beginning Piotr Andrevitch,"* said he, shaking his head. "And who dost thou take after? So far as I know, neither thy father, nor thy grandfather, were drunkards; to mention thy mother is unnecessary—she has never from her

* Peter, the son of Andrew.—Tr.

birth tasted anything stronger than *krass.** And whose
fault is it all ? That d——d *Monssié.* I fancy I see
him now, running to Antípievna ; ' Madame, *je vous prie,
vodka.'* There is *je vous prie* for you ! There is no
denying it; he has taught thee some nice things—that
son of a dog. And what was the use of engaging a
heathen for thy tutor, as if our master had not enough of
his own people about him to choose from ?"

I felt ashamed of myself; I turned to the wall, and
said to him—" Go away, Savelitch, I do not want any tea."

But it was difficult to stop Savelitch when he had once
begun to lecture.

"There, Piotr Andrevitch, thou seest what comes of tip-
pling ; one has a headache—one cannot eat anything. A
man who drinks is perfectly useless. Take a little
cucumber juice, with honey, or what is better still, half a
glass of spirits as a refresher. What sayest thou to it ?"

At that moment a boy entered and handed me a note
from Zourine. I opened it and read the following lines :—

"MY DEAR PIOTR ANDREVITCH,

" Please send me, by my boy, the hundred roubles
which thou losedst yesterday. I stand in great need of
money.

" Ready, and at thy service,

" IVAN ZOURINE."

There was no help for it; I tried to look unconcerned
and turning to Savelitch, who kept my money and

---

* A fermented liquor made from barley malt, wheat, rye, wheat
flour, and buck wheat.—Tr.

clothes and disposed of my affairs, ordered him to give a hundred roubles to the boy.

" How ? why ?" asked the astonished Savelitch.

" I owe them to him," I answered, in the coolest manner possible.

" Thou owest them ?" reiterated Savelitch, more and more astonished ; " whenever didst thou find the time to get into debt ? This business is not clear. Do what thou wilt, sir, but I shall not give the money."

I felt that unless I made the obstinate old man give in to me at this decisive moment, I would thereafter find it difficult to free myself of his tutelage, and looking proudly at him, said—

" I am thy master, and thou my servant. The money is mine. I lost it because I chose to do so ; but I advise thee not to argue the point, and to do what thou art told."

Savelitch was so taken aback, that he raised his arms, and remained motionless.

" What dost thou stand there like that for ?" I shrieked angrily.

Savelitch burst into tears.

" Oh, my little father,* Piotr Andrevitch," he murmured, " do not kill me with grief. My light! do listen to an old man ! Write to that scoundrel to say it was a joke, that we never possessed so much money ! One hundred roubles ! Good gracious! Tell him that thy parents have strictly forbidden thee playing for anything but nuts. . . ."

" Leave off lying," I interrupted severely ; " let me have the money, or I shall kick thee out."

* *Bátyoushka*, a term of endearment.—Tr.

Savelitch looked at me sorrowfully, and went for the money. I pitied the poor old man, but I wanted to get the upper hand, and to show him that I was a child no longer. The money was sent to Zourine. Savelitch hastened to "get me out of the d—d inn." He came to announce that the horses were ready. I left Simbirsk with an uneasy conscience, repenting silently, without bidding my master good-bye, and never expecting to see him again.

CHAPTER II.

THE GUIDE.

MY reflections on the way were none of the pleasantest. My loss was not insignificant, considering the value of money at that period. I could not but acknowledge in my inmost soul that my conduct at the inn at Simbirsk had been very foolish, and I felt myself guilty towards Savelitch. These thoughts tormented me. The old man sat behind, gloomy and silent, accasionally turning away his face and murmuring to himself. I wished at any price to make my peace with him, but I scarcely knew how to begin. At last I said—

" Well, well, Savelitch ; let us make it up; I beg thy pardon ; I see that I was in the wrong. I was foolish yesterday; I offended thee without cause. I promise to behave better in future, and to listen to thee. There now, do not be angry, and let us make it up."

"Ah, my little father, Piotr Andrevitch!" answered he, with a deep sigh. "I am angry with myself; it is all my own fault throughout. How could I ever leave thee all alone at the inn? What is to be done? I was tempted. I bethought myself of going to the deacon's wife, to see my *Koumā*.* Well, so it was; I went to my *Koumā*, and thus have got into trouble. A bad business! How shall I ever be able to look my master and my mistress in the face again? What will they say when they find out that their child drinks and gambles?"

I promised, in order to console poor Savelitch, that I should never henceforth dispose of a single kopeck with; out his consent. He gradually calmed down, but still kept grumbling to himself occasionally, as he nodded his head: "A hundred roubles!—no joke!"

I was nearing the place of my destination. Dreary plains, intercepted by mounds and hollows, stretched around me. All was covered with snow. The sun was setting. The *kibitka* was driving along a narrow road; or, more correctly speaking, a track made by the peasants' sledges. Suddenly, the *yemstchick*† began to look around him, and taking off his cap, he said to me—

"Wilt thou not order me to turn back, sir?"

"What for?"

"The weather is threatening—the wind is rising gradually. See how it sweeps the early snow?"

"Well, where is the harm?"

---

* A godfather and a godmother stand in the relation of *Koum* (m.) and *Koumā* (f.) to each other.—Tr.

† The driver of a travelling carriage.—Tr.

" And look what is going on there."

(The *yemstchick* pointed with his whip to the east.)

"I don't see anything except a white steppe, and a clear sky."

" And there—there !—that little cloud !"

I did indeed perceive on the horizon a small white cloud, which I at first took for a distant mound. The *yemstchick* explained to me that that small cloud presaged a snow storm.

I had heard of the snow storms in those regions, and was aware that entire trains of waggons were sometimes overwhelmed by them. Savelitch was of the *yemstchick's* opinion, and advised our returning. But I did not imagine that the wind was very high ; I hoped to reach the next station in time, and gave orders to drive faster.

The *yemstchick* went off at full spead, but still kept looking at the east. The horses were doing their work well. The wind was, however, rising fast. The small white speck had become a dense white cloud, which, as it heavily rolled onwards, stretched out, enveloping the whole sky. A little snow began to fall, which soon increased to heavy flakes. The wind commenced to howl, and we were in for a snowstorm. In an instant the dark sky and the white sea of snow had blended into one. Everything had disappeared from sight.

" Well, sir," shouted the *yemstchick*, " we are done for; this is a snow-storm !"

I looked out of the *kibitka ;* all was darkness and tempest. One might have mistaken for human sounds, what were but the fierce and expressive howlings of the wind. Savelitch and I were covered with snow; the horses slackened their pace and soon stood quite still.

"Why dost thou not go on ?" I asked the *yemstchick,* impatiently.

"Where is the use of going on ?" answered he, leaving his seat; "as it is, goodness knows where we have got to : there is no road, and darkness everywhere."

I was about to rebuke him. Savelitch took his part: "Why did'st thou not listen ?" said he angrily: "thou mightest have gone back to the inn, had tea, thou could'st have slept until the morning, the storm would have abated, and we should have been able to have gone on farther. Where do we hurry to now ? Had we been going to a wedding !"

Savelitch was right. What was to be done. The snow still fell. A drift was forming round our *kibitka.* The horses stood with bent heads, starting occasionally. The *yemstchick* walked round and round, and not being able to do anything else, kept adjusting the harness. Savelitch grumbled. I kept looking in all directions, in the hope of discovering some trace of a dwelling or of a road, but could discern nothing but the confused chasing of the snow-flakes. . . . Suddenly I perceived something black.

"There, *yemstchick !*" I cried; "look; what is that black object there ?"

The *yemstchick* strained his eyes.

"Goodness knows, sir," said he, taking his seat; "it is neither a waggon nor a tree, for it appears to move. It must be either a wolf or a man."

I ordered him to drive in the direction of the indistinct

object, which was also advancing towards ourselves. In a couple of minutes we met a man:

"Halloa! my good man!" shouted the *yemstchick;* "canst thou tell me which way the road lies?"

"The road is here; I am standing on hard ground," answered the traveller; "but of what use can it be?"

"Listen, my little *moujik,*"* said I; "art thou acquainted with this part of the country? wilt thou undertake to conduct me to some place where we can pass the night?"

"I know the country," said the wayfarer; "thank goodness it has been walked and driven over in all directions. But thou seest what the weather is like; how easy it is to lose one's way. It would be safer to wait here. The snow-storm may blow over, and the sky clear up; then we shall find our way by the stars."

His assurance supported me; I had already made up my mind to trust myself to God's mercy, and to spend the night in the midst of the steppe, when of a sudden the wayfarer took his seat by the side of the *yemstchick* saying:

"God be praised, a dwelling is not far off; turn to the right, and go on."

"And why should I turn to the right?" asked the *yemstchick,* with a dissatisfied air. "Where dost thou see a road there? I dare say thou thinkest: 'The horses are somebody else's, the harness is somebody else's, so drive on and don't stop.'"

It struck me that the *yemstchick* was right.

"And really," said I, "what makes thee think that a dwelling is not far off?"

* Peasant.—Tr.

"Because the wind blew from thence," answered the stranger; "I perceived the smell of smoke; it means that a village is near."

His quick perception and acute sense of smelling astonished me; I directed the *yemstchick* to drive on. The horses were stepping heavily over the deep snow. The *kibitka* advanced slowly, now rising over a hillock, then plunging into a ditch; again turning over from side to side. It was like the motion of a ship on a stormy sea. Savelitch groaned, and was continually striking against me. I let down the *tzynooka,** wrapped myself up in my pelisse, and dozed, lulled by the music of the storm and the rocking of the slow motion.

I dreamt a dream, which I *never could* forget, and in which, even now, I see something prophetic when I associate it with the peculiar events of my life. The reader will make every allowance for me, for he probably knows by experience how prone one is to give way to superstition, notwithstanding every feeling of contempt for such prejudices.

I was in that state when reality, giving place to fancies, is mingled with them in the dim visions of first sleep. I fancied the storm was still raging, and that we were still straying over the snowy steppe. . . . Suddenly I saw a gate, and I drove into the court of our house. My first thought was a dread lest my father should be angry with me for my involuntary return to the parental roof, and lest he should consider such to be an act of premeditated disobedience. . In my uneasiness, I jumped out of the

---

* A bass matting let down in front of the hood.—Tr.

kibitka and saw my mother, who ran to meet me at the threshold with a look of deep grief. " Gently," she said, " thy father is ill and at death's door, and desires to take leave of thee." Struck with terror, I followed her into the bedroom. It is dimly lit; people with sorrowful faces stand at the bedside. I approach the bed noiselessly; my mother raises the curtains and says : " Andrey Petrovitch, Petrousha has come ; he has returned on hearing of thy illness; bless him." I knelt and fixed my eyes on the patient. And what ? . . . instead of my father, I see a *moujik* with a black beard stretched on the bed, who looks pleasantly at me. In my perplexity I turn to my mother and say : " What does this mean ? This is not my father. And what should I ask a *moujik's* blessing for ?" " It is the same thing, Petrousha," replies my mother ; " this is thy nuptial sponsor: kiss his hand and let him kiss thee . . ." I didn't consent. Here the *moujik* jumps out of bed, draws an axe from behind his, back,* and commences to swing it about ; I seek to fly from him . . . and cannot ; the room is strewn about with corpses ; I stumble over them, and slip in pools of blood . . . the dreadful *moujik* calls me affectionately, saying, " Do not fear, come and receive my blessing ;" . . . terror and anxiety seize hold of me . . . and at that moment I awoke ; the horses stood still ; Savelitch held me by the hand and said :

" Get out, sir ; we have arrived."

" Arrived where ?" I inquired, rubbing my eyes.

* The Russian peasant wears his axe behind his back, stuck into his belt.—Tr.

"At the inn. God came to our aid; we ran right up against a paling. Get out quickly, sir, and warm thy self."

I stepped out of the *kibitka*. The storm continued, though with less severity. It was pitchy dark. The landlord met us at the gate, holding a lantern under the skirt of his coat, and led me into a room, which, though small, was tolerably clean; it was lit by a rush-light. A gun and a high Cossack hat were suspended to the wall.

Our host, a Cossack of the Yaïk,* was a man of about sixty, but hale and strong. Savelitch brought in the cellarette after me, and asked for a fire, in order to prepare some tea, of which I had never stood so much in need. The host left to make the necessary preparations.

"Where is our guide?" I said to Savelitch.

"Here, your honour," answered a voice from above.

I looked up at the loft, and saw a black beard and two sparkling eyes.

"Well, art thou frozen?"

"How is one not to be frozen with nothing to wear but a worn *armyak*?† I had a *touloup*—but why should I conceal the truth?—I pledged it last night at the public-house; the frost did not seem to be very severe."

At that moment the host returned with the boiling *samovar*,‡ I offered our guide a cup of tea; the *moujik* descended from the loft. His exterior struck me as being remarkable. He was about forty, of middle height, lean and broad-shouldered. A few gray hairs mingled with

* Or River Oural, flowing into the Caspian.—Tr.
† A smock.—Tr.   ‡ Russian tea-urn.—Tr.

his black beard ; his large, lustrous eyes were ever restless.   The expression of his face was pleasant enough, but
it was roguish. His hair was evenly cut all round ; he wore
a ragged *armyak* and capacious Tartar trousers. I handed
him a cup of tea; he tasted it and made a grimace.
" Your honour, do oblige me . . . order a glass of wine to
be given me ; tea is not a drink for us Cossacks."

I readily acceded to his wish.   The host produced a
bottle and tumbler from the cupboard, approached him,
and looking him in the face :

" Oho !" said he, " thou art again in our neighbourhood :
Where dost thou come from ?"

My guide winked significantly and answered with a
parable :

" *I flew about the kitchen-garden, picked hempseed, the
old woman threw a pebble at me, but missed.   Well, how
are all your people ?*"

" What, how are our people !" replied the landlord,
continuing the parabolical dialogue ; " *they were about to
ring for vespers, but the priest's wife forbid them : the
priest is absent on a visit, the devils are in the parish.*"

" Be quiet, uncle," said the vagabond ; " *when the rain
falls mushrooms will be there ; when there are mushrooms there will also be baskets ; but at present*" [here he
winked again] " *hide thy axe behind thy back ; the forester
is walking about.   Your honour, your health !*"

With these words he took the tumbler, made the sign
of the cross, and drained it at a draught ; he then bowed
to me and returned to the loft.

I could make nothing of this cut-throat conversation at

that time, and it was only subsequently I guessed that it referred to the army of the Yaïk, which had but recently been subdued after the mutiny of 1772. Savelitch was listening with an air of great displeasure. He looked with suspicion from the host to the guide. The inn, or, as it is there called, the *oumet*, was situated in the steppe, at a distance from any village, and much resembled a robber's retreat. But there was no help for it. To think of continuing the journey was unseen. Savelitch's agitation amused me much. I made myself comfortable for the night, stretching myself on a bench. Savelitch made up his mind to sleep on the stove, and our host lay on the floor. Everybody was soon snoring, and I fell into a deep sleep.

Awaking at a late hour on the following morning, I found the storm had ceased. The sun was shining. The dazzling white snow stretched like a sheet over the boundless steppe. The horses were ready; I settled with our host, who took from us so moderate a sum that even Savelitch did not grumble, nor did he attempt to bargain as was his wont, and his suspicions of the previous day were quite forgotten. I called our guide, thanked him for his aid, and desired Savelitch to give him half a rouble as a tip.

Savelitch frowned. "Half a rouble as a tip!" said he; "what for? Is it because thou hast given him a lift to the inn? No, sir, we have no spare money to waste. If we are to give a tip to everybody, we shall soon *ourselves have to starve.*"

I could not argue the point with Savelitch. The money had remained as I had promised, in his sole charge. I felt vexed, however, at not being able to show my gratitude to a man, who, if he had not saved me from actual danger, had at least extricated me from a very unpleasant predicament.

"All right," said I, coolly; "if thou wilt not give him half a rouble, find something for him amongst my things. He is too thinly clad. Give him my *touloup*, of hareskin."

"For pity's sake, my little father, Piotr Andrevitch!" said Savelitch, "what does he want thy hareskin *touloup* for? The cur will barter it away at the first public-house."

"It need not trouble thee, my little man," said the vagabond, "whether I shall barter it or not. His honour does me the favour to give me the pelisse off his back; it is his honour's will, and thy business as a serf is not to discuss, but to obey."

"Thou dost not fear God, robber that thou art!" answered Savelitch in an angry tone. "Thou seest that the child has not come to years of discretion, and thou art glad to take advantage of his simplicity and rob him. What good is a gentleman's *touloup* to thee? thou canst not even get it over thy d—d shoulders."

"I beg of thee not to moralize," said I to my servant; "let him have the *touloup*, immediately."

"Good gracious!" moaned Savelitch. "The *touloup* is all but new! I would not mind it, but that a tattered drunkard gets it!"

The *touloup* was produced. The *moujik* proceeded to try it on. And, indeed, the *touloup*, which even I had grown out of, fitted him rather tightly. He managed, however, to get it on somehow, bursting it open at the seams. Savelitch almost howled when he heard the threads part. The vagabond alone was delighted with my present. He accompanied me to the *kibitka*, and said with a bow :

" Many thanks, your honour ! God reward you for your good deed. I shall never forget your kindness."

He went his way, and I continued my journey, not heeding Savelitch, and soon forgot yesterday's storm, my guide, and my *touloup*.

Upon arriving at Orenburg, I directly went to the general. I beheld a tall man, already bent by age. His long hair was perfectly white; his old faded uniform reminded one of a warrior of the days of the Empress Anne, and his pronounciation was very German. I handed my father's letter to him. Upon his name being mentioned, he threw a sudden glance at me. " Mein Gott !" he said, " is it long since Andrey Petrovitch vos of dye age himself, and now he hass such a fellow as dee for a zohn ? Yes, time flies !" He opened the letter, and began to read it in an undertone to himself, making his remarks: " ' Dear sir, Ivan Karlovitch; I hope that your excellency !' . . . . Dear me, what formalities ! Pfouy ! is he not ashamed of himself ? Certainly, discipline pefore all, but is dis dee vay to write to an old comrate ? . . . . ' Your excellency has not forgotten !' . . . . him ! . . . .

'and ' . . . . when ? . . . . 'under the late Field-Marshal Münich . . . . during the march . . . . also little
Cardina ?' Ha ! ha ! bruder ! so he still remembers our
old frolics ? 'Now to business . . . . I send you my
mad-cap ' . . . . h'm ! . . . . 'hold him with porcupine
gloves !' . . . . Vat are porcupine glofes ? Dis must be a
Rooshan saying . . . . vat does it mean to holt vit porcupine glofes ?" he repeated, turning to me.

"That means," replied I, assuming the most innocent
air imaginable, "to treat him gently, without too great
severity; to give him a good deal of liberty; to hold him
with porcupine gloves."

"H'm; I understand . . . . and do not let him have
too much liberty . . . . no; to hold vit porcupine glofes
must have another signification ! . . . . 'enclosed is his
passport !' . . . . vy vere is it ? Ah ! here it is . . . .
'to attach him to the Semionoffsky Regiment.' All right,
all right, it shall all tonn . . . . 'thou must allow me,
laying rank aside, to embrace thee as an old friend and
comrade.' . . . . Vell, at last; . . . . and so on, and so
on . . . . Vell, sir," said he, having concluded the letter,
and laying aside my passport, "it shall all pe tonn ; dow
shalt join dee * * * Regiment, vit dee rank of officer,
but so as not to loose any time, dow shalt go to-morrow
to dee fortress of Byĕlogorsk, vere dow shalt pe unter dee
orders of Captain Mironoff, a goot and honest man. Dere
dow shalt know vat real service is; it will teash_ dee
discipline. At Orenburg dere is no-ting for dee to too ;
amusements are prejuticial to a young mann. To-day, I
beg dow wilt dine vit me."

"From bad to worse," thought I to myself. "Of what service has it been to me, to have been a sergeant in the Guards, almost from my mother's womb? What has it led to? To my being attached to the * * * Regiment, and having to serve in a lonely fortress, on the frontier of the Khirghis-Kasak Steppe!" .... I dined with Andrey Karlovitch, in company with his old aide-de-camp. The strictest German economy was observed at his table, and I think that the dread of occasionally seeing an extra visitor at his bachelor's board, was partly the reason of my hasty removal to the garrison. The following day I took my leave of the general, and repaired to my destination.

CHAPTER III.

THE FORTRESS.

THE fortress of Byělogorsk was situated at a distance of forty versts from Orenburg. The road led along the steep banks of the Yaïk. The river was not yet frozen over, and its leaden-coloured waves contrasted gloomily with the monotonous snow-covered shores. Beyond them stretched out the Khirghis Steppe. I was lost in reflections, which were mostly of a sad nature. A garrison life offered little enough attraction to me; I endeavoured to picture to myself the person of Captain Mironoff, my future chief, and I conceived him to be a strict, morose old man, without an idea beyond his duties, and who would be ready to put me under arrest, on bread and water, for every trifling offence. It was now getting dark; we were driving pretty fast. "Is the fortress far off?" I asked the *yemstchick*. "Not far," answered he; "there it is." I looked in all directions, expecting to view proud bastions, towers, and a ditch, but I could only see a small village, encircled by a wooden palisade. On one side stood three or four haystacks, partly covered with snow, upon the other was a sorry windmill, with bass fans which were in repose. "But where is the fortress?" I asked, in astonishment.

"Here it is," said the *yemstchick*, pointing at the village which we were about to enter. I observed at the gates an old bronze gun; the streets were narrow and crooked; the huts were low, and the greater number were thatched. I gave orders to drive to the commandant's residence, and in a few minutes the *kibitka* stopped in front of a small wooden house, which stood upon high ground near the church, also built of wood.

Nobody came to meet me. I walked through the hall, and let myself into the ante-room. An old invalid, seated on a table, was fitting a blue patch to the elbow of a green uniform. I desired him to announce me.

"Come in, sir," said the invalid; "our people are at home."

I entered an old-fashioned and clean little room. In a corner stood a cupboard which contained crockery. An officer's commission, framed and glazed, hung on the wall; close to it were some coarse engravings, representing the taking of Kystrin and Otchakoff, "The Choice of a Bride," and "The Burial of the Cat." At the window sat an old woman in a warm jacket; her head bound up with a kerchief. She was winding a skein of thread, which was being held by a one-eyed old man, in an officer's uniform.

"What is it you want, sir?" she asked, continuing her occupation.

I replied that I had come to enter the service, and had hastened to report myself to the captain, as in duty bound, and was about to address myself to the one-eyed man, whom I took for the commandant; but the old lady anticipated the speech I had prepared.

"Ivan Kouzmitch* is not at home," she said; "he is gone to Father Gherassim. But it does not matter, sir; I am his wife. I beg you to love and be gracious to us.† Sit down, my little father."

She called a maidservant, and told her to send the orderly. The little old man with the solitary eye kept looking at me with curiosity.

"Dare I ask," said he, "in what regiment you have served?"

I satisfied his curiosity.

"And dare I ask," he continued, "why you have left the Guards for this garrison?"

I replied that such was the will of my superiors.

"Probably in consequence of your conduct not being creditable to an officer in the Guards?" continued the indefatigable questioner.

"Leave off talking nonsense," said the captain's wife to

* John, the son of Cosmas.—Tr.

† A friendly mode of greeting.—Tr.

him; "thou seest that the young man is fatigued after his journey; he has other things to think about. . . . Hold thy hands out straighter. . . . And thou, my little father," continued she, turning to me; "don't fret at being banished to our wilderness. Thou art not the first, nor wilt thou be the last. *One learns to love what one has to endure.** It is now five years since Shvabrine, Aleksey Ivanovitch† Shvabrine was sent here for manslaughter. Goodness knows what possessed him; he went, thou seest, into the country with a sub-lieutenant; they both took up their swords, and began to poke at each other, until Aleksey Ivanovitch run the sub-lieutenant through, and that in the presence of witnesses! What's to be done! *Sin has not found its master.*"*

At that moment, the orderly, a young good-looking Cossack, came into the room.

"Maksymitch!"‡ said the captain's wife; "show this officer to his billet, and see that all is clean."

"I obey, Vassilissa Yegorovna,"§ answered the orderly. "Would it not do to place his honour with Ivan Polejaeff?"

"Nonsense, Maksymitch," said she; "Polejaeff has no room to spare; besides, he is my *koum*, and does not forget that we are his superiors. Conduct the officer. . . . What is your and your father's name, sir?"

"Piotr Andrevitch."

"Take Piotr Andrevitch to Semion Koúzoff. The rascal

---

* Russian proverbs.—Tr.   † Alexis, the son of John.—Tr.
‡ Son of Maximus.—Tr.
§ Vassilissa, the daughter of Gregory.—Tr.

has let his horse loose into my vegetable garden. Well, Maksymitch, is everything in order ?"

"All's correct, God be praised," answered the Cossack, quietly; "only Corporal Próhoroff has had a fight with Oustynaja Pezoulin in the bath house about a pail of hot water."

"Ivan Ignatitch !"* said the captain's wife, to the one-eyed little man; "find out which one of them is right, and who is wrong, and mind that thou punishest them both. Very well, Maksymitch, God be with thee. Piotr Andrevitch, Maksymitch will show you to your billet."

I took my leave. The orderly led me to a hut, situated on the upper part of the river's bank, at the very limits of the fortress. One half the hut was occupied by the family of Semion Koúzoff, the other half was given up to me. It consisted of one room, which was tolerably clean, and divided in two by a partition. Savelitch began to put things in order. I looked out of the narrow window. Before me lay a dreary steppe; on one side stood a few huts; some hens were wandering about the streets. In the porch was an old woman with a pail, calling her pigs, who responded with friendly grunts. And this was the place in which I was doomed to spend my youth! I felt sadly depressed. I left the window and laid myself down to sleep supperless, notwithstanding Savelitch's entreaties, who repeated mournfully—

"Good God! he will not eat! What will my mistress say, if the child gets ill ?"

I had only just begun to dress on the following morn-

* John, the son of Ignatius.—Tr.

ing, when my door was opened, and in walked a young officer of middle stature with a dark and unmistakably plain, but lively face.

"Pardon me," said he, in French; "that I should come to make your acquaintance with so little ceremony. I heard yesterday of your arrival. The desire to see at last a new face, was so strong in me, that I could not hold out any longer. You will understand the feeling when you will have been here a little while."

I guessed that this was the officer who had been dismissed from the Guards for his share in the duel. We soon got acquainted. Shvabrine was a clever fellow. His conversation was witty and engaging. He gave me an amusing account of the commandant's family, his friends, and of the country to which fate had consigned me. I was laughing heartily, when the invalid, whom I had seen cleaning some uniform in the commandant's hall, came in with an invitation to dinner from Vassilissa Yegorovna. Shvabrine offered to accompany me.

As we approached the commandant's house, we saw on the small parade ground some twenty little old invalids with long pig-tails and cocked hats. They were standing in single file. In front of them was the commandant, a tall hale old man, in a night-cap and nankin dressing-gown. He approached upon perceiving us, addressed a few kind words to me, and resumed the drill. We proposed remaining to see the exercise, but he invited us to go to Vassilissa Yegorovna, promising to follow shortly.

"Here," added he; "there is nothing for you to look at."

Vassilissa Yegorovna received us without any ceremony, but with warmth, and treated me as if she had known me for years. The invalid and Paláshka were laying the table.

"Why, what makes my Ivan Kouzmitch stay out so long to-day?" said the commandant's wife. "Paláshka, call your master to dinner. But where is Masha?"

Here a chubby and rosy-cheeked maiden of about eighteen, with light-brown hair smoothly brushed down behind her ears, which seemed to blush and tingle, came in. She did not impress me favourably at first. I had been prejudiced against her. Shvabrine had described Masha, the captain's daughter, as being a thorough simpleton. Maria Ivanovna* retired to a corner, and took up her needlework. The *stcky*† was served. Vassilissa Yegorovna not seeing her husband, again despatched Paláshka after him.

"Tell thy master the guests are waiting—the *stcky* will get cold—thank goodness the drills won't run away—he will have plenty of time to shriek himself hoarse."

The captain soon appeared accompanied by the one-eyed old man.

"What's the matter, my little father?" said his wife; "dinner has been served some time, and we cannot get thee to come."

"The fact is, Vassilissa Yegorovna," answered Ivan Kouzmitch, "I was on duty; I was instructing the little soldiers."

"Oh! nonsense," reiterated his wife; "thou only

* Mary, the daughter of John.—Tr.   † Cabbage soup.—Tr.

boastest when thou talkest of teaching soldiers; they are
not suited for the service, nor dost thou know anything
about it thyself. It would be better if thou would'st
stay at home and say thy prayers. My esteemed guests,
pray be seated."

We took our places. Vassilissa Yegorovna was not
silent for an instant, and kept putting all manner of
questions to me: who were my parents? were they
alive? where did they live? what was their income?
Upon learning that my father possessed three hundred
peasants, "Is it possible!" she said; "well, there are
rich people in the world! we possess only one soul,* the
girl Paláshka, but, thank God, we manage to exist. We
are beset but by one trouble: Masha is a marriageable
girl, and what is her dower to be? a comb, a broom, and
a few pence wherewith to pay for her bath. 'Twere well
if some good man would take her with so much, otherwise she must remain an old maid."

I looked at Maria Ivanovna. She had blushed
crimson, and tears were dropping on her plate. I felt for
her and hastened to change the conversation.

"I have heard," I said, somewhat inopportunely, "it
is apprehended that the Bashkirs purpose attacking your
fortress."

"Who did'st thou hear that from, my little father?"
asked Ivan Kouzmitch.

"I was told so at Orenburg," answered I.

"Nonsense!" said the commandant, "we have not
heard anything about it for a long time. The Bashkirs

---

* By the term *soul* was understood a serf.—Tr.

have been intimidated, and the Khirghis have also learnt a lesson. Never fear, they will not touch us; and should they do so, I will punish them to such an extent as would compel them to keep still for the next ten years."

"And are you not afraid," I continued, addressing the captain's wife, "to remain in a fortress threatened by such dangers?"

"It is a matter of habit, my little father," said she "Twenty years ago we were transferred to this place from the regiment, and dear me, how frightened I used to be of those d—d heathens! It was enough for me to see their fur caps and to hear their yells, and my heart seemed to stop beating! And now I do not even stir when I am told that those wretches are groping about the fortress."

"Vassilissa Yegorovna is a wonderfully brave lady," observed Shvabrine, seriously, with a consequential air. "Ivan Kouzmitch can bear witness to the fact."

"Yes, certainly," said Ivan Kouzmitch, "she is not one of the timid ones."

"And Maria Ivanovna," asked I, "is she as brave as you are?"

"Masha brave?" answered her mother. "No, Masha is a coward. She cannot even hear a gun fired without trembling all over. And when, two years ago, Ivan Kouzmitch took it into his head to fire our cannon on my name's day, my little dove almost died of fright. Since then we have ceased to fire the d—d cannon."

We rose from the table. The captain and his wife

3

retired to enjoy their nap; I accompanied Shvabrine to
his quarters, where I spent the remainder of the evening.

CHAPTER IV.

THE DUEL.

SEVERAL weeks had elapsed, and my existence at the
fortress of Byělogorsk became not only bearable, but even
agreeable.   I was received at the house of the commandant as if I were one of the family.   Both husband
and wife were most excellent people.   Ivan Kouzmitch,
who had risen from the ranks, was simple-minded and
uneducated, but most honest and kind-hearted.   His
wife ruled over him, which accorded well with his indolent
disposition.   Vassilissa Yegorovna assumed the direction
of all matters connected with the service, as she did those
of her household, and governed the fortress as she
governed her own house.   Maria Ivanovna soon became
less shy of me.   We got to know each other better, and
I discovered her to be a sensible and feeling girl.   I
became imperceptibly attached to these good people,
including even Ivan Ignatitch, the one-eyed sub-lieutenant
of the garrison, whom Shvabrine accused of undue
familiarity with Vassilissa Yegorovna, although there
was not a shadow of truth in the statement; but this did
not trouble Shvabrine.

I attained my officer's rank.   The service did not weigh
heavily on me.   In this fortress, which owed its protec-

tion to God alone, parades, exercises, and guards were
dispensed with. The commandant instructed the soldiers
himself from time to time, as he felt disposed, but he had
not yet succeeded in teaching them to distinguish the
right from the left side. Shvabrine possessed a few
French books. I read them, and they awakened in me
a taste for literature. In the forenoon I read, translated,
and sometimes attempted the composition of verses. I
invariably dined at the commandant's, where I usually
passed the rest of the day, and occasionally Father
Gherassim, with his wife Akoulina Pamphylovna,* the
great tale-bearer in the neighbourhood, used to spend the
evening with us. Of course Aleksey Ivanovitch Shvabrine and I met daily; but his conversations became
more and more distasteful to me. I did not like his continuing to make a laughing-stock of the commandant's
family, and especially his cutting remarks about Maria
Ivanovna. Of other society there was none at the
fortress, nor did I wish for any.

In spite of the prophecy, the Bashkirs did not revolt.
Tranquillity reigned in our fortress. But this peace was
unexpectedly interrupted by intestine strife. I have
already said, that I was engaged in literary pursuits.
My efforts, for the times, were tolerably successful, and
were, a few years later, approved by Alexander Petrovitch Soumarokoff.† One song I wrote pleased me very
much. It is a fact that under pretext of seeking advice,

* Aquiline, the daughter of Pamphylius.—Tr.
† Alexander, the son of Peter. Soumarokoff, a Russian poet
and tragedian, 1718—77.—Tr.

3—2

writers arc frequently but in search of a well-disposed listener. Thus, copying my little song, I took it to Shvabrine, who alone in the fortress was able to appreciate a poetical production. After a short preface I drew forth my manuscript and read the following verses:

"In annihilating thoughts of love I seek to forget the fair one, and
Alas! it is in fleeing Masha, that I hope to win back my freedom!

" But the eyes which have enslaved me are for ever in my sight;
they
Have disquieted my spirit, they have destroyed my peace.

" Thou, Masha, who learn'st my woes, have pity upon me;
Thou seest my cruel state, and knowest I am thy captive."

" What dost thou think of this?" asked I of Shvabrine, in expectation of praise as a tribute to which I was entitled. But, to my great vexation, Shvabrine, whom I usually found indulgent, decidedly declared that my song was worthless. " Why so?" I asked, concealing my vexation.

" Because," he replied, " such verses are only worthy of my master Vassily Kyrylitch Trediakovsky,* and remind me very much of his amorous couplets." Here he took my manuscript and proceeded to pick each verse to pieces, unmercifully, taunting me the while in the most stinging manner. I could stand it no longer, so, tearing the paper out of his hands, I declared that I would never again show him any of my compositions. Shvabrine also mocked at my threat.

* Basil, the son of Cyril. Trediakovsky, a greatly reviled poet, during the reign of Catherine II.—Tr.

" We shall see," said he, " whether thou wilt keep thy word; a poet requires a listener, just as Ivan Kouzmitch requires the *vodka* decanter before dinner. Say, who is that Masha to whom thou declarest thy tender passion and thy woes in love ? Can it be Maria Ivanovna ?"

" It is no business of thine," I replied, frowning, " who this Masha is. I ask neither thy opinion nor thy suppositions."

" Oho ! conceited poet and cautious lover !" continued Shvabrine, irritating me more and more ; " but listen to a friendly piece of advice; if thou art anxious to meet with success I advise thee not to have recourse to songs."

" What does this mean, sir ? explain thyself."

" Willingly. This means that if thou will'st that Masha Mironoff should meet thee at twilight, thou must, instead of these tender verses, present her with a pair of earrings."

My blood boiled.

" And why hast thou formed that opinion of her ?" I asked, with difficulty suppressing my indignation.

" Because," answered he with a diabolical smile, " I know by experience her tastes and habits."

" Thou liest, blackguard !" exclaimed I furiously; " thou liest shamelessly."

Shvabrine's face altered.

" This cannot be passed over," said he, squeezing my hand ; " you will give me satisfaction."

" Very well; whenever you please," answered I, rejoiced.

At that moment I was ready to tear him to pieces. I

repaired at once to Ivan Ignatitch, and found him needle in hand: by order of the commandant's wife he was stringing mushrooms, which were to be dried for the winter.

"Ah! Piotr Andrevitch!" said he on seeing me; "you are welcome. What brings you here? What business, may I ask?"

In a few words I explained to him that I had had a row with Aleksey Ivanovitch, and asked him to be my second. Fixing his one eye on me, Ivan Ignatitch listened attentively.

"You say," said he, "that you are about to kill Aleksey Ivanovitch and wish me to be a witness! Is it so, may I ask?"

"It is so."

"Dear me, Piotr Andrevitch! What are you thinking of? You have had words with Aleksey Ivanovitch? There is no great harm in that. He insulted you, you insult him in return; he gives you a blow in the face, you give him a box on the ear—a second, and a third—and go your way; we will bring you together again. Instead of this, is it a right thing to do to kill one's neighbour, may I ask? At least, if you were sure of killing him, God be with him, with Aleksey Ivanovitch; I myself don't care much about him. But, supposing he makes a hole through you? what a business that would be. Who will be the fool then, may I ask?"

The good sub-lieutenant's reasoning did not move me. I did not swerve from my resolution.

"As you please," said Ivan Ignatitch, "please yourself; but why should I be a witness to the affair? What for? What is there strange, that people should choose to fight, may I ask? Thank goodness, I fought against the Swede and the Turk; there is nothing new in it." I endeavoured to explain the duties of a second, but Ivan Ignatitch was quite unable to comprehend me. "Do as you please," said he, "but if I were to assent to be mixed up in this affair, it would, perhaps, only be to go to Ivan Kouzmitch and report to him officially, that a crime is contemplated in the fortress, contrary to the interests of the Crown; and would the commandant be pleased to take the necessary measures . . . . ?"

I became alarmed, and entreated Ivan Ignatitch "not to say anything to the commandant;" I prevailed upon him, with great difficulty, and having exacted his promise, I left.

The evening was spent, as usual, at the commandant's house. I tried to appear cheerful and unconcerned, so as not to excite suspicion, and to escape importunate questions; but I own I did not feel as unconcerned as persons in my position usually boast themselves to be. That evening, I felt sentimental and impressionable. Maria Ivanovna pleased me more than ever. The thought that I was perhaps looking upon her for the last time, added something touching to her appearance in my sight. Shvabrine was also there. I took him aside and apprised him of my conversation with Ivan Ignatitch. "What should we want seconds for?" said he, dryly; "we can do without them." It was convened that we should fight behind the haystacks in the vicinity of the fortress, the following morning at six o'clock. We were to all appearances conversing so amicably, that the overjoyed Ivan Ignatitch almost betrayed himself. "That's how it ought to have been long ago," said he to me in a pleased countenance; "defective peace is better than a good row; if it is not honourable, at least it is attended with safety."

"What is it you are saying, Ivan Ignatitch?" said the commandant's wife, who was playing at cards in a corner. "I did not quite hear it."

Ivan Ignatitch, perceiving that I was displeased, and recollecting his promise, became confused and scarcely knew what reply to make. Shvabrine hastened to the rescue.

"Ivan Ignatitch," said he, "approves of our peace-making."

"And who did'st thou fall out with, my little father?"

"We had all but a serious row, Piotr Andrevitch and I."

"What about?"

"About a mere nothing; a song, Vassilissa Yegorovna."

"Could you find nothing better to quarrel about? a song! . . . . how did it happen?"

"In this way; Piotr Andrevitch has lately composed a song, which he sang to me to-day, and I replied by humming my favourite:

> "' *Captain's Daughter,*
> *Do not take thy walk at midnight.'*

Discord was the result. Piotr Andrevitch got quite angry, but upon reflection, he admitted that everybody was free to sing what he pleases; thus the affair ended."

Shvabrine's impudence almost enraged me; none but myself seemed to have understood his coarse allusions; at least no one took any notice of them. The subject of songs led to a discussion on the merits of poets, and the commandant observed that they were all useless creatures and dreadful drunkards, and advised me, as a friend, to leave off writing verses, an occupation prejudicial to the service, and leading to no good.

Shvabrine's presence was unbearable. I took an early leave of the commandant and his family; on my return home, I examined my sword, tried its point, and went to bed, having left orders with Savelitch to call me at six o'clock.

The next morning, at the appointed hour, I was already standing behind the haystacks, waiting for my adversary. He soon appeared. " We might be caught out," he said, "we must be quick." We laid aside our uniform, keeping on our waistcoats, and drew our swords. At that instant Ivan Ignatitch, at the head of five invalids, rushed from behind the stacks. He summoned us to the commandant. We were vexed, but obeyed, the soldiers surrounded us, and we followed Ivan Ignatitch, who led the way in triumph, stepping out with an air of great importance.

We entered the house, Ivan Ignatitch threw open the door, and exclaimed, with solemnity, "I have brought them !" Vassilissa Yegorovna met us. " Ah ! my little fathers! What does this mean? How! what! a premeditated murder in our fortress! Ivan Kouzmitch, they must immediately be placed under arrest. Piotr Andrevitch ! Aleksey Ivanovitch ! give me your swords;

give them up, give them up. Paláshka, take these
swords into the lumber-room. Piotr Andrevitch, I did
not expect this of thee. Art thou not ashamed of thyself? Aleksey Ivanovitch is different; was he not transferred from the Guards for having caused a soul to perish?
he does not even believe in our Lord; but thou! dost
thou want to do the same?" Ivan Kouzmitch fully
agreed with his spouse, and kept repeating: "Yes, yes,
Vassilissa Yegorovna is right. Duelling is especially
forbidden by the articles of war." Paláshka carried our
swords to the lumber-room. I could not help laughing;
Shvabrine preserved his equanimity. "With all due
respect to you," said he coolly, "I cannot but remark,
that you have given yourself unnecessary trouble in subjecting us to your judgment. Leave that to Ivan Kouzmitch; it is his business." "Dear me, my little father!"
replied the commandant's wife, "are not husband and
wife one spirit and one flesh? Ivan Kouzmitch! what
art thou gaping at? Put them immediately into separate
rooms, on bread and water, to knock all this nonsense out
of their heads. And let Father Gherassim make them
do penance, to the end that they should ask God's forgiveness, and show themselves repentant before man."

Ivan Kouzmitch could not make up his mind what to
do. Maria Ivanovna looked exceedingly pale. By
degrees, the storm abated; the commandant's wife
regained her composure, and ordered us to embrace each
other. Paláshka returned to us our swords. We left
the commandant apparently at peace with each other.
Ivan Ignatitch accompanied us. "How is it you are not

ashamed," said I, angrily, "of having denounced us to the commandant, after having promised me that you would not do so ?" "As God lives, I did not tell it to Ivan Kouzmitch," answered he. "Vassilissa Yegorovna drew it all out of me. She it was who made all arrangements without the commandant's knowledge. However, thank God that all has ended so well." With these words, he returned homewards, and Shvabrine and I remained alone. "The affair cannot end thus," said I to him. "Of course not," answered Shvabrine; "you must answer to me with your blood for your impertinence; but we shall probably be watched. We shall have to dissemble for a few days. Good-bye." And we separated, as if nothing had occurred.

On my return to the commandant's house, I took my seat next to Maria Ivanovna as usual. Ivan Kouzmitch was not at home; Vassilissa Yegorovna was busy with her housekeeping duties. We conversed in an under-tone. Maria Ivanovna reproached me tenderly for the anxiety I had caused them all by my quarrel with Shvabrine.

"My heart failed me," said she, "when we were told that you were going to fight with swords. How odd you men are! For a chance word which might most likely be forgotten in a week, you are ready to stab each other and to sacrifice, not only your lives, but also your consciences, and the happiness of those who . . . . But I feel sure that the quarrel was not of your seeking—the fault was surely that of Aleksey Ivanovitch."

"And what makes you think so, Maria Ivanovna ?"

" I scarcely know. . . . He is so fond of ridiculing
everybody. I do not like Aleksey Ivanovitch. I have
an antipathy for him, and yet it is strange, I should not
like to displease him. It would make me very anxious."

"And what do you think, Maria Ivanovna ? does he
like you or not ?"

Maria Ivanovna looked confused and blushed.

" I think," she said, " I think I do please him."

" But why do you think so ?"

" Because he proposed to me."

" Proposed ! he proposed to you ! when ?"

" Last year. Two months before your arrival."

" And you did not accept him ?"

" I did not, as you see. Aleksey Ivanovitch is, of
course, a clever man, of good birth, and some fortune ;
but when I think that I should have to kiss him in the
presence of everybody under the crown*—never ! not for
anything in the world."

Maria Ivanovna's words opened my eyes and explained
a great many things to me. I understood why Shvabrine
persisted in slandering her. He had probably noticed our
mutual liking, and wished to draw us away from each
other. The words which had given rise to our quarrel
appeared to me to be still more abominable, when I discovered in them a premeditated calumny, and not only a
coarse indecent joke. The desire to punish the daring
caluminator became stronger within me, and I impatiently
awaited a fitting opportunity.

* Crowns are held over the heads of the bride and bridegroom
during the marriage ceremony.—Tr.

I had not to wait long. The next day whilst I was writing an elegy, and biting my pen in search of a rhyme, Shvabrine rapped at my window. I dropped my pen, snatched up my sword, and went out to him.

"Why should we delay," said Shvabrine; "nobody is watching us. Let us go down to the river side. No one will hinder us there."

We walked away in silence. Having descended by a steep foot path, we stopped close to the river and bared our swords. Shvabrine was the most expert, but I was stronger and bolder, and M. Beaupré, who had once been a soldier, had given me some lessons in fencing, which had not been lost upon me. Shvabrine had not expected to find such a dangerous adversary in me. For a long time, neither of us could harm the other; at last, perceiving that Shvabrine was losing strength, I thrust at him quickly, and made him retire almost into the river. Suddenly I heard my name called out in a loud voice. I turned and saw Savelitch hurrying to me over the hillside path. . . . At that moment, I felt a sharp prick in the chest, a little below the right shoulder. I fell and lost all consciousness.

CHAPTER V.

LOVE.

Upon coming to myself again, I was not able for a long time to collect my thoughts, nor was I able to understand what had happened to me. I lay on a bed in a strange room, feeling great weakness. Savelitch stood by me, holding a candle. Somebody was carefully removing the bandages which enveloped my chest and shoulder. Little by little my thoughts became clearer. I remembered the duel, and guessed that I had been wounded. Just then the door creaked.

" Well, how is he ?" whispered a voice that made me start.

" Still in the same condition," answered Savelitch, with a sigh ; " still unconscious, and this is the fifth day !"

I essayed to turn, but could not.

" Where am I ? Who is here ?" said I, with an effort.

Maria Ivanovna approached my bed and bent over me.

" How do you feel ?" said she.

" Thank God," I answered, in a feeble voice ; " is it you, Maria Ivanovna ? Tell me——"

I had not the strength to proceed. Savelitch uttered an exclamation. His face beamed with joy.

" He has come to !—he has come to !" he repeated. " Glory to Thee, O Lord ! Well, my little father, Piotr Andrevitch ! thou hast frightened me ! It is no joke ; this is the fifth day ! . . . ."

Maria Ivanovna interrupted him.

" Do not talk to him much, Savelitch," said she ; " he is still weak !"

She left, and closed the door gently after her. My thoughts were disturbed. I was at the commandant's house. Maria Ivanovna had really come to me. I wished to ask Savelitch some questions ; but the old man shook his head and stopped his ears. I closed my eyes in vexation and soon fell asleep.

Upon awaking, I called Savelitch ; but instead of him, I saw Maria Ivanovna before me. Her angelic voice spoke to me. I cannot express the delightful sensation which overcame me at that moment. I seized her hand, and pressed my lips to it, bathing it in my tears. Masha did not withdraw it. . . . And suddenly her lips touched my cheek, and I felt their pure and warm impress. I was all on fire.

"My dear sweet Maria Ivanovna," said I; "be my wife ; consent to my happiness."

She recollected herself.

" For God's sake, be calm," she said, drawing her hand away. " You are still in danger ; the wound might open afresh. Do take care of yourself, were it but for my sake."

With these words she went away, leaving me enraptured. So much happiness resuscitated me. She will be mine ! She loves me ! This conviction filled my whole being.

From that time I mended hourly. I was attended by the regimental barber, for there was no medical man in the fortress, and thank God, he had no pretentions to too much wisdom. Youth and nature hastened my recovery. All the commandant's family nursed me. Maria Ivanovna never quitted me. As a matter of course, I resumed my unfinished declaration at the first opportunity, and Maria Ivanovna listened to me with greater patience. Without any affectation, she confessed her sincere attachment, and said that her parents would no doubt be rejoiced at her happiness.

"But reflect well," she added, "will there be no hindrance on the part of thy parents ?"

I became pensive. I could not entertain any doubt of my mother's tenderness for me; but knowing the disposition and mode of thinking of my father, I felt that my attachment would not affect him much, and that he would merely consider it a young man's fancy. I candidly admitted this to Maria Ivanovna, making up my mind, however, to write an eloquent letter to my father, to ask for his parental blessing. I showed my letter to Maria Ivanovna, who thought it so convincing and so touching, that she did not doubt its success, and gave herself up to the feelings of her tender heart in all the confidence of youth and love.

I made my peace with Shvabrine during the first days of my convalescence. When reprimanding me for fighting the duel, Ivan Kouzmitch said—

"Ah! Piotr Andrevitch! I ought to put thee under arrest; but thou art already sufficiently punished. As to Aleksey Ivanovitch, he is a prisoner in the bread-room with a sentry over him, and Vassilissa Yegorovna has his sword under lock and key. Let him have time to reflect and repent."

I was too happy to suffer any ill-will to dwell in my heart. I interceded in behalf of Shvabrine, and the good commandant, with his wife's consent, released him. Shvabrine came to me; he expressed his deep regret at what had taken place between us; confessed that the fault was entirely his own, and entreated me to forget the past. Not being naturally of a malicious disposition, I sincerely forgave him our quarrel, and the wound he had inflicted on me. I perceived in his slander, the vexation caused by wounded vanity and rejected love, and generously made allowances for my unhappy rival.

I soon became restored to health, when I removed to my own lodgings. I awaited with impatience a reply to my letter, not daring to hope, but trying to stifle my gloomy presentiments. I had not as yet entered upon any explanations with Vassilissa Yegorovna and her husband; but my proposal ought not to have astonished them. Neither of us sought to conceal our feelings in their presence, and we already felt assured of their consent.

At last Savelitch came to me one morning, bringing a letter. I snatched it tremblingly. It was addressed in my father's hand. This bid me prepare for something of importance, for letters were generally written by my mother, my father adding a few lines at the end. I could not decide upon breaking the seal for a long time, and kept reading the formal superscription: "To my son, Piotr Andrevitch Grieff, Government of Orenburg, Fortress of Byëlogorsk." I tried to guess by the handwriting what humour my father could have been in when he wrote the letter. At length I opened it, and saw by the first lines that the whole affair had gone to the· d—l.

The contents of the letter were as follows:—

" MY SON PIOTR,

"The letter in which thou askest our paternal

4

benediction and consent to thy marriage with Maria
Ivanovna, daughter of Mironoff, we received on the 15th
of this month, and not only do I not intend to give thee
my blessing or my consent, but, moreover, I mean to be
up to thee, and punish thee for thy follies like a naughty
boy, notwithstanning thy officer's rank; for thou hast
proved that thou art as yet unworthy of wearing a sword,
which was given thee for the defence of thy country, and
not for fighting duels with such scamps as thou thyself
art. I shall write without delay to Andrey Karlovitch
to ask him to remove thee from the fortress of Byëlogorsk,
and send thee further away, so that thou shalt shake off
such follies. Thy mother, upon hearing of thy duel, and
that thou wast wounded, fell ill of grief, and is still con-
fined to her bed. What is to become of thee? I pray
to God to effect a change in thee though I dare not hope
in His great mercy.

"Thy father,

"ANDREY GRIUEFF."

The perusal of this letter, awakened in me a variety of
sensations. The unkind expressions my father employed
so liberally, wounded me deeply. The contempt with
which he mentioned Maria Ivanovna, appeared to me as
unbecoming as it was unjust. The prospect of being
removed from the fortress of Byëlogorsk, alarmed me ;
but the news of my mother's illness pained me most. I
felt indignant towards Savelitch, never doubting that my
parents had heard of my duel through him. Pacing to
and fro in my little room, I stopped in front of him, and
looking at him fiercely, said, "Thou dost not appear to

be satisfied, that thanks to thee I was wounded, and that I lay for a whole month at death's door; thou wilt now kill my mother also."

Savelitch looked thunderstruck.

" For pity's sake, sir," said he, almost sobbing, " what dost thou say ? I the cause of thy being wounded ? God is my witness, that I was hastening to put my breast between thee and the sword of Aleksey Ivanovitch ? My d——d old age retarded me; and how have I harmed thy mother ?"

" How hast thou harmed her ?" I answered. " Who asked thee to write and denounce me ? Wast thou appointed as a spy over me ?"

" I ! denounce thee !" asked Savelitch, in tears. " Oh, Lord ! heavenly King ! There, take, read, what my master writes to me; thou wilt see how I have denounced thee."

" Shame upon thee, old cur that thou art, that notwithstanding my strict injunctions, thou hast not written to me about my son, Piotr Andrevitch, and that strangers should be obliged to acquaint me of his follies. Is that the way thou fulfillest thy duty and thy master's wishes ? I shall send thee, thou old cur, to feed swine, for hiding the truth and conniving with the young man. I order thee to give me immediate information, so soon as thou shalt receive this, upon the state of his health, which I am told is improved; also what part of the body he was wounded in, and whether he has been well attended to."

Savelitch was evidently guiltless, and I had incautiously hurt him by my reproaches and suspicions. I begged his pardon, but the old man was inconsolable.

"This is what I have lived to see," he kept repeating; "these are the thanks I get for serving my masters! An old cur, a swineherd, and it is again I who have caused thy wound! No, my little father, Piotr Andreitch, it is not I, but the d——d *monssié* who is to blame for it all. It is he who taught thee to flourish iron spits about, and stamp with thy foot, as if by flourishing and stamping one could defend oneself against a bad man! Yes, truly, it was necessary to engage *monssié*, and waste one's money!"

"But who could have taken the trouble to inform my father of my conduct? The general? He did not seem to care very much about me, and Ivan Kouzmitch had not considered it necessary to report my duel."

I was lost in surmises; my suspicion fell on Shvabrine. He alone could have benefited by such a denunciation, which might possibly have resulted in my removal from the fortress, and my separation from the commandant's family. I went to Maria Ivanovna to tell her all. She met me at the porch.

"What is the matter with you?" said she, on seeing me. "How pale you are!"

"Everything is at an end!" answered I, handing to her my father's letter.

It was now her turn to look pale. Having read it, she returned it with a trembling hand, and said in an agitated voice, "It is not my fate . . . . your parents do not wish to admit me into their family. God's will be done! He knows better what is good for us. There is no help for it; Piotr Andrevitch, may you at least be happy . . . ."

"It shall not be," exclaimed I, seizing her hand; "thou lovest me; I am prepared for everything. Let us go; let us kneel before thy parents; they are simple people, and not hardhearted and proud. . . . They will bless us, and we shall marry. . . . And then, in time, we shall, I feel certain, bend my father's will. My mother will be on our side—he will forgive me. . . ."

"No, Piotr Andrevitch," replied Masha, "I shall not marry thee without thy parents' blessing. Without thy parents' blessing, thou shalt have no happiness. Let us submit to God's will. Should'st thou find a bride, should'st thou love another—God be with thee, Piotr Andrevitch, and I shall pray for thee both. . . ."

Here she burst into tears and left me; I was about to follow her into the house, but felt that I was unable to master my emotion, so I returned home.

I sat in deep meditation, which was suddenly interrupted by Savelitch.

"Here, sir," said he, giving me a written sheet of paper; "see how I denounce my master, and how I try to set the father against the son."

I took the paper from his hand—it was Savelitch's answer to the letter he had received. Here it is, word for word:—

"ANDREY PETROVITCH, SIR, OUR MERCIFUL FATHER,

"I received your gracious writing, in which you deign to reproach me, your slave, for that I ought to be

ashamed not to obey my master's orders. I am not an
old cur, but your faithful servant, who obeys his master's
orders and has served him zealously up to his gray hairs.
I did not write anything about the wound of Piotr
Andrevitch, so as not to frighten you without cause, and I
hear that our mistress and mother, Avdotia Vassilievna,
has, as it is, taken to her bed from fear, and I shall pray
to God for her health. Piotr Andrevitch was wounded
below the right shoulder, in the breast just below the
rib, the wound being about half a *vershok** deep, and he
laid at the commandant's house, where we carried him
from the shore, and was attended to by the local barber,
Stepan Paramonoff, and now Piotr Andrevitch is, thank
God, well, and I have nothing to write of him but what
is good. The commandants are, I hear, satisfied with
him, and Vassilissa Yegorovna treats him as if he were
her own son. And that such an *occasion* did happen to
him, must not be reckoned as a reproach to the young
man—*a horse has four legs and yet he stumbles.* You
deign to write that you will send me to feed swine—I
submit if it is your lordship's will. Herewith I salute
you as a slave.

" Your faithful slave,

" ARHIPP SAVELITCH."

I could not help smiling occasionally whilst reading
the good old man's writing. I myself was not in a state
to answer my father's letter; I considered Savelitch's
sufficient for the purpose of tranquillizing my mother.

* A *vershok* = 1.75 English inch.—Tr.

From this period my position altered. Maria Ivanovna scarcely spoke to me, and tried to avoid me in every manner. The commandant's house became unendurable. Gradually, I accustomed myself to remain at home alone. Vassilissa Yegorovna reproached me for this, at first, but finding me obstinate, she left me in peace. I only saw Ivan Kouzmitch when on duty; Shvabrine I met seldom and reluctantly, the more so because I noticed his hidden dislike to me, which helped to confirm my suspicions. My existence became insupportable. I lapsed into a gloomy state of melancholy, fostered by my loneliness and inaction. This solitude intensified my love, which hourly became more burdensome to me. I lost all desire for reading and literature. My spirits sank. I feared lest I should either lose my reason, or abandon myself to dissolute habits. Unexpected events, which largely influenced my subsequent career, agitated my very soul violently and beneficially.

CHAPTER VI.

POUGATCHEFF.*

BEFORE entering on the account of the singular events

* Emilian Pougatcheff, a Cossack of the Don, who had served during the Seven Years' War in the armies of Russia, Prussia, and Austria ; returning to his own country, he incited a rebellion in 1773, assuming to be Peter III., who had been assassinated in 1762. Defeated on the banks of the Volga in 1774, and captured, he was beheaded at Moscow the following year.—Tr.

to which I was a witness, I must say a few words with respect to the conditions of the Government of Orenburg, at the close of the year 1773.

This vast and rich government was peopled by a large number of half-savage tribes, who had but recently acknowledged the supremacy of the Russian emperors. Their continual uprisings, their freedom from laws and a state of civilization, their levity and cruelty, necessitated constant watchfulness on the part of the government, in order to keep them in subjection. Fortresses were erected in suitable places, where Cossacks, who were the original possessors of the shores of the Yaïk, were permanently located. But the Cossacks of the Yaïk, whose duty it was to ensure the peace and safety of this territory, had for some time past become turbulent and dangerous subjects of the crown. In 1772 a tumult took place in their chief town. The cause of it originated in the severe measures adopted by Major-general Traubenberg to bring the troops into due submission. The result was, the barbarous murder of Traubenberg, a self-constituted change in the leadership, and finally, the suppression of the revolt by means of grape-shot and the infliction of cruel punishment.

This had happened shortly before my arrival at the fortress of Byĕlogorsk. Everything now was quiet, or appeared to be so. The authorities had too easily believed in the feigned repentance of the wily rebels, who were secretly nursing their hatred, and were only awaiting a fitting opportunity for the removal of disorders.

I return to my narrative.

Sitting alone one evening (this was in the beginning of October, 1773), I was listening to the whistling of the autumn wind, and looking through the window, watched the clouds which were passing rapidly across the moon. The commandant sent for me ; I instantly obeyed. I found Shvabrine, Ivan Ignatitch, and the Cossack orderly, assembled at his house. Neither Vassilissa Yegorovna nor Maria Ivanovna were in the room. The commandant saluted me in a disturbed manner. He closed the door, bid us all be seated, with the exception of the orderly, who remained standing, drew a paper from his pocket, and said, "Gentlemen, news of importacce! Listen to what the general writes." Here he put on his spectacles, and read as follows :

"TO THE COMMANDANT OF THE FORTRESS OF
BYELOGORSK,
"CAPTAIN MIRONOFF.
"*Confidential.*

"I herewith inform you that Emilian Pougatcheff, a Cossack of the Don, and a sectarian, has escaped from arrest, and having with unpardonable temerity assumed the name of the late Emperor Peter III., has gathered around him a band of wretches, has incited to sedition in the villages on the shores of the Yaïk, and has already taken and destroyed several fortresses, pillaging and massacring everywhere. You are therefore, captain, herewith commanded to adopt immediately, upon the receipt of this, the necessary measures for repelling the above-named wretch and pretender; and you are, if possible, to annihilate him entirely should he attempt to attack the fortress entrusted to your charge."

"To take the necessary measures !" said the commandant, removing his spectacles, and folding the paper. "It is very easy to say so. The rascal seems to be formidable, and we can only muster one hundred and thirty men, all told, without including the Cossacks, on whom we can scarcely rely; no offence meant, Maksymitch" (the orderly smiled). "However, let us be ready, gentlemen. Be on the alert, establish sentry posts and night rounds; in the event of an attack, shut the gates and assemble the soldiers. Thou, Maksymitch, must watch thy Cossacks closely. Let the gun be examined and properly cleaned. And above all things, let this be kept secret, so that no person in the fortress shall know anything about it before the time."

Having given these directions, Ivan Kouzmitch dismissed us. Shvabrine and I went away together, discussing what we had just heard.

" How dost thou think this will end ?" I asked.

" God knows," he answered; " we shall see. I see nothing alarming in all this as yet. But in case . . ."

Here he became thoughtful, absently whistling a French tune.

Nothwithstanding all our precautions, the news of Pougatcheff's appearance had spread in the fortress. Although Ivan Kouzmitch entertained the greatest respect for his wife, nothing on earth would have in-

duced him to confide to her a service report of a confidential nature. Upon receiving the general's letter, he
very cleverly disposed of Vassilissa Yegorovna, by telling
her that Father Gherassim had received astounding news
from Orenburg, which he mysteriously kept to himself.
Vassilissa Yegorovna immediately decided upon paying a
visit to the priest's wife, and acting upon the advice of
Ivan Kouzmitch, she took Masha with her, so that she
might not feel dull if left alone.

Ivan Kouzmitch left to himself, immediately sent for
us, having locked Paláshka up in the lumber-room to
prevent her from eavesdropping. ·

Vassilissa Yegorovna returned home without having
been able to gather anything from the priest's wife, and
learned that Ivan Kouzmitch had held a council of war
during her absence, Paláshka being in the meanwhile
locked up. Guessing that her husband had deceived her,
she commenced to question him. But Ivan Kouzmitch
was preparèd for the attack. He never lost his presence
of mind, and replied to the queries of his inquisitive helpmate courageously.

"You see, my little mother, our women here have
taken to light their stoves·with straw, and as an accident
may easily result, in consequence, I have given strict
orders that they shall henceforth be prohibited from doing
so, and that they should light their stoves with faggots
and brushwood."

"Then why didst thou lock up Paláshka?" asked the
commandant's wife. "For what offence did the poor girl
have to sit in the lumber-room until our return?"

Ivan Kouzmitch was not prepared for such a question. He got puzzled and muttered something incoherently. Persuaded of her husband's cunning, but knowing full well that she should learn nothing of him, Vassilissa Yegorovna ceased interrogating, and turned the conversation to salted cucumbers, which Akoulina Pamphylovna prepared in quite a peculiar manner. She could not sleep all night, unable to conceive what could possibly occupy her husband's mind, that she was not to know.

The next day, upon her return from mass, she saw Ivan Ignatitch busily engaged extracting from the gun the rags, pebbles, bits of wood, knuckle-bones, and all sorts of rubbish with which the children had crammed it.

" What can these warlike preparations mean ?" mused the commandant's wife. " Can it be possible that the Khirghis are expected to attack ? But is it likely that Ivan Kouzmitch conceals such trifles from me ?" She called Ivan Ignatitch, determined to coax out of him the secret which so tormented her female curiosity.

Vassilissa Yegorovna made some remarks having reference to housekeeping, like a judge who prefaces his interrogatory by putting irrelevant questions in order to throw the accused off his guard. After a momentary silence, she sighed deeply and said, shaking her head—

" Good God ! What news ! What will come of it ?"

" Well, my little mother!" answered Ivan Ignatitch, " God is merciful. We have a pretty good number of soldiers, plenty of powder, and I have cleaned out the gun. We may yet repulse Pougatcheff. *If God does not forsake us, the pig will not eat us !"**

"And what is this Pougatcheff like ?" asked the commandant's wife.

Here Ivan Ignatitch felt that he had betrayed himself, and stopped short. But it was too late. Vassilissa Yegorovna obliged him to confess everything, after having promised not to tell any one.

Vassilissa Yegorovna kept her word, and did not tell any one, except the priest's wife, and then she only did so because her cow was out grazing on the steppe, and might be carried off by the rascals.

Pougatcheff was soon in everybody's mouth. The rumours respecting him varied. The commandant despatched the orderly to the neighbouring villages and fortresses to gain all possible information about him. The orderly returned after a couple of days, and reported that he had seen, at a distance of about sixty versts from the fortress, a great many fires laid, and had heard from the Bashkirs that an innumerable host was advancing. He was not able, however, to affirm anything with certainty, for he was afraid to venture too far.

It was easy to notice the general excitement that prevailed among the Cossacks in the fortress ; forming themselves into little groups in the streets, they conversed in an undertone, and dispersed at the sight of a dragoon or of one of the soldiers. Spies were set on them. Youlaï, a baptized Kalmuck, made to the commandant an important disclosure. "The orderly's report,"

* Russian proverb.—Tr.

Youlaï said, "was false. On his return the stealthy Cossack had declared to his comrades that he had been with the rebels, had been conducted before their leader, who had given him his hand to kiss, and had conversed with him for a long time." The commandant immediately made a prisoner of the Cossack, and appointed Youlaï in his place. This news was received by the Cossacks with evident dissatisfaction. They murmured aloud, and Ivan Ignatitch, who carried the commandant's orders into execution, heard them say with his own ears : " Thou shalt catch it by-and-by, thou garrison rat !" It was the intention of the commandant to have interrogated the prisoner that very day; but the orderly had made his escape from confinement, probably by the aid of some accomplices.

A fresh occurrence increased the commandant's uneasiness. A Bashkir, upon whom were found seditious papers, had been seized. The commandant again deemed it necessary to assemble his officers, and again sought to get rid of Vassilissa Yegorovna under some plausible pretext. But being a straightforward and truthful man, Ivan Kouzmitch could think of no other plan but that to which he had already had recourse.

"Look here, Vassilissa Yegorovna," said he, coughing several times; "I am told that Father Gherassim has received from the town——"

"Leave off telling stories, Ivan Kouzmitch," interrupted his wife. "Thou art probably about to assemble a council to talk in my absence about Emilian Pougatcheff; but I shall not be taken in this time."

Ivan Kouzmitch stared at her.

"Well, my little mother," said he; "since thou dost know all about it, thou mayst remain; we shall talk it over in thy presence."

"That's it, my little father," she answered; "it is not for thee to be so sly; now, send for the officers."

We again met. Ivan Kouzmitch read to us in his wife's presence Pougatcheff's proclamation, written probably by some illiterate Cossack. The scoundrel declared it to be his intention to 'march on our fortress without delay; he invited the Cossacks and the soldiers to join his band, and advised the commandant not to resist, under pain of death. The proclamation was coarsely worded, but in strong terms, and would undoubtedly have produced a mischievous influence on simple-minded people.

"There's a blackguard!" exclaimed the commandant's wife. "What will he be demanding next? Does he require us to go out to meet him and lay the colours at his feet? Oh, the son of a dog! He does not know that we have served for forty years, and that, thank God, we have seen something during that time! Is it possible that there are commandants who have yielded to the rascals?"

"It should not be possible," answered Ivan Kouzmitch; "and yet I understand that the wretch has taken possession of many fortresses."

"He must indeed be strong," remarked Shvabrine.

"We shall soon know his real strength," said the commandant. "Vassilissa Yegorovna, give me the key of the store-room. Ivan Ignatitch, send the Bashkir here, and order Youlaï to bring the lash."

"Wait a bit, Ivan Kouzmitch," said the commandant's wife, rising. "Let me take Masha out of the house, or she will get frightened on hearing shrieks. And truth to tell, I myself am not fond of such investigations. Good-bye to you."

The system of torture was so deeply rooted in the administration of justice in the olden time, that the humane *ukase* which abolished it, remained disregarded for a considerable time. The prisoner's confession was considered indispensable, to establish his conviction, which is not only a false idea, but one also literally opposed to common sense in a judicial point of view; for if denial on the part of the culprit is not admissible as proof of his innocence, still less should his confession be accepted as evidence of guilt. Even at the present time do I occasionally hear old judges regret the abolition of that barbarous custom. But in those days no one doubted the absolute necessity for it; neither the judges nor yet the accused themselves. The commandant's orders, therefore, did not astonish or disquiet any of us. Ivan Igna-titch went for the Bashkir, who was locked up in the store-room, and in a few moments the prisoner was brought into the hall. The commandant directed that he should be conducted to his presence.

The Bashkir had some difficulty in stepping over the threshold (his feet were in stocks), and taking off his cap, he stood at the door. Looking up at him, I started. Never shall I forget that man. He appeared to be over seventy. He had no nose nor ears. His head was shaven; a few gray hairs on his chin replaced a beard; he was short, thin, and bent; but his narrow eyes sparkled like fire.

"Ah! ha!" said the commandant, having by these dreadful indications recognized one of the rebels who had been punished in 1741, "I see thou art an old wolf, who hast already been taken in our traps. It is not the first time thou playest the rebel, or thy head would not be so well shaven. Come nearer; speak; who sent thee?"

The old Bashkir remained silent and looked at the commandant with a vacant stare.

"Why dost thou not speak?" continued Ivan Kouzmitch. "Dost thou not understand Russian? Youlaï, ask him in your language, who sent him into our fortress?"

Youlaï repeated the question in Tartar. But the Bashkir looked at him with the same expression, not saying a word in reply.

"*Yashee!*"* said the commandant. "I shall make thee speak. Take off his fool's striped dressing-gown and pink his back. Youlaï, see that it is properly done."

Two invalids proceeded to strip the Bashkir. The unhappy man's face assumed an expression of anxiety. He looked about him like a poor little animal just caught by children. But when one of the invalids seized his hands, and putting them round his neck, lifted the old man on to his shoulders, and Youlaï took the lash and raised it then the Bashkir groaned in a feeble supplicating tone,

* Tartar for *good.*—Tr.

5

and, shaking his head, he opened his mouth, where, instead of his tongue, he moved a short stump.

When I call to mind that this has happened in my lifetime, and that I have lived to see the mild reign of the Emperor Alexander, I cannot but marvel at the rapid strides civilization has made, and at the diffusion of humane measures. Young man! should these pages fall into your hands, bear in mind that the best and most lasting reforms are those which emanate from the amelioration of morals without violent commotions.

We were all painfully overcome.

" Well," said the commandant, " I see we are not to expect anything from him; Youlaï, lead the Bashkir back to the store-room. And we, gentlemen, have still something to discuss."

We were beginning to consider our position, when Vassilissa Yegorovna rushed into the room breathless and agitated.

" What has happened ?" asked the astonished commandant.

" My little father—a calamity," answered Vassilissa Yegorovna. " The fortress of Nijneōzero has been taken this morning. Father Gherassim's workman has just returned from there. He saw them take it. The commandant and all the officers have been hanged. All the soldiers are made prisoners. The wretches will be here before one has time to turn."

This unexpected intelligence impressed me forcibly. I was acquainted with the commandant of the fortress of Nijneōzero, a quiet unassuming young man; he had been

with us two months previously on his way from Orenburg with his young wife, and had put up at the house
of Ivan Kouzmitch. The fortress of Nijncōzero was
twenty-five versts distant from us. We might expect
Pougatcheff's attack hourly. I vividly pictured to myself the fate of Maria Ivanovna, and my heart sank
within me.

"Listen, Ivan Kouzmitch," said I to the commandant,
"it is our duty to defend the fortress to our last breath;
nothing can be urged against this. But we must think
of the safety of the women. Send them to Orenburg if
the road is still free, or to a distant and safer fortress
where the wretches have not yet had time to penetrate."

Turning to his wife, Ivan Kouzmitch said : "See here,
my little mother, how would it do if you really went
away, until we have settled with the rebels ?"

"Oh, nonsense !" said the commandant's wife. "Where
is the fortress that is assured against bullets ? Why is
not Byělogorsk safe ? God be thanked, this is the
twenty-second year that we are in it. We have seen
Bashkirs and Khirghis; we may overcome Pougatcheff as
well !"

"Well, my little mother," reiterated Ivan Kouzmitch,
"thou mayest stay on, if thou puttest so much trust in
our fortress. But what are we to do with Masha? It
is well if we are victorious, or if we obtain relief in time;
but if the wretches capture the fortress ?"

"Well, in that case——"

Here Vassilissa Yegorovna became confused and stopped
short, greatly agitated.

"No, Vassilissa Yegorovna," continued the commandant, noticing that, perhaps for the first time in his life, his words had taken effect, " it is not fit that Masha should remain here. Let us send her to Orenburg to her godmother; enough guns and troops there, besides its stone walls. And I would advise thee also to go with her; although thou art an old woman, thou knowest not what may befall thee if the fortress should be carried by assault."

" Well," said the commandant's wife, " be it so. We shall send Masha. As to myself, do not think of asking me any more, for I shall not go. Why should I leave thee in my old age, and seek a lonely grave in a distant soil. We have lived together, we must die together."

" There is some sense in that," said the commandant. " But let us not delay. Go and prepare Masha for the journey. She shall leave at daylight to-morrow, and we shall even give her an escort, though in truth we can ill afford to spare our men. But where is Masha ?"

" With Akoulina Pamphylovna," answered his wife ; " she fainted when she heard that Nijneōzero had been captured. I fear that she may get ill. Good God ! that we should have come to this pass !"

Vassilissa Yegorovna went to prepare her daughter for her departure. The conference at the commandant's continued, but I no longer took a part in it, nor did I pay any further attention to it. Maria Ivanovna came to supper, looking pale, her face bearing traces of tears. We supped in silence, and rose from table earlier than usual ; having bid each other good-night, we separated.

But I had purposely forgotten my sword, and returned to fetch it; I had a presentiment that I should find Maria Ivanovna alone. Indeed, she met me at the door, and handed my sword to me.

"Good-bye, Piotr Andrevitch," said she, her eyes dim with tears; "I am sent away to Orenburg. May health and happiness attend you; perhaps, God willing, we may meet again, but if not——"

Here she broke into sobs. I embraced her.

"Good-bye, my angel," said I, "good-bye, my dear one. Happen what may to me, believe that my last thought, my last prayer, will be for thee!"

Masha wept on my breast. I kissed her passionately, and hurried out of the room.

CHAPTER VII.

THE ASSAULT.

I DID not sleep that night, nor indeed did I take off my clothes. It had been my intention to proceed at daylight to the gate of the fortress, at which Maria Ivanovna was to leave, and there bid her a last farewell. I felt that a great change had come over me; the agitation of my soul was far less painful to me than that depression which I had so recently experienced. An undefined but sweet sensation, the impatient expectation of danger and a noble ambition, were all mingled with my sorrow at parting. The night passed away imperceptibly. I was already about to leave the house, when my door was opened, and a corporal appeared, who reported that our Cossacks had fled during the night, carrying away Youlaï by force, and that strange people were seen riding around the fortress. The idea that Maria Ivanovna would not have time to leave, filled me with dread; I hurriedly gave the corporal some directions and hastened to the commandant's house.

It was already dawn. I was rapidly going down the street when I heard my name called out. I stopped.

"Where are you going to?" asked Ivan Ignatitch, overtaking me; "Ivan Kouzmitch is on the ramparts, and has sent me for you. *Pougatch** is come."

"Is Maria Ivanovna gone?" I asked, with heartfelt trepidation.

"She has not had time," answered Ivan Ignatitch; "the road to Orenburg is cut off; the fortress is surrounded. It is a bad business, Piotr Andrevitch!"

We mounted the rampart, an eminence of natural formation, and defended by a palisade. All the inhabitants of the fortress had already assembled there. The garrison stood under arms. The gun had been removed thither the previous day. The commandant was pacing in front of his small force. The approach of danger seemed to inspire the old warrior with extraordinary bravery. About twenty horsemen were scattered over the steppe within a short distance of the fortress. They appeared to be Cossacks, but there were also some Bash-

* *Pougatch, s.* a fright; a play upon the name of Pougatcheff. —Tr.

kirs among them, who were easily distinguished by their fur caps and quivers. The commandant walked round the lines exhorting the soldiers : " Come, boys, let us stand up for our mother empress to-day, and let us prove to the world that we are a brave and loyal people !"

The soldiers demonstrated their zeal by loud shouts. Shvabrine stood beside me, watching the enemy closely. On becoming aware of the movement in the fortress, the men we had seen on the steppe assembled in a cluster, and consulted with each other. The commandant ordered Ivan Ignatitch to lay the gun at the enemy, and himself applied the match. The ball whistled and flew past them without occasioning any harm. The horsemen separated and galloped out of sight, clearing the steppe.

At that moment, Vassilissa Yegorovna appeared on the rampart, accompanied by Masha, who was unwilling to quit her side.

" Well," asked the commandant's wife, " how does the battle progress ? Where is the enemy ?"

" The enemy is not far off," answered Ivan Kouzmitch; " please God all will be well. What, Masha, art thou afraid ?"

" No, papa," replied Maria Ivanovna; " I feel more frightened sitting at home."

She looked at me and made an effort to smile. I involuntarily grasped the hilt of my sword, remembering that I had received it from her own hands the night before, as if for the protection of the one I loved best. My heart burned within me ; I fancied myself her chosen knight. I longed to prove that I was worthy of her trust, and impatiently awaited the decisive moment.

Fresh troops of horsemen now appeared from behind an eminence half a verst off, and soon the steppe became covered with people armed with spears and cross-bows. Amongst them was a man in a red caftan, riding a white horse, and holding a drawn sword; it was Pougatcheff himself. He halted, and was at once surrounded, when four men, evidently carrying out his instruction, rode up to the fortress at full speed. We recognized our deserters. One held a sheet of paper high above his cap; another had Youlaï's head stuck on his lance, which he threw at us over the palisade. The head of the poor Kalmuck had rolled to the commandant's feet. The traitors shouted :

. "Do not fire! surrender to the emperor! The emperor is here!"

"I shall teach you!" cried Ivan Kouzmitch. "Boys, fire!"

Our soldiers fired. The Cossack who held the letter reeled and fell off his horse; the rest galloped back. I looked at Maria Ivanovna. Horrified at the sight of Youlaï's gory head, deafened by the discharge, she looked lifeless.

The commandant summoned a corporal, and ordered him to take the paper from the dead Cossack's hand. The corporal went and returned leading the horse of the fallen man by the bridle. He handed the letter to the commandant; Ivan Kouzmitch tore it to pieces after having silently read it. The rebels, however, were evidently preparing for action. Bullets soon began to hiss past our ears, and several arrows struck into the ground and the palisade near us.

"Vassilissa Yegorovna," said the commandant, "this is no place for women; take Masha away; thou seest the girl is half dead!"

Vassilissa Yegorovna, who had become meek under fire, cast a look at the steppe, on which a great movement was noticeable; then turning to her husband, she said:

"Ivan Kouzmitch, life and death are in God's hands; bless Masha. Masha, come to thy father."

Masha, pale and trembling, approached Ivan Kouzmitch, knelt down before him, and bowed herself to the earth. The old commandant made the sign of the cross over her three times; he then raised and kissed her, saying, in an altered voice:

"Be happy, Masha. Pray to God. He will not abandon thee. If thou should'st find a good man, may God bless your attachment. Live together as thy mother and I have lived. Well, good-bye, Masha; Vassilissa Yegorovna, lead her away quickly."

Masha threw herself on his neck, weeping.

"Kiss me also," said the commandant's wife, bursting into tears; "good-bye, my own Ivan Kouzmitch. Forgive me if ever I have displeased thee in anything."

"Good-bye, good-bye, my little mother!" said the commandant, embracing his old companion. "That will do! Go home quickly, and if thou canst find time, dress Masha in a *sarafan*."*

The commandant's wife and daughter left. I watched the retreating Masha; she looked round and nodded to me. Ivan Kouzmitch now turned to us, and all his attention became concentrated on the enemy. The rebels gathered around their chief, and suddenly dismounted.

"Stand fast now," said the commandant, "they are about to attack——"

Dreadful shouts and shrieks followed; the rebels were running at the fortress. Our gun was loaded with grape. The commandant allowed them to approach, and fired again. The shot had taken effect in the midst of the crowd. The rebels divided, and fell back a little. Their leader alone remained in the front. He was waving his sword, and appeared to be encouraging his men with energy. The shouts and shrieks which had ceased for but a moment, were renewed.

"Now then, boys," said the commandant, "open the gates, beat the drum. Advance! follow me!"

The commandant, Ivan Ignatitch, and I were in an instant without the palisade; but the terrified garrison did not stir.

"Why do you stand there, boys?" shouted Ivan Kouzmitch. "If we are to die, let us die. Our duty requires it."

The rebels rushed at us, and invaded the fortress. The drum ceased. The garrison dropped its arms. I was

* The costume of female peasants, in which the girl might be disguised.—Tr.

knocked off my legs, but I rose to my feet again, and followed the rebels into the fortress. The commandant, who was wounded in the head, was surrounded by the wretches, who demanded the keys of him. I was about to rush to his succour, but was seized by a few lusty Cossacks, who bound my hands with their belts, saying:

"Stop a bit, you will catch it by-and-by, you traitors to the emperor!"

We were dragged into the streets. The inhabitants had come out of their houses, carrying bread and salt.* The bells began to peal. A loud voice in the crowd announced that the emperor was awaiting the prisoners in the square, prepared to receive their oaths of allegiance. The mob rushed to the square; we were also led thither.

Pougatcheff sat in an arm-chair in the porch of the commandant's house. He wore a handsome Cossack *caftan*,† richly braided. The high sable hat, from which hung a golden tassel, came down to his sparkling eyes. I fancied I knew his face. He was surrounded by Cossack chiefs. Near the porch, pale and trembling, cross in hand, as if silently interceding on behalf of the victims which were to be, stood Father Gherassim. A gibbet was being hurriedly erected in the square. At our approach the Bashkirs quickly dispersed the crowd, and we were led before Pougatcheff. The ringing of bells had ceased; deep silence reigned.

"Which is the commandant?" asked the Pretender.

---

* A peace offering.—Tr.
† A long coat, worn by the lower classes.—Tr.

Our orderly stepped to the front, from the crowd, and pointed to Ivan Kouzmitch. Pougatcheff looked sternly at the old man, and said :

"How didst thou dare to oppose me ; *me*, thy emperor ?"

The commandant, weakened by his wound, summoned his failing strength, and replied in a firm voice :

" Thou art not my emperor ; thou art a robber and a usurper, that is what thou art !"

Pougatcheff frowned gloomily, and waved a white kerchief. Several Cossacks seized the old captain, and dragged him to the gibbet. Astride the cross beam, was the mulilated Bashkir, whom we had examined the previous day. He was holding the rope, and in another minute I saw poor Ivan Kouzmitch dangling in the air. Ivan Ignatitch was next led before Pougatcheff.

"Swear allegiance," said Pougatcheff, "to the emperor Piotr Feodorovitch !"*

"Thou art not our emperor," replied Ivan Ignatitch, repeating his captain's words ; "thou, uncle, art a robber and a usurper !"

Pougatcheff again waved the kerchief, and the kind-hearted sub-lieutenant was hanged by the side of his old chief.

My turn had come. I looked boldly at Pougatcheff, prepared to repeat the answer given by my brave com-

* Peter, son of Feodor ; Peter III. was son of Anna, daughter of Peter the Great, by Charles Frederick, Duke of Holstein-Gottorp. The name of Frederick does not exist in the Russian calender, and is substituted by Feodor (Theodore).—Tr.

rades, when, to my indescribable astonishment, I saw amongst the rebel heads Shvabrine, with his hair evenly cut round, and wearing a Cossack *caftan*. He approached Pougatcheff, and whispered a few words to him.

" Let him be hanged !" said.Pougatcheff, without looking at me.

A noose was thrown around my neck; I silently repeated a prayer, bringing sincere repentance for all my sins before God, and imploring the salvation of all dear to me. I was hurried to the gibbet.

" Do not fear—do not fear," repeated my executioners; perhaps really seeking to encourage me.

Suddenly I heard a cry; " Hold on, you cursed fellows ! —hold on !"

The executioners paused. I looked back. Savelitch lay at Pougatcheff's feet.

" My father !" my poor servant was saying, " of what use can the death of that gentleman's child be to thee ? Let him go ; thou canst obtain a ransom for him ; and, if thou dost want to make an example, and inspire fear, then let me, an old man, be hanged !"

Pougatcheff made a sign, my bonds were loosened, and I was set free.

" Our father pardons thee," was said to me.

I could not at that moment declare that I was overjoyed at my deliverance, though I did not regret it. My sensations were too confused. I was again conducted to the Pretender, and made to kneel before him. Pougatcheff extended his veined hand towards me.

" Kiss his hand—kiss his hand !" everybody repeated.

I should have preferred the most violent of deaths to such abject humiliation.

" My little father, Piotr Andrevitch," whispered Savelitch, who stood behind, nudging me, " do not be obstinate! What does it cost thee? Spit, and kiss the rob—— (tfu!) Kiss his hand!"

I did not move. Pougatcheff dropped his hand, saying, with a sneer—

" His lordship would appear to have become foolish through joy. Raise him."

I was raised, and let go. I looked on at the continuation of this horrible cruelty.

The inhabitants were being sworn in. They approached one by one, kissed the crucifix, and bowed before the Pretender. The soldiers of the garrison followed. The regimental tailor, armed with his blunt scissors, cut off their queues. They gave their heads a shake, kissed Pougatcheft's hand, who extended to them his pardon, and enlisted them in his army. This continued for three hours. At last Pougatcheff rose and left the porch, accompanied by his chiefs. A white horse, richly caparisoned, was led to him. Two Cossacks seized him under the arms and lifted him into the saddle. He informed Father Gherassim that he would dine with him. At that moment a woman's shriek was heard. Several of the scoundrels had dragged Vassilissa Yegorovna, dishevelled and almost stripped, into the porch. One of them had already managed to put on himself her *dooshegreyka.** Others were drawing after them feather-

---

* " Soul-warmer," a coat lined with fur, worn by females.—Tr.

beds, boxes, the tea-service, linen, and all sorts of things.

"Oh, my little fathers!" cried the poor old' woman, "have pity on me, my fathers; let me go to Ivan Kouzmitch." She looked at the gibbet, and recognized her husband. "Wretches!" she exclaimed, distracted, "what have you done to him? My light, my Ivan Kouzmitch, brave soldier's heart! The bayonets of the Prussians did not touch thee, neither did the Turkish bullets; thou hast not laid down thy life in an honourable fight—thou hast perished at the hands of an escaped convict——"

"Let the old witch be quieted!" said Pougatcheff.

A young Cossack struck her on the head with his sabre, and she fell dead on the house-steps. Pougatcheff rode away, the crowd rushing after him.

CHAPTER VIII.

THE UNINVITED GUEST.

THE square became deserted. I remained on the same spot, unable to collect my thoughts, disturbed as they had been by such terrible events. The uncertainty of Maria Ivanovna's fate tortured me most. Where was she? What had happened to her? Had she had time to conceal herself? Was her refuge a safe one? Filled with anxiety, I entered the commandant's house. It was empty; chairs, tables, boxes, were all destroyed; the

crockery lay broken; everything was strewn about. I
ran up the little stair which led to Maria Ivanovna's
room, and entered it for the first time. I saw her bed,
which the villains had searched; the cupboard had been
broken open and robbed of its contents. The lamp was
still burning before the empty *kyoott.** A little mirror
hanging on the wall had also remained uninjured.
Where was the mistress of the simple, virginal chamber ?
A fearful thought flashed across me: I fancied her in the
hands of the robbers. My heart ached. I burst into
bitter, bitter tears, and called aloud the name of my beloved one. I heard a slight noise, and Paláshka, pale
and trembling, issued from behind the cupboard.

"Ah! Piotr Androvitch!" said she, raising her arms.
"What a day! what horrors——"

"And Maria Ivanovna," I asked, impatiently; "what
about Maria Ivanovna ?"

"The young lady is alive," answered Paláshka. "She
is hiding at Akoulina Pamphylovna's."

"At the priest's house!" exclaimed I with terror.
"My God! Pougatcheff is there."

I rushed out of the room, reached the street in an instant, and hastened, regardless of everything, to the
priest's house. Noises, laughter, and songs issued from
it. Pougatcheff was feasting with his companions.
Paláshka had followed me. I bid her send Akoulina
Pamphylovna to me secretly. In a few minutes the

---

* A glass case made to contain images, and thus becoming a
shrine.—Tr.

priest's wife came out to the lobby, with an empty bottle in her hand.

"For God's sake where is Maria Ivanovna?" I asked, with indescribable agitation.

"My poor little dove is lying on my bed, behind the partition," answered the priest's wife. "Ah! Piotr Andrevitch, we have had a narrow escape; but, thank God, all has gone off well: the wretch was just about to sit down to dinner, when she, poor thing, coming to herself, groaned. I felt a chill all over. He heard it. 'Who is it moaning there, old woman?' I bowed down low before the thief: 'My niece, sire, has been taken ill, and has been laid up a fortnight.'—'And is thy niece young?'—'Yes, sire.'—'Then let me see thy niece, old woman.' My heart leapt within me; but what could I do? 'Welcome, sire; only the girl is not able to rise and come before your grace.'—'Never mind old woman; I shall go to her myself!' And he did go behind the partition, the d—d rascal! what dost thou think of that? He drew aside the curtain, looked in with his vulture's eyes—and that was all! God was with us. Wilt thou believe me, the Father and I were quite prepared to suffer a martyr's death? Fortunately, my little dove did not recognize him. Oh! Lord God, what a day we have lived to see! Poor Ivan Kouzmitch!—who would have believed it! And Vassilissa Yegorovna! and Ivan Ignatitch!—what had he done? How is it that you escaped? And what do you say of Shvabrine? He has had his hair cut, and here he is now, feasting with them! He has been sharp about it, I must say. And when I happened to mention

6

my sick niece, wilt thou believe it, he looked daggers at me ? However, he did not betray me ; let us thank him even for so much."

Drunken shouts and the voice of Father Gherassim reached our ears. The guests were clamouring for wine, the host was calling after his helpmate. The priest's wife fidgeted.

"Go home, Piotr Andrevitch," said she. "I have no time to think about you just now ; we must entertain the wretches. Harm may befall you, if you get into their drunken hands. Good-bye, Piotr Andrevitch ; what is to be, will be. Let us hope that God will not forsake us."

She left me. I returned home, my anxiety being slightly relieved. Passing by the square, I saw several Bashkirs gathered at the foot of the gallows, and drawing the boots off the corpses that were hanging ; I restrained, with difficulty, an outburst of indignation, feeling that any interference on my part would have been useless. The fortress was in the possession of the robbers, who were plundering the officers' houses. In all directions were heard the shouts of the tipsy rebels. I reached home. Savelitch met me at the threshold.

"God be praised !" exclaimed he, on seeing me. "I began to think that the wretches had again got hold of thee. Well, my little father, Piotr Andrevitch ! Canst thou believe it ! the rascals have plundered us of every-thing—clothes, linen, crockery—nothing is left to us. But that does not matter ! Thank God that they let thee off with thy life! Well, sir, and hast thou recognized the ataman ?"*

" No, I have not. Who is he ?"

" How, sir ? hast thou forgotten the drunkard who coaxed the *touloup* out of thee at the inn ? The little bran new hare-skin *touloup;* and he, the beast, split it by forcing himself into it !"

I was amazed. Indeed the resemblance between Pougatcheff and my guide was startling. I became convinced that Pougatcheff and he were the same persons, and was now able to understand why I had been dealt with so mercifully. I could not but marvel at the circumstances so strongly linked together—a boy's *touloup,* made a present of to a vagabond, had saved me from the noose, and a drunkard who had hung about wayside inns, was now besieging fortresses, and shaking the empire !

" Wilt thou take something to eat ?" asked Savelitch, unchanged in his habits. "There is nothing at home. I shall go out, and if I can find something, it shall be got ready for thee."

Left alone, I gave myself up to reflection. What was there for me to do ? To remain in a fortress that had fallen into the power of the wretch, or to join his band, was equally impossible for an officer. Duty bade me go where I might still be of service to my country in the present embarrassing circumstances. . . . But my attachment urged me strenuously to stay near Maria Ivanovna to be her protector and guardian. And although I fore-

---

* Cossack chieftain.—Tr.

saw a speedy and inevitable change in these circumstances, still, I could not rid myself of a feeling of alarm,
when I considered the danger of her situation.

My reflections were interrupted by the entrance of a
Cossack, who had come with the announcement that the
great emperor required me to appear before him.

" Where is he ?" I asked, preparing to obey.

" In the commandant's house," answered the Cossack.
" After dinner our father went to take a bath, and now,
he is having his rest. Well, your lordship, everything
proves that he is an important personage. At dinner he
deigned to eat up two roasted sucking pigs, and he bore
the hot steam so well, that even Tarass Koúrotchkine
could not stand it, being obliged to give the birch broom
to Tomka Bichbayeff, and only recovered from its effects
after having a quantity of cold water thrown over him.
It is impossible not to admit that all his ways are very
grand. And I was told that in the bath-room he showed
the marks of a Tzar on his breasts—on one side he has
the two-headed eagle of the size of a *pyaláck,** and on
the other he has the likeness of his own person."

I did not think it necessary to dispute the point with
the Cossack, so I followed him to the commandant's
house, endeavouring to imagine beforehand, my interview
with Pougatcheff, and wondering how it would end. My
reader will easily understand that I did not feel perfectly
indifferent to its result.

It was getting dusk when I approached the command-

* Five copeck piece.—Tr.

ant's house. The gibbet with its victims loomed hideously
in the dark. The body of the poor captain's wife was
still lying in the porch, in front of which two Cossacks
stood on sentry. The Cossack by whom I had been
escorted went to announce me, and returning immediately,
conducted me into the room, where, on the previous
day, I had taken such an affectionate leave of Maria
Ivanovna.

A strange spectacle presented itself. Pougatcheff and
the Cossack chiefs in coloured shirts and caps, their red
faces heated by wine, their eyes glittering, sat at a table,
which was covered with a cloth, and laden with bottles
and tumblers. · Shvabrine and our orderly, those newly-
sworn traitors, were not of the number.

" Ah ! your lordship !" said Pougatcheff, on seeing me·
" You are welcome ; honour and placd to you."

The guests made room for me. I took my seat in
silence at the end of the table. My neighbour, a young
Cossack, slight and handsome, poured me out a glass of
wine ; which, however, I did not touch. I scanned the
assembly with curiosity. Pougatcheff sat at the post of
honour, leaning on the table, and supporting his black
bearded chin with his broad fist. His regular and almost
agreeable features had nothing of cruelty about them.
He frequently turned towards a man of about fifty, now
addressing him as count, then Tymofeitch, and sometimes
uncle. Everybody seemed to treat his neighbour as a
comrade, and none showed any special respect to their
leader. They conversed on the assault of that morning,
of the success of the rebellion, and of their future plans of

action. Each boasted of his own doings, offered his opinion, and freely contradicted Pougatcheff. And it was at this extraordinary council of war, that it was decided to attack Orenburg—a bold move, which was very nearly being crowned by a fatal success! The march was fixed for the morrow.

"Well, boys!" said Pougatcheff, "let us sing before we retire for the night, my favourite song. Tchoumakoff, begin!"

My neighbour began the sorrowful song in a small shrill voice, the rest joining in the chorus—

> " Do not murmur green wood, my mother !
> Do not hinder me from thinking my thoughts.
> To-morrow, I must hie me to judgment
> Before a fierce judge, before the Tzar himself.

> " The Lord Tzar will ask of me ;
> ' Tell me, tell me, thou child, thou peasant's son,
> With whom hast thou thieved, with whom hast thou robbed.
> Hast thou many associates ?'
> ' I shall tell thee, my hope, my Orthodox Tzar,
> The whole truth shall I tell thee the whole verity,
> That I have but four associates.
> That my first associate, is the dark night,
> That my second associate, the steel blade,
> And my third associate, my good steed,
> And my fourth associate, my mighty bow ;
> That my messengers are red hot arrows.'
> What will my hope, the Orthodox Tzar say !
> ' Well done ! thou child, thou peasant's son ;
> Thou hast known how to steal, thou hast known how to reply.
> I shall make thee a gift, child,
> Of a lofty palace in the midst of the field
> A palace of two posts, and a cross beam.' "

It is scarcely possible to convey an idea of the impression produced upon me by this popular song, with the gallows for its subject, sung as it was by people destined for them. Their ferocious looks, their ringing voices, the dismal tone in which these sufficiently expressive words were sounded, all filled me with a sort of undefined terror.

The revellers drained another glass, and then rose and took leave of Pougatcheff. I was about to follow out after them, but Pougatcheff said—

" Stay, I have to speak to thee."

We remained alone. We were silent for some minutes. Pougatcheff watched me, now and then closing his left eye with an extraordinary expression of roguery and derision. At last he burst into such a genuine merry laugh, that, as I looked at him, I also laughed, without knowing why.

" Well, your lordship !" said he, " thou wast frightened —admit it, when my boys threw the rope round thy neck ? I suppose the sky must have appeared to thee of the size of a sheepskin. . . . And thou would'st have swung from the cross-beam, had it not been for thy servant. I recognized the old owl immediately. Well, sir, could'st thou have supposed that the man who guided thee to the inn, was the great emperor himself ?" (here he assumed an important and mysterious air). " Thou art very guilty towards me," he continued ; " but I showed thee mercy for thy good deed, for thou didst me a service at a time when I was forced to hide myself from my enemies. But this is not all ! I shall show thee greater favour when I recover my empire. Dost thou promise to serve me zealously ?"

The rogue's question and his impudence appeared to me so amusing, that I could not repress a smile.

"What art thou laughing at ?" asked he, frowning. "Or is it thou dost not believe that I am the great emperor ? Answer me frankly."

I was perplexed. I could not acknowledge the vagabond as being the emperor; it would have been unpardonable cowardice. To call him an imposter to his face, would have been to expose myself to destruction, and to utter what I had been prepared to say at the first outburst of indignation in sight of the gallows, and in the presence of the multitude, would have amounted to vain bragging. I hesitated. Pougatcheff awaited my reply in stern silence. At last (and I think of that moment with self-satisfaction to this day), a sense of duty triumphed over human weakness. I said to Pougatcheff—

"Listen! Shall I tell thee the whole truth ? Just reflect whether it is possible for me to acknowledge thee as the emperor. Thou art a reasonable being; thou thyself would'st know that I was shamming."

"Who am I then, according to thy opinion ?"

"God knows; but whoever thou mayest be, thou playest a dangerous game."

Pougatcheff threw a quick glance at me.

"Then thou dost not believe," said he, "that I am the Emperor Piotr Feodorovitch? Very well! But is there

no success for the daring? Did not Grishka Otrepieff*
reign in days gone by? Think what thou pleasest of me,
but do not leave me. What does it matter to thee?
Who is not a priest is a father. Serve me 'in faith and
in truth' and I shall make thee a field-marshal and prince.
What dost thou think of this?"

"No," I answered, firmly. "I am a nobleman by birth.
I swore to serve the empress; I cannot serve thee. If
thou really wishest me well, permit me to go to Orenburg."

Pougatcheff reflected.

"And if I do let thee go," said he, "dost thou at least
promise not to take up arms against me."

"How can I promise thee so much?" I replied. "Thou
thyself knowest that it cannot be as I wish. If I receive
orders to march against thee, I must do so; I cannot help
myself. Thou art now a chief thyself; thou exactest
obedience of thy people. What would it look like, should
I refuse to serve when called upon to do so? My life is
in thy hands; if thou lettest me free, thou shalt have my
thanks; if thou executest me, God is thy judge; as to
myself, I have told thee the truth."

Pougatcheff was struck by my sincerity.

"Be it so," he said, slapping me on the shoulder; "one
must either execute or fully pardon. Go—the four

---

* Gregory Otrepieff, a runaway monk of Ischoudoff, was the
first of the impostors who personated Dmitri V., son of John the
Terrible, put to death in his infancy by Boris Godounoff, 1591.
Supported by Sigismund II., King of Poland, he overthrew Boris,
and reigned at Moscow in 1605. His marriage to a Pole and a
Catholic, led to his massacre by the multitude in 1606.—Tr.

quarters are open to thee, and do as seemeth thee best. Come and bid me good-bye to-morrow, and now get thee to bed, for sleep also oppresses me."

I left Pougatcheff and emerged into the street. The night was still and frosty. The moon and stars shone brightly, illuminating the square and the gallows. All was quiet and dark within the fortress. In the public-house only were there lights, whence issued the shouts of lingering idlers. I looked up at the priest's house. The shutters were closed, everything appeared quiet there.

Entering my lodging, I found Savelitch bewailing my absence. The news of my having been set at liberty, rejoiced him greatly.

"God be praised!" said he, crossing himself. "We must leave the fortress as soon as it is day, and follow whither luck leads us. I have prepared some food for thee, my little father; thou must then go to bed and sleep till morning, safe as in Christ's bosom."

I followed his advice, and, having supped heartily, fell asleep on the naked floor, worn out morally and physically.

CHAPTER IX.

THE SEPARATION.

I WAS awakened at an early hour by the beat of the drum. I proceeded to the place of assembly. Pougatcheff's mob was already mustering in the vicinity of the gallows, from which yesterday's victims were still suspended. The Cossacks were on horseback, the foot soldiers under arms. The standards were unfurled. Several guns, among which I noticed our own, had been mounted on field carriages. The inhabitants had also assembled in expectation of the Pretender. At the porch of the commandant's house stood a Cossack, holding a beautiful white horse of the Khirghis breed by the bridle. I looked for the body of the commandant's wife. It had been moved a little on one side, and covered with a piece of matting. Pougatcheff appeared. The crowd uncovered. Pougatcheff stopped in the doorway and saluted it. One of the chiefs handed to him a bagful of coppers, which he scattered in handfuls. The people rushed in a noisy scuffle to pick them up. Pougatcheff was surrounded by his principal accomplices. Shvabrine was one of the number. Our eyes met; he probably read contempt in mine, for he turned away with a look of genuine malice, and feigned derision. Perceiving me in the crowd, Pougatcheff nodded his head, and beckoned me to come to him.

"Listen," said he; "go at once to Orenburg, and tell the governor and all the generals that they are to expect me in a week. Recommend them to welcome me with childlike love and obedience; otherwise, they shall not escape a cruel death. A happy journey to you, your lordship!" Turning to the people, and pointing to Shvabrine, he said: "Here, my children, is your new commander. Obey him always; he is responsible for you and for the fortress."

I heard these words with horror. Once in command of the fortress, Maria Ivanovna was in his power! My God! what would become of her? Pougatcheff descended the steps. The horse was led to him. He flung himself quickly into the saddle, before the Cossacks who were in attendance had time to assist him.

Of a sudden, my Savelitch stepped out of the crowd, approached Pougatcheff, and handed to him a sheet of paper. I could not conceive what it was all about.

"What is this?" asked Pougatcheff, with dignity.

"If thou wilt but read, thou shalt know," replied Savelitch.

Pougatcheff took the paper and examined it for a long time, with a significant air.

"Why dost thou write so elaborately?" he inquired at last. "Our bright eyes are able to decipher nothing of this.* Where is my chief secretary?"

A young man, in a corporal's uniform, was quickly at Pougatcheff's side. "Read aloud," said the Pretender, giving him the paper. I felt very curious to know what my servant had found to write to Pougatcheff about. The chief secretary spelled out in a stentorian voice, the following:—

"'Two dressing gowns, one of cotton, the other of striped silk; value six roubles.'"

"What does this mean?" said Pougatcheff, frowning.

"Order him to read on," replied Savelitch, quietly.

The chief secretary proceeded:—

* *Il ne sait ni lire, ni écrire, mais c'est un homme extrêmement hardi et déterminé.*—Catherine II. to Voltaire, 22 October, 1774.

" ' A uniform coat of fine green cloth, value 7 roubles.

" ' White cloth trousers . . „ 5 roubles.

" ' Twelve shirts of Dutch linen, with ruffles, 10 roubles.

" ' A case containing a tea service „ 2½ roubles.' "

" What rubbish !" interrupted Pougatcheff. " What do I care about tea cases and trousers with ruffles !"

Savelitch cleared his throat, and proceeded to explain.

" Deign to understand, my little father, that it is an inventory of the gentleman's property, stolen by the wretches . . ."

" What wretches ?" said Pougatcheff, angrily.

" I beg your pardon, a slip of the tongue," replied Savelitch. " The wretches are not wretches ; but thy boys have, for all that, rummaged and plundered. Do not get angry : *a horse has four legs, and yet he stumbles.* Now order him to read on."

" Read to the end," said Pougatcheff.

The secretary continued :—

" ' One cotton counterpane, another of wadded silk, value 4 roubles.

" ' A fox fur pelisse, covered with red ratteen, value 40 roubles.

" ' Also, a hare-skin *touloup*, given to thy grace at the wayside inn, value 15 roubles.' "

" What is that ?" exclaimed Pougatcheff, with fire in his eyes.

I felt alarmed for the safety of my poor servant. He was about to resume his explanations, but Pougatcheff interrupted him.

"How dost thou dare to come to me with such rubbish as this!" he exclaimed, tearing the paper out of the secretary's hands, and throwing it in Savelitch's face. "Stupid old man! you have been plundered—what a great misfortune! Know, old owl, that you must pray to God unceasingly for me and my boys, for that thou and thy master are not hanging up there by the side of the rebels. . . Hare *touloup!* dost thou not know that I might have thee skinned alive, to make *touloups* of ?"

"As thou pleasest," answered Savelitch; "but I am not a free man, and must give an account of my master's property."

Pougatcheff was evidently in a generous mood. He turned and rode away, without adding another word. Shvabrine and the chiefs followed him. The forces left the fortress in military order. The crowd rushed out to escort Pougatcheff. I and Savelitch only remained in the square. He was holding his inventory, which he looked at regretfully.

Sensible of the good understanding existing between Pougatcheff and myself, he thought of turning it to advantage; but his ingenuity was ill rewarded. I was about to scold him for his misplaced zeal, but had some difficulty in suppressing my laughter.

"Laugh, sir," said Savelitch, "laugh; we shall see whether it is a laughing matter when we have to provide a new outfit."

I hurried away to the priest's house, to see Maria Ivanovna. The priest's wife met me with a sad announcement. Maria Ivanovna had been attacked during the night with a violent fever. She lay unconscious and delirious. Conducted to her room, I gently approached her bed. I was alarmed at her altered appearance. She did not recognize me! I stood and looked at her for a long time, regardless of Father Gherassim and of his good-natured wife, both of whom endeavoured to comfort me. I was agitated by gloomy thoughts. The condition of the poor, unprotected orphan, in the midst of lawless rebels, and my own helplessness in her behalf, terrified me. But Shvabrine, Shvabrine it was that most tormented me. Invested with authority by the Pretender, in command of the fortress where the unhappy girl, the innocent object of his hatred, would be left—he was capable of doing anything. Of what avail was I? What assistance could I render? How was I to free her from the villain's power? There was but one way; I decided upon going to Orenburg immediately, with the object of hastening and co-operating in the recovery of the fortress of Byĕlogorsk. I bid the priest and Akoulina Pamphylovna farewell, eagerly entrusting to their charge, her whom I already looked upon as my wife. I seized the poor girl's hand, my tears flowing fast as I kissed it.

"Good-bye," said the priest's wife, accompanying me to the door, "good-bye, Piotr Andrevitch. We must hope to meet in better times. Do not forget us, and mind you write often. Poor Maria Ivanovna has no one left now but yourself to protect her."

Returning to the square, I stopped an instant to look up at the gibbet, and inclined my head before it, then leaving the fortress, took the Orenburg road, accompanied by Savelitch.

I was walking on in deep meditation, when suddenly I heard behind me the tramping of a horse. I looked back A Cossack, galloping out of the fortress, and leading a Bashkir horse, was making signs to me. I awaited him, and soon recognized our orderly. Riding up to me, he dismounted, and handing over the bridle of the other horse, he said :—

" Your lordship! our father makes you a present of a horse, and of a pelisse off his own back " (a sheepskin *touloup* was secured to the saddle), " also . . . . . ." muttered hesitatingly the orderly, " he also sends you . . . . half a rouble, ... but I have lost it on the way : I entreat that you will generously forgive me."

Savelitch looked askance at him, and murmured :—

" Lost on the way! And what is it that jingles in thy breast ? thou shameless fellow !"

" What jingles in my breast ?" said the orderly, not in the least abashed : " God be with thee, little old man ! It is the bridle that jingles, and not the half rouble."

" Very well," I said, interrupting the altercation ; " thank him who sent thee, in my name; try to find the lost money on thy way back, and keep it for a *vodka.*"

" Much obliged to you, your lordship," he answered, turning his horse's head : " I shall ever pray to God for you."

So saying, he galloped back, keeping one hand inside his breast, and in a few minutes was out of sight.

I put on the *touloup,* and mounted the horse, Savelitch getting up behind.

"There, sir," said the old man, "dost thou not see that I have not uselessly bowed down before the rascal? Thief though he be, he has felt somewhat ashamed, although this huge Bashkir nag and the sheepskin *touloup* are not worth one half of what the vagabonds have stolen, and what thou thyself hadst given him; and yet they may prove of service, *even a few hairs off a vicious dog!*"

CHAPTER X.

THE SIEGE.

As we approached Orenburg, we passed a crowd of convicts with shaven heads, and faces disfigured by the tongs of the executioner. They were at work on the fortifications, under an escort of garrison invalids. Some were employed carting away the rubbish which filled the ditch, others, with spades, digging the earth; on the ramparts were masons carrying bricks and repairing the walls. We were stopped by the sentries at the gate, who demanded our passports. Upon hearing that I had come from the fortress of Byĕlogorsk, the sergeant conducted me straight to the general's residence.

I found him in the garden. He was examining the apple-trees which had been ripped by the blasts of autumn, and, assisted by his gardener, was carefully enveloping them in straw. His countenance was serene,

7

good-natured, and healthy. He was delighted to see me, and proceeded to make inquiries respecting the lamentable events of which I had been a witness. I related all to him. The old man listened with attention, removing meanwhile the dead branches.

"Poor Mironoff!" said he, when I had ended my sad recital; "what a pity! He was a good officer, and Madame Mironoff was a good lady, and so clever at salting mushrooms! And what about Masha, the captain's little daughter?"

I replied that she remained at the fortress in charge of the priest's wife.

"Ay, ay, ay!" observed the general, "that's bad, very bad. One cannot possibly rely on the discipline of the robbers. What will become of the poor girl?"

I replied that Byĕlogorsk, being at no great distance, his excellency would probably not delay in sending troops for the relief of its poor inhabitants.

The general shook his head, doubtfully; "We shall see, we shall see," said he. "We shall have time enough to talk it over. I beg you will do me the favour to come and take a cup of tea. I hold a council of war to-day. You will be able to give us correct information about the miscreant Pougatcheff and his army. In the meantime, go and rest."

I repaired to the rooms assigned to me, where I found Savelitch already engaged putting things in order, and I impatiently awaited the appointed time. The reader will easily understand that I did not fail to appear at the council which was to have such an influence on my

future career. I proceeded to the general's, at the hour
fixed. There I found one of the civil authorities of the
town, if I remember aright, the Director of Customs, a
stout, red-faced, little old man, in a watered silk *caftan*.
He questioned me regarding the fate of Ivan Kouzmitch,
whom he called his *koum*, and frequently interrupted me
with extraneous questions, and moral reflections, which
if they did not prove him to be a man versed in military
matters, at least evinced his natural intellect and sagacity.
The other members soon assembled. After having taken
our places, and the tea having been handed round, the
general laid before us very distinctly, and in detail, the
state of affairs.

"Now, gentlemen," he continued, "we must decide our
course of action towards the rebels : the *defensive* or the
offensive ? Both modes have their advantages and dis-
advantages. To act on the offensive offers greater chances
for the speedy destruction of the enemy ; to remain on
the defensive is surer and safer. . . . . Therefore, let
us put it to the vote in legal order, that is to say, beginning with the juniors. Ensign !" he continued, turning
to me, "pray give us your opinion."

I rose, and after having in a few words described
Pougatcheff and his band, confidently affirmed that
the Pretender had no means of withstanding regular
forces.

My opinion was received by the members with evident
dissatisfaction. In their judgment it was the rash and
impertinent notion of a young man. In the muttering
which ensued, I distinctly overheard the word "green-

horn " pronounced in a whisper. The general turned to me, and said with a smile,

"Ensign ! the first votes at councils of war are usually given in favour of offensive measures: that is the usual procedure. Let us now continue to collect other votes. *Kallejsky Savetnik,** tell us your opinion."

The little old man in the watered silk *caftan* quickly emptied his third cup of tea, mixed with a fair proportion of rum, and replied:—

"My opinion, your excellency, is, that we must act neither defensively nor offensively."

"How is that, *Kallejsky Savetnik?*" reiterated the astonished general. "Military tactics offer no alternative ; action must be either defensive or offensive . . . ."

"Your excellency ! try subornation."

"Eh! Eh ! your opinion is a very reasonable one Subornation is allowable in military tactics, and we may take advantage of your advice. We shall be able to offer for the miscreant's head . . . . seventy, or even one hundred roubles, ... from the secret fund . . . ."

" And," interrupted the Director of Customs, "may I, in that case, be a Khirghis ram, and not a *Kallejsky Savetnik*, if those robbers do not deliver up to us their leader, bound hand and foot ?"

" We must reflect and talk it over," answered the general; " in any case, however, we must adopt military measures. Gentlemen, give your votes in legal order."

Every opinion was opposed to mine. All the officials

* Conseiller de Collége. An employé of the sixth class.—Tr.

urged the little reliance to be placed in the troops, the uncertainty of success, and the necessity for prudence, and the like. All concurred in its being more reasonable to remain under cover of guns inside strong stone walls, than to try the fortune of war on the open field. Having heard every opinion to the end, the general shook the ashes from his pipe, and pronounced the following speech :—

"Gentlemen! I must declare to you, that so far as I am concerned, I am quite of the ensign's opinion; for that opinion is founded on all the rules of wholesome tactics, which invariably give the preference to offensive over defensive action."

Here he stopped, and proceeded to fill his pipe. I felt triumphant in my vanity. I looked proudly at the officials, who whispered to each other, and looked displeased and anxious.

"But, gentlemen," he continued, emitting a thick cloud of tobacco smoke with a deep sigh, "I dare not take upon myself so great a responsibility, considering that the safety of the province intrusted to me by her imperial majesty, my gracious sovereign, is at stake. I therefore cede to the majority, which has decided that it is more prudent and safer to await the siege within the city walls, and to repel the attacks of the enemy by the force of artillery, and (if it be possible) to discomfit them also by sorties."

It was now the turn of the officials to look ironically at me. The council ended, I could not help lamenting the weakness of the worthy warrior, who, in spite of his own convictions, allowed himself to be influenced by the opinions of ignorant and inexperienced men.

A few days after this remarkable council had been held, we received intelligence that Pougatcheff, true to his word, was approaching Orenburg. I espied the rebel army from the city walls. Its number seemed to have increased tenfold since the last assault, which I had witnessed. The enemy also had the pieces of artillery, which Pougatcheff had captured from the small fortresses he had subdued. Bearing in mind the decision of the council, I foresaw a long confinement within the walls of Orenburg, and almost cried with vexation.

I shall not describe the siege of Orenburg, which belongs to history, and not to notes of a private nature. I shall briefly observe that this siege, owing to the imprudence of the local authorities, became fatal to the inhabitants, who suffered hunger and every misery imaginable. It will be readily understood that life at Orenburg became most unbearable. Everybody sorrow-fully awaited the decision of his destiny; lamentations were universal by reason of the dearth, which was really terrible. The people were beginning to get accustomed to the shells, which flew into their court-yards; even the assaults of Pougatcheff ceased to attract general attention. I felt bored to death. Time sped on, I received no letter from the fortress of Byëlogorsk. All the roads were cut off. My separation from Maria Ivanovna was becoming unendurable. My only recreation consisted in warlike sallies. Thanks to Pougatcheff, I had a good horse with which I shared my scant portion of food, and on which I rode out daily to exchange a few shots with Pougatcheff's archers. The advantage in these encounters remained generally with the wretches who were tipsy, well fed, and well mounted. Our miserable cavalry could not withstand them. Our famished infantry would occasionally go out, but the deep snow impeded their movements, and rendered their evolutions against the scattered horsemen ineffectual. The artillery on the ramparts thundered in vain, and when on the field, it was unable to advance, owing to the extenuated condition of the horses. This was our mode of action. And this was what the Orenburg officials termed prudence and sound judgment.

Having upon one occasion succeeded in dispersing a goodly mass of the enemy, I rode up to a Cossack who had remained behind, and was about to cut him down with my Turkish sabre, when he suddenly took off his cap, and shouted,

. " Good-day, Piotr Andrevitch; how do you do ?"

'I looked at him, and recognized our orderly. I felt unspeakably rejoiced to see him.

"Good-day, Maksymitch," said I; "how long is it since thou hast left Byělogorsk ?"

" Not long, Piotr Andrevitch, I returned only yesterday. I have a letter for you."

" Where is it ?" I exclaimed, agitated.

"I have it here," replied Maksymitch, putting his hand in his bosom. "I promised Paláshka that I should let you have it somehow."

He handed to me a folded paper, and instantly galloped

away. I opened it, and read with trepidation the following lines :—

"It has pleased God to deprive me suddenly of my father and mother : I have no relations nor any protectors on earth. I have recourse to you, knowing that you have always been my well-wisher, and that you are prepared to assist everybody. I pray to God that this letter may reach you. Maksymitch has promised to deliver it to you. Paláshka has heard from Maksymitch that he often sees you at a distance in the sorties, and that you do not take the least care of yourself, and do not think of those who pray with tears for you. I was ill a long time; and when I got well, Aleksey Ivanovitch, who commands here instead of my late father, forced Father Gherassim to deliver me to him, threatening him with Pougatcheff's displeasure. I live in our own house a prisoner. Aleksey Ivanovitch wants to force me to marry him. He says he saved my life by keeping up Akoulina Pamphylovna's deception, who told the wretches that I was her neice. But I would rather die than become the wife of such a man as Aleksey Ivanovitch. He treats me very cruelly, and threatens, should I not change my mind and consent, to take me into the wretches' camp, where, he says, the fate of Elisaveta Harloff awaits me. I have begged of Aleksey Ivanovitch to give me time to think over it, and he has consented to wait three days longer; but if I do not marry him at the end of the three days, I am to expect no pity. My little father, Piotr Ardrevitch, you are my only protector; save me, poor girl. Entreat the general and all the chiefs to lead help to us as soon as possible, and come yourself, if you can. I remain your devoted and poor orphan,

"MARIA MIRONOFF."

I almost lost my senses on reading this letter. I rode off into the town, spurring my poor horse unmercifully. On the way I thought of one plan and then of another, for the liberation of the unhappy girl, without being able to come to any decision. Reaching the town, I went straight to the general's, and rushed into his room.

The general was pacing it to and fro, smoking his meerschaum pipe. He stopped on seeing me. He was probably startled at my appearance, for he asked, with concern, the object of my over-hasty visit.

"Your excellency," I said, "I come to you, as I would to my own father; for God's sake do not reject my supplication: my life-long happiness is at stake."

"What is it?" asked the old man, astonished. "What can I do for thee? Speak!"

"Your excellency! order me to take a battalion of troops and fifty Cossacks, and let me clear out the fortress of Byĕlogorsk."

The general looked fixedly at me, thinking probably that I had lost my reason (in which he was not entirely mistaken).

"What do you say? clear out the fortress of Byĕlogorsk?" said he, at last.

"I answer for success," I continued, with warmth; "only let me go."

"No, young man," said he, shaking his head; "at so great a distance the enemy might easily cut you off from communication with the chief strategical point, and obtain a complete victory over you. The intercepted communications . . . ."

I became alarmed when I perceived that he was about to enter into deliberations of a military character, and hastened to interrupt him.

"The daughter of Captain Mironoff," said I, "writes a letter to me; she asks for help; Shvabrine forces her to marry him."

"Indeed! Oh! that Shvabrine is a great rascal, and if he falls into my hands, I shall order him to be tried within twenty-four hours, and he will be shot on the rampart of the fortress! but, until then, we must have patience . . . ."

"Have patience!" I exclaimed, beside myself; "and in the meanwhile he will marry Maria Ivanovna!"

"Oh!" reiterated the general, "there is no great harm in that; it is better she should be Shvabrine's wife in the meanwhile; he will thus be able to protect her, and when he is shot, why, then, please God, we shall find a bridegroom for her. Pretty little widows do not long remain single; at least, what I mean to say is, that a young widow will sooner find a husband than would a young girl."

"I should sooner consent to die," I said, enraged, "than cede her to Shvabrine."

"Bah! bah! bah! Ha!" said the old man. "Now I understand; thou art evidently in love with Maria Ivanovna. Oh! that is another affair! Poor fellow; but for all that, I cannot possibly give thee a battalion of troops and fifty Cossacks. Such an expedition would be injudicious, and I cannot possibly take the responsibility upon myself."

I bowed. I was seized with despair. A sudden thought flashed in my mind. What it was my reader will learn in the following chapter, as old novel writers say.

CHAPTER XI.

THE REBEL CAMP.

I LEFT the general and hurried to my lodgings. Savelitch met me with his usual admonition: "What pleasure canst thou find, sir, in conferring with the tipsy robbers? Is it a gentlemanly occupation? All times are not alike; thou shalt perish heedlessly. Well, it would be different if thou foughtest against the Turk or the Swede; but just now, it is a sin even to name who the enemy is."

I interrupted him by asking how much money I had altogether.

"Enough for thee," he answered, with a satisfied air. "However well the robbers searched for it, still I managed to conceal it." With these words he pulled out of his pocket a long knitted purse full of silver.

"Well, Savelitch," I said, "give me one-half and take the rest thyself. I go to the fortress of Byëlogorsk."

"My little father, Piotr Andrevitch," said the good servant, in a trembling voice; "do not tempt God! How art thou to travel now, when all the roads are blocked up by these robbers ? Have pity upon thy parents, if thou hast none for thyself. Where dost thou want to go to? What for ? Wait a short time; the troops will soon be here and capture the rascals, then thou mayest go wherever thou pleasest."

But my resolution was not to be shaken.

"It is too late now for reflection," said I to the old man. "I must go. I cannot help going. Do not grieve, Savelitch : God is merciful, we may meet again. Do not scruple to make use of the money, and do not stint thyself. Buy whatever thou mayest need, even if the price be risen threefold. I make thee a present of the money. If I do not return within three days . . . ."

"What dost thou say, sir ?" interrupted Savelitch ; "dost thou think it possible that I should let thee go alone ? No; do not expect such a thing, even in thy dream. If thou hast really decided upon going, I shall follow thee even on foot. I shall not desert thee ! 'That I should sit behind a stone wall without thee.' Dost thou think me mad ? No, sir, I shall not remain behind."

I knew that it was useless to argue the point with Savelitch, and allowed him to prepare for the journey. In half an hour I had mounted my good horse, and Savelitch a lean lame nag which one of the inhabitants had given him *gratis*, not having the means left wherewith to keep it. We reached the town gates ; the sentries allowed us to pass, and we rode out of Orenburg. It was getting dark. My road lay past the village of Berd, Pougatcheff's retreat. The high road was snowed over, but the tracks of horses' hoofs, daily renewed, were

visible over the whole steppe. I rode at a quick trot,
Savelitch could hardly follow me, and was continually
shouting—

"Slower! for God's sake slower! My cursed little nag
cannot keep up with thy long-legged imp. Where is
the hurry? Well enough if we were going to a feast!
As it is, we are making for the edge of the axe. . . .
Piotr Andrevitch. . . . My little father, Piotr Andrevitch!
. . . Good God! the master's child is going to perdition."

The fires of Berd were sparkling before us. We neared
the deep ditches, the natural fortifications of the village.
Savelitch kept up with me, continuing, however, his
pitiful supplications without intermission. I was hoping
to go round the village without an accident, when
suddenly I perceived in front of me in the dark, five
mujiks armed with clubs—they were Pougatcheff's
advanced sentinels. We were hailed. Not knowing the
pass-word, I meant to ride by in silence; but they
instantly surrounded me, and one of them seized the
bridle of my horse. I drew my sabre, and struck the
mujik over the head; his cap saved him, but he staggered
and let go the bridle. The others, becoming confused,
made off. I took advantage of this, and, putting spurs to
my horse, gallopped onwards.

The ever-increasing darkness might have ensured me
from all danger, but, upon looking behind, I perceived
that Savelitch was not with me. The poor old man on
his lame horse, was unable to effect his escape out of the
hands of the robbers. What was to be done? Having
waited some few moments, and become persuaded that

he had been detained, I turned to deliver him. As I approached the ditch, I heard a noise in the distance— shouts and Savelitch's voice. Hurrying on, I soon found myself again in the midst of the *mujiks* on guard, who had stopped me a few minutes previously. Savelitch was amongst them. They threw themselves upon me with loud cries, and dragged me off my horse in an instant. One of them, evidently the man in charge, declared that he would take us before the emperor immediately.

" And our father is free to order," he added, " whether you are to be hanged at once, or whether you are to await God's daylight."

I offered no resistance. Savelitch followed my example, and the sentinels led us away in triumph.

We crossed the ditches and entered the village. Fires were burning in all the huts. Shouts and noises resounded everywhere. I met a crowd in the streets; but no one noticed us in the dark, nor was I recognized as being an officer from Orenburg. We were taken straight to a hut, which stood at a crossing. In front of it were several wine casks and two cannon.

" Here is the palace," said one of the *mujiks*. " I shall announce you at once."

He entered the hut. I looked at Savelitch; the old man was crossing himself, and muttering a prayer. I had to wait a long time; at last the *mujik* returned, and said to me—

" Go in, our father has ordered the officer to be admitted."

I entered the hut, or the palace as the *mujiks* had called it. It was lit up by two tallow candles, and its walls were covered with gilt paper; with this exception, the benches, the table, the wash-hand basin suspended by a cord, the towel hanging on a nail, the oven-fork in the corner, and the broad shelf upon which stood flower-pots, all was the same as in an ordinary hut. Pougatcheff sat under the holy images, in a red *caftan*, a high cap, his arms akimbo, looking remarkably important. By his side stood several of his chief companions, with an assumed air of servility. It was evident that the news of the arrival of an officer from Orenburg had excited great curiosity among the rebels, and that they were preparing to receive me pompously. Pougatcheff recognized me at first sight. His assumed look of importance disappeared at once.

"Ah! your lordship!" said he, quickly. "How art thou? Why has God brought thee here?"

I replied that I was riding past on private affairs, and that his men stopped me.

"What affairs?" he asked.

I did not know what answer to make.

Concluding that I did not wish to enter into explanations in the presence of witnesses, Pougatcheff turned to his comrades, and ordered them out. All obeyed with the exception of two, who did not stir.

"Thou canst speak boldly before them," said Pougatcheff. "I do not conceal anything from them."

I looked askance at the pretender's confidants. One, a

thin and bent old man, with a small gray beard, had nothing remarkable about him, excepting a blue ribbon which he wore over his gray coat across his shoulder. But I shall never forget his fellow. He was tall, powerful, and broad-shouldered, and appeared to be about five-and-forty. His thick red beard, his gray sparkling eyes, his nose without nostrils, and the red spots on his forehead and cheeks, gave his pock-marked broad face an indefinable expression. He wore a red shirt, a Khirghis dressing gown, and Cossack trowsers. The first (as I afterwards learned), was the deserter, Corporal Byělobaródoff; the second, Aphanasy Sakaloff (surnamed *Hlopousha*), a banished convict, who had escaped from the mines of Siberia on three different occasions. The society I so unexpectedly found myself in, for a time diverted my thoughts from the feelings that exclusively agitated me. But Pougatcheff's question recalled me to myself.

"Speak; upon what business hast thou left Orenburg?"

A strange thought struck me. I fancied that Providence, which for the second time had confronted me with Pougatcheff, was affording me the opportunity of carrying out my intentions. I decided upon taking advantage of this, and without giving myself time for reflection, I answered Pougatcheff's question.

"I go to the fortress of Byělogorsk, to free a poor insulted orphan."

Pougatcheff's eyes flashed.

"Who of my people has dared to offend the orphan?" he cried. "Were his forehead seven spans high, he shall not escape my judgment. Speak! who is the guilty one?"

"Shvabrine," answered I. "He keeps in confinement the girl which thou sawest sick at the priest's home, and wishes to force her to marry him."

"I shall teach Shvabrine!" said Pougatcheff, sternly. "He will learn what comes of indulging his own fancies, and oppressing my people. I shall hang him."

"Let me have a word to say," said Hlopousha, in a hoarse voice. "Thou wert in too much haste, when thou didst appoint Shvabrine commandant of the fortress, and now thou art equally in a hurry to hang him. Thou hast already offended the Cossacks by nominating a nobleman to be their chief; do not offend the noblemen in like manner, by executing them on the first accusation!"

"There is no necessity for having pity on them, and for showing them mercy," said the old man with the blue ribbon. "There is no harm in hanging Shvabrine; but it would be just as well to question this officer further. Why has he come? If he does not acknowledge thee to be his emperor, he has no right to seek justice at thy hands; and if he does acknowledge thee, why has he then up to this day remained at Orenburg with thy enemies? Wilt thou not order me to take him into the office and light a fire there? I begin to suspect that his grace is sent over to us by the Orenburg commanders."

The old wretch's logic struck me as being very convincing. A cold shiver ran through me as I thought of the hands into which I had fallen. Pougatcheff noticed my perturbation; "Well, your lordship," said he with a

8

sneer, "the field-marshal is, I fancy, stating the truth. What dost thou think ?"

At Pougatcheff's sneer, my courage returned. I answered quietly, that I was in his power, and that he might do with me as he thought proper.

"Very well," said Pougatcheff. "Now, tell me; in what condition is your town ?"

"Thank God," I answered, "all is well."

"Well!" repeated Pougatcheff; "and the people dying of starvation ?"

The pretender was speaking the truth; but, bound by my allegiance, I kept assuring him that all such were empty rumours, and that Orenburg was well supplied with all sorts of provisions.

"Thou seest," quickly observed the little old man, "that he deceives thee to thy face. All the deserters affirm unanimously that hunger and the plague are at Orenburg, that the people eat carrion, and even that is an honoured dish ; and his grace assures thee that they have enough of everything. If thou wilt hang Shvabrine, thou mayest as well hang this fellow on the same gallows, to prevent either of them from feeling envious."

The cursed old man's words seemed to shake Pougatcheff. Fortunately Hlopousha began to cavil with his companion.

"Be quiet, Naoumitch," said he; "thou only thinkest of strangling and stabbing. What sort of a hero art thou ? One has but to look at thee to wonder what holds thy soul and body together! Thou art with a foot in the grave thyself, and wouldst cause others to perish. Hast thou not enough blood on thy conscience yet?"

"And thou, what kind of saint art thou? reiterated Byĕlobaródoff. "Where hast thou taken thy pity from?"

"Of course," answered Hlopousha, "I am also a sinner, and this hand" (here he clenched his bony hand, and turning up his sleeve showed his hairy arm) "also is guilty of having shed Christian blood. But I slew my enemy and not my guest; on the free highway and in the dark wood, and not at home, behind the stove; with the mace and the axe, and not with old women's tales."

The old man turned away and muttered the words: "Cut nostrils! . . . ."

"What is it thou art whispering there, old owl?" exclaimed Hlopousha. "Cut nostrils; mayest thou get them; thy turn is to come; please God thou also shalt have a smell at the tongs. . . . . But till then, take care lest I pluck out thy ugly beard!"

"Generals!" said Pougatcheff with dignity: "leave off quarrelling. It would be no great misfortune if all the Orenburg curs were to dangle from the same cross-beam; but it would be a misfortune if our dogs were to eat each other up. There now, make it up."

Hlopousha and Byĕlobaródoff said not a word, and scowled at each other. I felt the absolute necessity for changing the conversation, which might have ended very disadvantageously, so far as I was concerned, and turning to Pougatcheff, I said cheerfully:—

"Ah! I was very nearly forgetting to thank thee for the horse and the *touloup*. But for thee I would never have

8—2

reached the town, and should have been frozen to death by the way."

My bait took. Pougatcheff brightened up.

"*A debt is rendered honourable by payment,*" said he, with a wink. "Tell me now, what is the girl, whom Shvabrine has offended, to thee? Is thy heart perchance caught, young man? Eh?"

"She is my affianced bride," I replied, seeing that the sky had cleared, and that there was no necessity for concealing the truth.

"Thy affianced bride!" exclaimed Pougatcheff. "Then why didst thou not say so before? We shall assist thee to get married, and shall feast at thy wedding!" Then, turning to Byĕlobarόdoff: "Listen, field-marshal! His lordship and I are old friends. Let us sit down to supper; *the morning will bring wiser counsels.* We shall consider what is to be done."

I would gladly have declined the proffered honour; but there was no help for it. Two young Cossack women, the daughters of the proprietor of the *isba,** spread a white cloth, placed a loaf of bread, a dish of *ouha,†* and several bottles of wine and beer on the table, and I found myself for the second time at the same board with Pougatcheff and his terrible comrades.

The orgies, of which I was an involuntary witness, continued until late at night. At last a state of intoxication began to overpower the revellers. Pougatcheff dozed in his chair; his companions rose and made me a sign to

* Cottage.—Tr.   † A fish-soup.—Tr.

leave him. We went out together. By Hlopousha's arrangements, the sentry led me into the office, where I found Savelitch, and where I was locked up with him. Savelitch was so wonder-struck at all that was happening, that he never asked a single question. He lay down in the dark, and sighed and groaned for a long time; he then began to snore, and I gave myself over to reflections, which kept me awake throughout the night.

The next morning Pougatcheff sent for me. I went to him. His *kibitka*, to which a *troika* of Tartar horses was harnessed, stood ready at the gate. The streets were crowded with people. I met Pougatcheff in the passage; he was dressed for a journey, in a pelisse and Khirghis cap. His companions of the previous day surrounded him, assuming an appearance of servility—a strong contrast to all I had witnessed overnight. Pougatcheff welcomed me cheerfully, and directed me to sit by his side in the *kibitka*.

We took our places. "To the fortress of Byëlogorsk," said Pougatcheff to the broad-shouldered Tartar who, in a standing position, drove the *troika*. My heart beat fast. The horses started, the bells tinkled, our *kibitka* flew. . . .

"Stop! stop!" cried a voice I knew too well, and I saw Savelitch running towards us. Pougatcheff ordered the *yemstchick* to pull up. "My little father, Piotr Andrevitch," cried my servant; "do not leave me in my old age amongst these ras . . . ."

"Ah! it is thou, old owl!" said Pougatcheff. "God

has brought us together again. All right; jump up behind."

"Thank you, sire, thank you, my father!" Savelitch repeated, taking his seat. "May God grant thee health for a hundred years, because thou hast looked down upon me, old man that I am, and hast comforted me. I shall ever pray for thee, and shall never even mention the hare-skin *touloup* again."

This hare-skin *touloup* might have seriously angered Pougatcheff in the end. Fortunately the pretender either did not hear, or pretended not to hear the misplaced allusion. The horses were again off. The people in the streets stopped as we passed, and bowed low. Pougatcheff nodded to them on both sides. In a few minutes we were out of the village, and hurrying along the level road.

It is easy to imagine what my feelings were at that moment. In a few hours I was to see her whom I had already considered as lost to me. I pictured to myself our re-union; I also thought of the man upon whom my fate depended, and who, by a curious chain of circumstances, was so mysteriously connected with me. I recalled to mind the hasty cruelty, the bloodthirsty habits of him who had constituted himself the deliverer of the one I loved. Pougatcheff was not aware that she was Captain Mironoff's daughter; the enraged Shvabrine was capable of revealing all to him; Pougatcheff might also discover the truth from other sources. . . . . What would then befall Maria Ivanovna? I felt a cold tremor, and my hair stood on end. . . . .

Suddenly Pougatcheff interrupted my meditations, turning to me with the question :—

"What is it that makes your lordship thoughtful?"

"How am I not to be thoughtful?" I answered. "I am an officer and a nobleman; but yesterday I fought against·thee, and to-day I drive with thee in the same *kibitka*, and the happiness of my life depends upon thee."

"Well, what then?" asked Pougatcheff. "Art thou afraid?"

I replied, that having once been spared by him, I counted, not only upon his forbearance, but upon his assistance.

"And thou art right; by God thou art right!" said the pretender. "Thou sawest that my boys looked askance at thee; and the old man has insisted, even this day, upon thy being a spy, and that thou should'st be tortured and hanged; but I would not consent," he added, lowering his voice, so as not to be overheard by Savelitch and the Tartar; "for I recollected thy glass of wine and thy *touloup*. Thou seest I am not yet such a bloodsucker as thy people make me out to be."

I remembered the taking of the fortress of Byĕlogorsk, but did not think it necessary to contradict him, and did not answer a word. "What do they say of me at Orenburg?" asked Pougatcheff, after a short pause.

"Why, they say that thou art difficult to manage; and in truth, thou hast given us work to do."

The pretender's face expressed that his vanity was satisfied.

"Yes!" said he with a pleased look; "I am a good one to fight. Have they heard at Orenburg of the battle of Youzeiff? Forty generals killed, four armies made captive.

What thinkest thou ?   Will the Prussian king be able to withstand me ?"

The robber's bragging amused me.

"What dost thou thyself think," said I; "wouldst thou be able to stand up against Frederick ?"

"With Feodor Feodorovitch ?* and why not ?   Don't I manage your generals, and they have beaten him ?   Up to the present time, my arms have been successful.   Give me but time, and thou wilt see still other things, when I advance upon Moscow."

"And so thou thinkest of advancing upon Moscow ?" The pretender reflected for a moment, and then said in a low tone of voice :—

"God knows.   My road is narrow, my will is limited. My boys have too much to say; they are scoundrels.   I must keep my ears open; at the first mishap they will buy off their necks with my head."

"Just so !" said I to Pougatcheff.   "Would it not be better if thou wert thyself to leave them, whilst it is yet time, and throw thyself on the clemency of the empress ?"

Pougatcheff smiled a bitter smile.

"No," he replied, "it is too late for repentance.   There, can be no mercy for me.   I shall continue as I have begun.   Who knows ?   I may yet succeed !   Did not Grishka Otrepieff reign over Moscow ?"

"But dost thou know what his end was ?   He was pitched out of a window, killed, burned, and his ashes were blown away from a gun !"

* Name given to Frederick the Great, by the Russian soldiers.—Tr.

"Listen," said Pougatcheff, with a sort of wild inspiration. "I shall narrate to thee a tale which was told me by an old Kalmuck woman in my childhood. Once upon a time, an eagle inquired of a raven: 'Tell me, raven, why dost thou live three hundred years in this bright world, and I only thirty-three years in all?' 'Because, my little father,' answered the raven, 'thou drinkest living blood, and I feed off carrion.' The eagle thought: 'Well, let us try to feed upon the same.' So the eagle and the raven flew away. Suddenly they spied the carcass of a horse. They let themselves down upon it. The raven began to peck and to extol it. The eagle pecked once, pecked twice, flapped his wings, and said to the raven: 'No, brother raven, 'tis better to drink the living blood once, than to feed for three hundred years upon carrion; and trust to God for the rest!' What sayest thou to the Kalmuck tale?"

"It is ingenious," I answered. "But to live by murder and plunder is, according to my views, to peck at carrion."

Pougatcheff looked at me with astonishment, and made no reply. We became silent, each absorbed in his own meditations. The Tartar struck up a doleful song. Savelitch was nodding sleepily in the rumble. The *kibitka* flew over the smooth wintry road. . . . Of a sudden I perceived a small village on the steep banks of the Yaïk, encircled by a palisade, and showing a church steeple; a quarter of an hour later, we drove into the fortress of Byĕlogorsk.

CHAPTER XII.

THE ORPHAN.

OUR *kibitka* stopped at the commandant's house. The people had recognized the sound of Pougatcheff's bells, and came out in a throng to meet him. Shvabrine received the pretender at the very threshold. He wore a Cossack uniform, and had allowed his beard to grow. The traitor helped Pougatcheff to alight with fawning demonstrations of joy and zeal. He looked confused upon seeing me, but soon recovered himself and stretched out his hand, saying:—

"And thou also art one of us? That's right. It should have been so long ago!"

I turned away without making any reply.

My heart ached when I found myself in the old familiar room where the late commandant's commission still hung from the wall, a sad epitaph on times gone by. Pougatcheff seated himself on the sofa where Ivan Kouzmitch used to doze, lulled to sleep by his consort's grumbling Shvabrine himself carried a glass of *vodka* to him. Pougatcheff drank it off, and said, pointing to me:—

"Offer some to his lordship as well."

Shvabrine approached me with the tray; but I turned away from him a second time. He did not look like himself. With his usual perspicacity, he could not have failed to observe Pougatcheff's displeasure. He quailed before him, and looked at me mistrustfully. Pougatcheff made inquiries as to the condition of the fortress, as to the prevalent rumours in regard to the enemy, and such like, when suddenly and unexpectedly he asked :—

"Tell me, my little brother, who is the girl thou holdest here imprisoned ? Let me see her."

Shvabrine turned deadly pale.

"Sire," said he in a trembling voice, ... "Sire, she is not imprisoned . . . . she is ill . . . . she is in bed."

"Lead me to her chamber then," said the pretender, rising. Refusal was impossible. Shvabrine conducted Pougatcheff to Maria Ivanovna's room. I followed them.

Shvabrine stopped on the staircase.

"Sire !" said he, "you have it in your power to demand whatever you please of me, but do not permit a stranger to enter my wife's bedroom."

I shook all over.

"Then thou art married !" said I to Shvabrine, prepared to tear him to pieces.

"Silence !" interrupted Pougatcheff, "that is my business. As to thee," he continued, addressing Shvabrine, "I will have no subtilty and no shamming : she may be thy wife or not, but I take who I please into her room. Your lordship, follow me."

Shvabrine again stopped when we had reached the bedroom door, and said falteringly :

"Sire, I warn you, she is in a high state of fever and has been delirious these three days."

"Open the door," said Pougatcheff.

Shvabrine searched his pockets and said he had forgotten the key. Pougatcheff kicked the door, the lock gave way, the door flew open, and we entered.

On looking about me, I felt ready to faint. On the floor sat Maria Ivanovna, clad in a peasant's dress, pale, haggard, and dishevelled. A jug of water, covered with a lump of bread, was by her side. On seeing me she started and screamed. I cannot express what my feelings were. . . .

Pougatcheff looked at Shvabrine, and said with a bitter sneer :

" Thy hospital is not bad !" He then approached Maria Ivanovna. " Tell me, my little dove, why does thy husband punish thee ? How hast thou wronged him ?"

" Husband !" she repeated. " He is not my husband. I shall never be his wife ! I prefer to die, and I shall die, if I am not rescued."

Pougatcheff looked at Shvabrine menacingly.

" And thou hast dared to deceive me !" said he. " Dost thou know, thou good for nothing, what thou deservest ?"

Shvabrine dropped on his knees. . . . At such a sight, contempt overcame every feeling of hatred and wrath within me. I looked with loathing upon the nobleman who was writhing at the feet of a Cossack deserter. Pougatcheff relented.

" I pardon thee this time," said he to Shvabrine ; " but know that the first time thou offendest, this also will be reckoned against thee." He then turned to Maria Ivanovna, and said to her kindly : " Come away, my pretty girl ; I grant thee thy freedom. I am the Tzar."

Maria Ivanovna threw a quick glance at him, and guessed that it was the murderer of her parents who stood before her. She covered her face with her hands, and fell senseless to the floor. I rushed to her side; at that moment my old acquaintance Paláshka slipped boldly into the room, and began to busy herself about her mistress. Pougatcheff left the chamber, and we three descended into the sitting-room.

" Well, your lordship," said Pougatcheff, laughing, " now that we have freed the pretty girl, what dost thou think of our sending for the priest to marry his niece ? I shall give her away if thou wishest; Shvabrine will be the best man; we shall feast, and drink, and shut the gates !"

What I had so much dreaded now came to pass. On hearing Pougatcheff's proposal, Shvabrine quite lost his head.

" Sire !" he exclaimed, enraged; " I am guilty, I have lied to you ; but Griueff also is deceiving you. This girl is not the priest's niece ; she is the daughter of Ivan Mironoff, who was executed at the taking of the fortress."

Pougatcheff fixed his fiery eyes on me.

" What does this mean ?" he asked, perplexed.

" Shvabrine has told thee the truth," I answered with firmness.

" Thou didst not tell me of this," observed Pougatcheff, whose face clouded over.

" Judge thyself," I replied; " how could one, in the presence of thy people, declare that Mironoff's daughter

was in existence ?   They would have torn her to pieces!
Nothing could have saved her !"

" Thou art right again," said Pougatcheff, laughing.
" My drunkards would not have spared the poor girl.
The priest's wife has done well to deceive them."

" Listen," said I, upon seeing how well-disposed he
appeared to be. " I do not know, and do not wish to
know, by what name I am to address thee. . . . But God
is my witness, that I should be happy to pay thee with
my life for what thou hast done for me.   Only do not
demand what is against my honour and my conscience as
a Christian.   Thou art my benefactor.   Complete what
thou hast commenced : let me go with the poor orphan
whithersover God may lead us.   And we shall, wherever
thou mayest be, whatever thy lot, pray to God daily for
the salvation of thy sinful soul. . . ."

Pougatcheff's untamed heart seemed touched.

" Let it be as thou desirest," said he.   " If one must
execute, let execution be complete, and if one has to
pardon, let pardon be complete : such is my custom.
Take thy little beauty ; lead her wherever thou pleasest,
and may God bless your love and guide you."

Here he turned to Shvabrine, and ordered him to pro- '
vide me with passes for all the barriers and fortresses
subject to him.   Completely humilitated, Shvabrine stood
petrified.   Pougatcheff then proceeded to inspect the
fortress, accompanied by Shvabrine, and I remained
behind, under the pretext that I had to get ready for my
journey.

I rushed to the bedroom.   The door was closed.   I

knocked. " Who is there ?" asked Paláshka. I announced myself. Maria Ivanovna's dear voice was heard behind the door. " Wait a little, Piotr Andrevitch ; I am dressing. Go to Akoulina Pamphylovna. I shall be there directly."

I complied, and went to Father Gherassim's house. His wife and he ran out to meet me. Savelitch had fore-stalled me.

" Good-day, Piotr Andrevitch," said the priest's wife. " God has brought us together again. How are you ? We have never let a day pass without thinking of you. And Maria, my poor dove, has suffered so much during your absence ! . . . But tell me, my little father, how have you managed Pougatcheff ? how is it that he has not done away with you ? Well, we have to thank the wretch."

" Leave off, old woman," interrupted Father Gherassim. " Do not blab out all thou knowest. There is no salvation in tale-telling. My little father, Piotr Andrevitch ! come in, pray come in. What a time it is since we last saw you !"

His wife set before me what they happened to have in the house, talking incessantly the while. She related how Shvabrine had compelled them to deliver Maria Ivanovna to him ; how Maria Ivanovna cried, and would not leave them ; how Maria Ivanovna communicated with them through Paláshka (a sharp lass, who knew how to make the orderly even dance to her pipe); how she had advised Maria Ivanovna to write to me, &c., &c. I, in my turn, told her my story in a few words. The priest and his wife crossed themselves, when they learned that Pougatcheff knew of their deception. "The power of the cross be with us!" said Akoulina Pamphylovna. "Do Thou, O God! let the cloud pass away from us! Well, Aleksey Ivanovitch, thou art a cunning fox indeed!" At that moment the door opened, and Maria Ivanovna entered, a smile playing on her pale face. She had laid aside her peasant's garb, and was dressed as usual, simply and becomingly.

I seized her hand, and for a long time was unable to say a word. We were both silent, our hearts being too full. Our hosts felt that they were in the way, and left us. We remained alone. All was forgotten. We talked, and it seemed that we were not able to say enough. Maria told me all that had happened to her from the time of the taking of the fortress, describing all the horrors of her position, and all the trials to which the base Shvabrine had subjected her. We also recalled the happy past. . . . We were both crying! . . . . At last I exposed my plans to her. To remain in the fortress, in Pougatcheff's power, and under the command of Shvabrine, would be impossible. One could not think of Orenburg then undergoing all the calamities of a siege. She had no relatives living. I advised her to go to my parents' property. At first she hesitated: the prejudice manifested against her by my father alarmed her. I tranquillized her. I knew that my father would consider it a happiness, and would make it his duty to receive the daughter of a worthy warrior who had perished in the service of his country. "Dear Maria Ivanovna!" I said, "I look upon thee as I would upon my wife. Extraordinary circumstances have united us indissolubly; nothing on earth can separate us." Maria Ivanovna listened to me with gentleness, without any affectation of reserve, and without inventing any excuses. She felt that her destiny was bound up with mine. But she repeated that she would only become my wife with the consent of my parents. I said nothing in opposition to this. We exchanged a passionate ardent kiss, and thus all was settled between us.

An hour afterwards, an orderly brought to me a pass, signed with Pougatcheff's hieroglyphics, and informed me that Pougatcheff desired to see me. I found him ready to start. I cannot express what I felt at parting from this dreadful man, this monster, this miscreant towards everybody excepting myself. Why should I not speak the truth? At that moment I felt drawn towards him by strong sympathies. I eagerly longed to tear him away from the gang of wretches, whose leader he was, and save his head whilst there was yet time. I was hindered from expressing to him what filled my heart to overflowing, by the presence of Shvabrine and the people who were gathered about us.

We parted as friends. Seeing Akoulina Pamphylovna in the crowd, Pougatcheff shook his finger at her, and winked significantly. He then entered the *kibitka*, gave the order to drive to Berd, and when the horses had already started, he leant out of the *kibitka*, and shouted out to me : " Good-bye, your lordship; we may perhaps meet again some day." We did indeed meet—but under what circumstances ! . . . .

9

Pougatcheff was gone. I gazed long at the white steppe over which his *troïka* sped. The crowd dispersed, Shvabrine withdrew. I returned to the priest's house. All was ready for our departure ; I was anxious not to delay. Our luggage had been placed in the commandant's old travelling carriage. The *yemstchick* quickly put the horses to. Maria Ivanovna went to take a last farewell of the graves of her parents, which stood behind the church. I offered to accompany her, but she begged that I should let her go alone. She returned in a few minutes, weeping silently. The carriage drove up, Father Gherassim and his wife came out. We three, Maria Ivanovna, Paláshka, and I, took our places inside the *kibitka.* Savelitch scrambled into the rumble. "Farewell, Maria Ivanovna, my little dove ! farewell Piotr Andrevitch, our falcon bird !" the good priest's wife said. "A happy journey to you and God bless you both !" We left. I saw Shvabrine standing at a window of the commandant's house. His look was one of dark hatred. I had no desire to triumph over a humiliated foe, and turned my face away. We emerged from the fortress, and left Byĕlogorsk behind us for ever.

CHAPTER XIII.

THE ARREST.

I WAS so unexpectedly united to the dear girl regarding whose safety I had been even that very morning so anxiously concerned, that I could not believe my senses,

and fancied that all that was occurring was an empty
dream. Maria Ivanovna looked pensively, now at me,
now at the road, and seemed unable to realize her
position. We were silent, our hearts had been too
severely tried. Time passed away imperceptibly, and in
two hours we were already entering the nearest fortress,
also in Pougatcheff's power. Here we changed horses.
I saw by the haste with which they were put to by the
eager officiousness of the bearded Cossack raised to the
post of commandant by Pougatcheff, that, thanks to the
loquaciousness of our *yemstchick*, I was taken for a court
favourite !

We continued our journey, night began to close around
us. We approached a small town, where, according
to the statement of the Cossack, we should find a
detachment, about to join the pretender. We were
stopped by the sentry. To the challenge, "Who goes
there ?" the *yemstchick* answered in a loud voice : "The
emperor's *koum*, with his lady." In an instant, a troop
of Hussars surrounded us, using fearfully abusive
language. "Get out, thou devil's *koum !*" said a mou-
stachoed sergeant-major. "Thou shalt catch it presently,
thou and thy lady !"

I alighted and demanded to be taken to the officer in
command. On perceiving my uniform, the soldiers
desisted from abusing us. The sergeant-major conducted
me to the major. Savelitch followed close after me,
muttering to himself, "There is the emperor's *koum*
for you. Out of the frying pan into the fire. . . . Good

9—2

God! how is it all to end?" The *kibitka* came after us, at a slow pace.

A five minutes' walk brought us to a small house, brightly lit up. The sergeant-major put a sentry over me, and went to report me. He immediately returned, and stated that his lordship had no time to receive me, but that he had ordered that I should be conveyed to the prison, and the lady to his house.

"What does this mean?" I cried beside myself. "Has he lost his senses?"

"I cannot say, your lordship," answered the sergeant-major. "Only his high lordship has ordered your lordship to be taken to the prison, and her ladyship is to be taken to his high lordship, your lordship."

I rushed into the porch. The sentries did not attempt to hold me back, and I ran straight into a room where six Hussar officers were playing at cards. The major was dealing. What was my astonishment, when on looking at him I recognized Ivan Ivanovitch Zourine, who had once cheated me at the inn in Simbirsk.

"Is it possible?" I exclaimed, "Ivan Ivanovitch? is it thou?"

"But! ha! ha! Piotr Andrevitch? What brings thee here? Where art thou from? How art thou? Wilt thou take a card?"

"Thank you, no. Give directions that I should be taken to lodgings somewhere."

"What lodgings? Stay here."

"I cannot; I am not alone."

"Well, then, let thy comrade come also."

"I am not with a comrade; I am .... with a lady."

"With a lady! Where didst thou hook her? Aha! sir!"

With these words, Zourine whistled in such an extra-ordinary manner, that all burst out laughing. I got quite confused.

"Very well," continued Zourine, "thou shalt have a lodging. But it is a pity .... We should have feasted as in old times .... I say, boy! why don't they bring Pougatcheff's *kouma* here? Or is she capricious? Tell her not to be afraid; the master is a kind man, he will not offend her—lead her in by the shoulders."

"What art thou talking about?" said I to Zourine. "What *kouma* of Pougatcheff? It is the daughter of the late Captain Mironoff. I delivered her out of captivity, and am now taking her to my father's house, where I shall leave her."

"What? then it was thee they reported just now? Gracious! what is the meaning of it all?"

"I shall tell thee by-and-by; but at present, for God's sake, come and reassure the poor girl, whom thy hussars have frightened."

Zourine immediately made the necessary arrangements. He went out himself to apologise to Maria Ivanovna for the involuntary misunderstanding, and ordered the sergeant-major to take her to the best lodgings in the town. I remained his guest for the night.

We supped, and when we were left alone I related to him my adventures. Zourine listened very attentively. When I had concluded, he shook his head and said:—

"All well enough; one thing only is not well; why the devil dost thou want to marry? I am an honest man, I do not wish to deceive thee; believe me when I tell thee that marriage is all nonsense. What dost thou want to drag a wife about for, and nurse brats? Spit upon such a notion. Listen to me: break with the captain's daughter. The road to Simbirsk has been cleared by me, and is now safe. Send her alone to-morrow to thy parents; and remain in my detachment. There is no necessity for thee to return to Orenburg. If thou wert to fall again into the hands of the rebels, thou wouldst hardly get away. Thus this amorous trash will wear itself out, and all will be well."

Although I did not quite agree with all he said, still I felt that honour and duty required my presence in her majesty's army. I decided upon following Zourine's advice; to send Maria Ivanovna to my parents, and to remain with the detachment.

Savelitch came to assist me to undress. I desired him to be prepared the next day to accompany Maria Ivanovna. He was about to rebel.

"What dost thou say, sir? How am I to leave thee? Who is to look after thee? What will thy parents say?"

Well aware of his obstinate disposition, I resolved upon winning him over with kind and confidential words.

"My good friend, Arhipp Savelitch!" said I, "do not refuse to be a benefactor to me; I shall not need a servant, but I shall be uneasy if Maria Ivanovna were to leave without thee. In serving her, thou shalt serve me because I have made up my mind to marry her so soon as circumstances will permit."

Here Savelitch clasped his hands in indescribable amazement.

"Marry!" he repeated. "The child wants to marry! What will his father say? What will his mother think of it?"

"They will consent, they will certainly consent," I replied, "when they know Maria Ivanovna. I also rely upon thee. My father and mother have faith in thee; thou wilt speak in our behalf, wilt thou not?"

The old man was moved.

"Oh! my little father, Piotr Andrevitch!" answered he. "Although thou hast taken it into thy head to marry too early, still Maria Ivanovna is such a dear young lady, that it would be a sin to miss such an opportunity. Then let it be as thou sayest. I shall accompany the angel of God, and shall humbly submit that such a bride need not have a dowry."

I thanked Savelitch, and laid me down in the same room with Zourine. Being very excited, I grew talkative. At first Zourine conversed readily, but by degrees his speech became indistinct, and he finally answered me with a snore. I ceased talking, and soon followed his example.

The next morning I went to Maria Ivanovna. I communicated to her my plans. She admitted that they were wise, and at once agreed with me. Zourine's detachment was to quit that same day. No time was to be lost. I bid Maria Ivanovna "good-bye" on the instant, entrusting her to Savelitch, and giving her a letter to my parents. Maria Ivanovna burst out crying :—

"Good-bye, Piotr Andrevitch," said she in a low voice. "God alone knows whether we shall meet again, but I shall never forget you; thou alone shalt live in my heart to my dying hour."

I was not able to say anything. We were surrounded by people. I wished to avoid giving way, in their presence, to the feelings by which I was agitated. At last she was gone. I returned to Zourine, sad and silent. He tried to cheer me up, and I endeavoured to divert my thoughts. We spent the day noisily and in feasting, and in the evening we marched out.

We had got to the end of February. Winter, which had impeded military movements, was drawing to its close, and our generals were preparing for concerted action. Pougatcheff was still under the walls of Orenburg. But our forces were uniting and drawing near the robber's lair on all sides. Insurgent villages surrendered upon sight of our troops; the villain's bands were everywhere flying before us, and everything foretold a speedy and successful termination of the revolt.

Shortly after this, Prince Galitzin beat Pougatcheff, who had advanced upon the fortress of Tatishscheff, dispersed his troops, relieved Orenburg, and to all appearances struck the final and decisive blow. Zourine had been detached and sent against a band of rebel Bashkirs, who had however dispersed before we got up with them. Spring overtook us whilst we were in a small Tartar village. The rivers overflowed, and the roads became impracticable. We consoled ourselves during our inactivity with the thought of a speedy termination to this tiresome and petty warfare with robbers and savages.

But Pougatcheff had not been captured. He made his appearance at the mines of Siberia, where he assembled fresh bands, and renewed his ravages. Rumours of his successes again spread about. We learnt of the destruction of several Siberian fortresses. Soon the news of the taking of Kazan and of the advance of the pretender on Moscow, alarmed the commanders of the military forces, who were listlessly enjoying repose in the fond hope that the despised rebel had been reduced to subjection. Zourine received orders to cross the Volga.

I shall not describe our march and the termination of the war. I shall briefly observe that wretchedness had reached its climax. All authority was at an end; landed proprietors were hiding in the woods. Insurgent bands pillaged in every direction. The officers in command of detached forces, punished and remitted at will; the condition of this large territory which had become a prey to the flames, was dreadful to contemplate! . . . . May Heaven spare us from witnessing a Russian rebellion; it is senseless and pitiless !

Pougatcheff had fled, and was pursued by Ivan Ivanovitch Mihelson. We soon heard of his complete annihilation. At length Zourine received intelligence of the capture of the pretender, and at the same time orders to halt. The war was at an end. I should now be able to go to my parents. The prospect before me, that I should embrace them, that I should see Maria Ivanovna, of whom I had had no news, filled me with delight. I danced about like a child. Zourine laughed and said, shrugging his shoulders :—

" No, no; no good will come of it! Thou shalt marry —and thou shalt be lost!"

But a strange feeling envenomed my joy : I thought of the wretch whose hands had been steeped in the blood of so many innocent victims, and of the execution that awaited him, and felt disturbed in spite of myself. " Why," thought I with vexation, " why didst thou not run up against a bayonet, or fall under a shower of grape ? Thou could'st not have done better." How was I to feel otherwise ? I never should forget his merciful consideration towards me at one of the most terrible moments of my life, and to him I owed the deliverance of my betrothed out of the hands of the hateful Shvabrine.

Zourine granted me leave of absence. In a few days I was again to be in the bosom of my family. I was again to see my bride. An unexpected storm burst over me.

On the appointed day of my departure, at the very moment that I was about to start on my journey, Zourine entered my hut, holding a paper and looking much disturbed. Something pricked me at the heart. I feared I knew not what. He sent my servant out of the room, and said that he had some business to transact with me.

" What is it ?" I asked, alarmed.

" An unpleasant matter," said he, giving me the paper. " Read what I have just received."

I read it: it was a confidential order, directing all

officers in command of detachments to arrest me wherever I should be found, and to send me without delay under an armed escort to Kazan, before the commission appointed to investigate the charges laid against Pougatcheff.

The paper almost dropped out of my hands. "I can do nothing," said Zourine. "My duty is to carry out the order. The rumours of thy friendly journeys with Pougatcheff have somehow reached the ears of the authorities. I hope there will be no evil consequences and that thou wilt justify thyself before the commission. Do not be downhearted, and go."

My conscience was clear. I did not fear a court-martial; but I was alarmed at the prospect of the probability of a delay, for months to come, in the happy meeting I had anticipated. The *telega** was ready. Zourine bid me a friendly adieu. I mounted the *telega.* Two hussars with drawn sabres sat upon either side of me, and I soon found myself on the high road.

CHAPTER XIV.

JUDGMENT.

I FELT convinced that my wilful departure from Orenburg was the cause of my arrest. I was able to exculpate myself easily enough; reconnoitring had not been prohibited; but on the contrary, was greatly encouraged. I

* A cart.—Tr.

might be charged with over zeal, but not with disobedience. My friendly intercourse with Pougatcheff,
however, could be proved by a multitude of witnesses,
and would appear, to say the least, very suspicious. I
thought much over the inquiry that awaited me, framed
my replies, and made up my mind to speak the whole
truth, believing such a course to be the simplest, and at
the same time the most hopeful.

I reached Kazan, deserted and consumed by fire.
Where once had stood the houses, lay heaps of ashes on
either side the streets, while blackened walls, windowless
and roofless, stood out here and there. Such were the
traces Pougatcheff had left behind him. I was taken to
the fortress, which alone had escaped the conflagration.
The hussars handed me over to the officer on guard. He
sent for the blacksmith. Chains were put on my feet
and soldered together. I was then conveyed to prison,
and left alone in a small and dark cell, with bare walls
and a window secured with iron bars.

Such a beginning forebode no good. However, I lost
neither courage nor hope. I sought refuge in the consolation of all who are heavy laden ; and having for the
first time tasted the sweetness of prayer, issuing from a
pure though broken heart, I sank into a quiet sleep, unconcerned as to what awaited me.

I was awoke by the jailer the next morning, who
announced to me that my presence was required before
the commission. A couple of soldiers escorted me across
the court-yard into the commandant's house; they
remained in the hall, and I was suffered to enter alone.

I found myself in a tolerably spacious room. At a table, strewn with papers, sat two men; an old general with a stern and cold countenance, and a young captain of the Guards of about eight and twenty years of age, of prepossessing exterior, and pleasing and easy manners. Near the window, at a separate table, sat the secretary, a pen behind his ear, bending over his papers, ready to note my deposition. The inquiry commenced. I was asked my name and surname. The general inquired whether I was the son of Andrey Petrovitch Griueff, and upon my replying in the affirmative, roughly remarked: " Pity that such an honourable man should have such an unworthy son !" I answered quietly, that whatever the nature of the charges about to be preferred against me, I hoped to be able to meet them by a sincere declaration of the truth. My self-assurance displeased him. " Thou art sharp, my good fellow," said he frowning, " but we have seen the like of thee before this !"

The young man then asked, upon what occasion and at what period I had entered Pougatcheff's service, and upon what duties I had been employed by him ?

I replied with indignation, that as an officer and a nobleman, I could neither have entered Pougatcheff's service nor have accepted any employment under him.

" How is it then," reiterated my interrogator, " that the nobleman and officer alone was spared by the pretender, when all his comrades were cruelly put to death ? How is it that that same officer and nobleman feasted amicably with the rebels, and accepted from the chief of the vagabonds, a pelisse, a horse, and half a rouble in money ?

How did such a strange friendship originate, and upon what was it based, if not on treachery, or, at least, on base and criminal cowardice ?"

I was deeply hurt at the officer's words, and proceeded to exculpate myself with warmth. I related in what manner my acquaintance with Pougatcheff had begun in the steppe, during a snowstorm, and how he recognized and spared me at the taking of the fortress of Byělogorsk. I admitted that I did not scruple to accept the *touloup* and the horse from the pretender, but that I had defended the fortress of Byělogorsk against the rebel, to the last extremity. I concluded by referring him to my general, who could testify to my zeal during the calamitous siege of Orenburg.

The stern old man took up an open letter and read it aloud :

" With reference to the inquiry made by your excellency in regard to Ensign Griueff, supposed to be implicated in the present uprising, and to have entered into communication with the insurgent, a proceeding contrary to the rules of the service, and in violation of the oath of allegiance; I have the honour to report, that the said Ensign Griueff was on duty at Orenburg from the beginning of October of the past year, 1773, to the 24th of February of the present year, at which date he absented himself from the town, and has not served under my command since. Deserters from the enemy are reported to have stated that he has been in Pougatcheff's camp, and that he drove with him to the fortress of Byělogorsk, in which he had formerly served ; with

regard to his conduct, I can only . . ." Here he stopped
and said in a severe tone of voice: "What canst thou
say to this, in thy defence?"

It was my intention to have continued as I had begun,
and to have declared my connection with Maria Ivanovna as frankly as I had narrated the rest, but I suddenly felt an irrepressible aversion to doing so. It
struck me that the commission would call for her as a
witness were I to mention her, and the idea of mixing
up her name with the vile evidence of the wretches, and
also confronting her with them face to face—this dreadful
consideration so shocked me that I became confused, and
lost my presence of mind.

My examiners, who had apparently begun to listen to
me with a certain amount of consideration, became again
prejudiced upon noticing my indecision. The officer of
the Guards required that I should be opposed to my
principal accuser. The general ordered *that wretch of
yesterday* to be summoned. I turned abruptly towards
the door, in expectation of my accuser. In a few minutes
the clanking of chains was heard, the door was opened,
and Shvabrine appeared. I was astonished at the change
that had taken place in him. He was painfully thin and
pale. His hair, so recently of a jet black, had turned
quite gray; his long beard was matted. He repeated his
accusations in a faint but firm voice. He stated that I
had been sent off to Orenburg by Pougatcheff as a spy;
that I daily rode out reconnoitring with the object of
having written reports conveyed, of all that was passing
in the town; that I at last joined the pretender, accom-

panying him from fortress to fortress, and seeking by every
means to injure my fellow-traitors, with the view of
usurping their places, and of benefiting by the rewards
showered by the pretender.   I listened in silence and felt
at ease in one respect.   Maria Ivanovna's name had not
been uttered by the base wretch, either because his
vanity suffered at the remembrance of her who had
rejected him with scorn, or perhaps because a spark of
the same feeling which forced me to silence still lingered
in his breast.   However that may be, the name of the
daughter of the commandant of the fortress of Byëlogorsk
was not mentioned in the presence of the commission.   I
felt strengthened in my resolution, and when the officers
asked me how I could refute Shvabrine's evidence, I
replied that I held to my first deposition, and had nothing
further to offer in my defence.   The general ordered us
to withdraw.   We went out together.   I looked at
Shvabrine without saying a word to him.   He smiled
viciously, and lifting his chains, stepped quickly past
me.   I was reconducted to jail, but was not again taken
before the commission.

I was not a witness of all that now remains to be related to the reader ; but I have so often heard it described,
that the smallest details have, as it were, been graven in
my memory, and I feel as though I had been myself
present.

Maria Ivanovna was received by my parents with that
sincerity and good-will so characteristic of people in days
gone by.   They considered it a divine favour, that the
opportunity was afforded them of welcoming and com-

forting the poor orphan. They soon became truly attached to her, for it was impossible to know and not to love her. My father no longer looked upon my attachment as a piece of folly; and as to my mother, her only wish was that her Petrousha should marry the captain's dear little daughter.

The rumours of my arrest painfully astonished my parents. Maria Ivanovna had narrated to them so innocently my acquaintance with Pougatcheff, that, far from being disquieted, they were frequently induced to laugh heartily. My father would not believe that I was implicated in the despicable rebellion, which had for its object the overthrow of the throne and the abolition of nobility. He examined Savelitch narrowly on this point. The old man did not conceal the fact that his master had visited Emilian Pougatcheff, and that the wretch made a great deal of him; but he at the same time swore that he had never heard of any treason. The old people were reassured, and anxiously awaited favourable news. Maria Ivanovna was much agitated, but said little, for her disposition was in the highest degree a retired one.

Several weeks elapsed . . . . and my father received a letter concerning myself, from our relative Prince * * * at Petersburgh. After the usual preliminaries, he wrote that the suspicion of my share in the schemes of the insurgents had unfortunately proved only too well founded; that my execution had been deemed necessary for the sake of example, but that the empress, in consideration of my father's meritorious services and advanced years, had decided upon extending her pardon to

10

the criminal son, and, sparing him from an ignominious death, had commanded that he should be sent to a distant part of Siberia, an exile for life.

This unexpected blow almost killed my father. He lost his habitual firmness, and vented his (usually mute) grief in bitter lamentations.

"What!" repeated he, beside himself. "That my son should have plotted with Pougatcheff! Oh, heavens! that I should have lived to see this! The empress delivers him from death! Am I the better for that? It is not execution that is dreadful; my great-grandfather died on the scaffold because he would not violate the dictates of his conscience; my father suffered with Volinsky* and Aroushtcheff. But that a nobleman should break his oath of allegiance, that he should unite himself with robbers, murderers, and runaway serfs! . . . It is a shame and a disgrace to our race! . . . ."

Alarmed at his despair, my mother dared not weep in his presence, and endeavoured to restore to him his courage by suggesting the probability of the rumours being false, and popular opinion divided. My father was inconsolable.

Maria Ivanovna suffered the most. Feeling persuaded that I might have exculpated myself had I wished to do so, she guessed the truth, and accused herself as being the cause of my misfortunes. She tried to conceal her tears

---

* Volinsky had presented to the Empress Anna a paper, having for its object the overthrow of Biron; he and his friends subsequently fell victims to the vengeance of that favourite.—Tr.

and her anguish, and was incessantly devising means for obtaining my deliverance.

One evening my father sat on the sofa turning over the leaves of the "Court Calendar," but his thoughts were far away, and the perusal did not produce its wonted effects. He whistled an old march. My mother was silently knitting a woollen jacket, an occasional tear dropping on it. Maria Ivanovna, who was at her work by their side, informed them, without any preface, that she was under the necessity of going to Petersburg, and begged they would furnish her with the requisite means for the journey. My mother felt much grieved.

" Why dost thou want to go to Petersburgh ?" said she. " Is it possible, Maria Ivanovna, that thou wishest to abandon us ?"

Maria Ivanovna answered that her future depended upon the journey ; that she was going to seek the protection and assistance of people of influence, as the daughter of a man who had suffered for his loyalty.

My father drooped his head; he was pained at every word that reminded him of his son's imputed crime, and felt it as a poignant reproach to himself.

" Go," said he, with a sigh. " We do not wish to stand in the way of thy happiness. May God grant thee a good man for thy husband, in the place of a sullied traitor !"

He rose, and left the room.

Alone with my mother, Maria Ivanovna partly disclosed her intentions. My mother embraced her with tears, praying to God for a happy issue to the precon-

10—2

ceived project. Maria Ivanovna started upon her journey a few days after this, accompanied by the faithful Paláshka and the trusty Savelitch, who consoled himself, during his forced separation from me, with the reflection that he was at least serving my bride-elect.

Maria Ivanovna arrived safely at Sofia, and, on learning that the court happened to be at Tzarskoe-Selo, she decided upon remaining. A little room behind a partition was got ready for her at the station. The station-master's wife immediately entered into conversation with her, informed her that she was the niece of a fire-lighter at the palace, and initiated her into all the mysteries of court life. She told her at what hour the empress usually rose, drank her coffee, took her walk; what great gentlemen were with her at such times; what she had deigned to say yesterday at dinner, and whom she had received in the evening. In a word, Anna Vlassievna's accounts would have filled a volume of historical notes, and would have been highly prized by the coming generation!

Maria Ivanovna listened attentively. She strolled into the garden. Anna Vlassievna* had a story to tell of each alley, each little bridge; and, after a long walk, they returned to the station quite pleased with each other.

The following morning Maria Ivanovna woke early, dressed, and quietly went out into the garden. It was a lovely morning. The sun was shining brightly through the lime-trees, already seared by the fresh autumnal breezes, the smooth surface of the broad lake glittered in

* Anne, daughter of Blase.—Tr.

the sunshine, the swans emerged proudly from under the overhanging bushes. Maria Ivanovna passed by the beautiful lawn, upon which a monument had been lately erected in commemoration of the recent victories of Count Piotr Alexandrovitch Roumiantgoff. Suddenly a little white dog, of an English breed, barked and rushed at her. Maria Ivanovna started, and at the same moment she heard a pleasant female voice say:

"Do not fear, she does not bite."

And Maria Ivanovna saw a lady on the bench in front of the monument. Maria Ivanovna sat herself down at one end. The lady eyed her sharply, and Maria Ivanovna on her part had time, in a few side glances, to scan her from head to foot. She was in a white morning dress, a cap, and a *doushegreyka*. She appeared to be about forty years of age. Her full, blooming face was expressive of dignity and calm, and her blue eyes and smiling lips added an inexpressible charm. The lady was the first to break the silence.

"You are probably a stranger?" she said.

"Yes; I arrived yesterday only, from the country."

"You have come with your parents?"

"No, I have not. I have come alone."

"Alone! But you are so young."

"I have no father or mother."

"You are here on business, probably?"

"Yes, I have come to present a petition to the empress."

"You are an orphan, and probably have to complain of injustice or insult?"

"No. I have come to seek mercy, and not justice."

"Permit me to inquire who you are?"

"I am the daughter of Captain Mironoff."

"Captain Mironoff!—the one who commanded one of the Orenburg fortresses?"

"The same."

The lady seemed moved.

"Excuse me," said she, in a still more friendly tone, "if I meddle in your affairs; but I am occasionally at court: explain to me what your petition consists in, and I may perhaps be able to help you."

Maria Ivanovna rose, and thanked her respectfully. Everything about the unknown lady attracted her heart involuntarily, and inspired her with confidence. She took a folded paper from her pocket, and handed it to her unknown protectress, who read it over to herself.

She perused it first with attention and interest; but of a sudden her face changed, and Maria Ivanovna, whose eyes watched all her movements, was startled by the severe expression on that face, which, a moment before, had been so pleasant and calm.

"You petition for Griueff?" said the lady, coldly. 'The empress cannot pardon him. He joined the pretender, not from ignorance or credulity, but as a debased and dangerous vagabond!"

"Oh! it is not true!" exclaimed Maria Ivanovna.

"How not true?" continued the lady, wrathfully.

"Not true—I swear to God it is not true! I know all, and will tell you everything. It is for my sake alone that he has subjected himself to all that has befallen him. And if he has not justified himself before the commission, it has only been because he has not wished to introduce my name."

Here she narrated with warmth what my reader already knows.

The lady listened attentively.

"Where are you staying?" she asked, when Maria Ivanovna had concluded ; and, upon learning that it was at Anna Vlassievna's, added, with a smile—"Ah! I know. Good-bye ;, do not mention our meeting to any person. I hope that you will not have to wait long for an answer to your letter."

With these words she rose, and entered a covered walk. Maria Ivanovna returned to Anna Vlassievna full of hope.

Her hostess scolded her for taking so early a walk in autumn—so noxious, she said, to a young girl's health. She brought in the *samovar*, and, sipping a cup of tea, was just about to recommence her endless relations about the court, when a court carriage stopped at the door, and a chamber-groom entered with the announcement that the empress was pleased to invite Maria Ivanovna Mironoff to the palace. Anna Vlassievna became terribly fidgety in her astonishment.

"Dear me!" she exclaimed : "the empress requires you at court. How has she ever heard of you? And how are you, my dear, to appear before her majesty? Methinks you do not even know how to walk in court fashion. Had I not better accompany you? I could at all events give you a hint occasionally. And how are

you to go in your travelling dress? Had we not better
send to the midwife for her yellow gown?"

The chamber-groom said that her majesty had been
pleased to command that Maria Ivanovna should go
alone, and just as she was. There was no alternative.
Maria Ivanovna took her seat in the carriage, and drove
off, taking Anna Vlassievna's counsels and blessings.

Maria Ivanovna had a presentiment that our fate was
about to be decided ; her heart beat fast, and sank within
her. In a few minutes the carriage stopped at the palace.
Maria Ivanovna, much agitated, ascended the staircase.
The doors flew open before her. She passed through a
succession of gorgeous apartments, the chamber-groom
leading the way. They finally reached a closed door,
where he left her, with the assurance that she should be
immediately announced.

The prospect of being brought face to face with the
empress frightened her so much, that she found some
difficulty in supporting herself. The doors were opened,
and she entered her majesty's dressing-room.

The empress sat at her toilet-table, attended by several
ladies, who respectfully stood aside to make way for
Maria Ivanovna. The empress turned to her kindly, and
Maria Ivanovna recognized the lady with whom she had
but recently so freely conversed. She motioned her to
come nearer, and said, with a smile—

"I am glad that I was able to keep my word, and
grant your request. Your business is settled. I am convinced of your lover's innocence. Here is a letter, which
you will be good enough to deliver yourself into the
hands of your future father-in-law."

Maria Ivanovna took the letter with a trembling hand, and fell weeping at the empress's feet, who raised and kissed her.

"I know that you are not rich," she said; "but I must acquit myself of a debt I owe to the daughter of Captain Mironoff. Have no anxiety for the future. I take it upon myself to provide for you."

Having reassured the poor orphan, the empress dismissed her. Maria Ivanovna returned in the same court-carriage; Anna Vlassievna, who was impatiently awaiting her return, poured out question upon question, to which Maria Ivanovna replied anyhow. Anna Vlassievna was not pleased at her want of memory, but ascribed it to her provincial shyness, and was generous enough to excuse her. That same day Maria Ivanovna left on her way homewards, without a thought even of seeing Petersburg.

Here end the memoirs of Piotr Andrevitch Griueff. It is asserted from family traditions that, by an edict signed by the sovereign, he was liberated about the end of the year 1774; that he was present at the execution of Pougatcheff, who recognized him in the crowd, and nodded to him with the head which, a few minutes later, was held up bleeding to the people. Soon after, Piotr Andrevitch and Maria Ivanovna were married. Their descendants are settled in the government of Simbirsk. Thirty versts from —— is a village, the property of ten persons. In the house of one of the proprietors is

shown, framed and glazed, an autograph letter of Catherine II. It is addressed to the father of Piotr Androvitch,
and records the justification of his son, and eulogises the
intelligence and goodness of heart of the daughter of
Captain Mironoff.

THE LADY-RUSTIC.

THE possessions of Ivan Petróvitch Beréstoff lay in one of our remote provinces. He had served in the Guards in his youth, but had retired early in the year 1797, and settled on his property, which he never again quitted. He had married a lady of noble birth, but in indigent circumstances, who died in child-bed during his absence when on a visit to one of his distant estates. He soon found consolation in his house occupations. Having built a house according to a design of his own, and established a cloth manufactory, he put his money matters in order, and began to consider himself the cleverest man in the place,—an opinion which was never disputed by his neighbours, who used to visit him accompanied by their families and their dogs. He wore on week-days a plush jacket, and on holidays a surtout of home-spun; he kept his own accounts, and read nothing but *The Senate News*.

He was generally liked, though people thought him proud. It was only his nearest neighbour, Grigory Ivánovitch Múromsky, who could not get on with him. He was a thorough Russian country gentleman. Having squandered at Moscow the greatest part of his fortune,

and having become a widower at about the same time,
he retired to one of his remaining estates, where he continued his extravagances, though they now took a different course.   He laid out an English garden, upon which
he wasted almost all that remained of his income.   His
stable-boys were dressed as English jockeys.   His daughter's governess was an Englishwoman.   His agricultural
labours were conducted on the English principle.

But " Russian bread is not begotten of foreign culture,"
and notwithstanding a considerable decrease in his expenditure, the income of Grigory Ivánovitch did not
increase.   He had found means to contract new debts,
though he lived in the country.   Nevertheless, nobody
considered him a fool, for he was the first of the landowners in the province who thought of mortgaging his
property at the Court of Trustees,—a transaction which
at that period was considered very hazardous.   Amongst
those who censured him was Beréstoff, who expressed
himself in the strongest terms.   Hatred to innovations
formed a prominent trait in his character.   He could not
speak with equanimity of his neighbour's Anglomania,
and sought every opportunity to criticize him.   If he
chanced to show a guest over his premises, and if his
household arrangements elicited approbation, he was sure
to say, with a malicious smile : " Oh ! yes ; my place is
not like my neighbour's, Grigory Ivánovitch's.   How
could we squander after the English fashion !   We are
thankful if we can manage to keep off hunger in the
Russian way !"   These and such like sarcasms came to
Grigory Ivánovitch's knowledge, exaggerated and embel-

lished according to the tale-bearer's zeal. The Anglomane stood criticism as badly as our own journalists do. He raged, and called his calumniator a bear and a provincialist.

This was the footing they were upon when Beréstoff's son arrived. He had been brought up at the ——— University, and intended entering the army; but his father would not give his consent. For the Civil Service the young man had no taste. Neither would give in, and the young Aleksèy in the meanwhile led the life of a private gentleman, having, however, allowed his moustache* to grow, ready for any emergency.

Aleksèy was really a good fellow, and it would have been a pity indeed were his well-proportioned figure never to be seen in a uniform, and were he, instead of showing himself off on horseback, to spend his youth bending over office-papers. The neighbours who saw him lead on the hunting-field, reckless of the way he followed, all agreed in saying that he would never turn out a creditable head of a department. All the young ladies watched him, and ·sometimes would take a furtive look at him; but Aleksèy took little notice of them, and they attributed his indifference to some love affair. The copy of the address on one of his letters was actually being handed about amongst them: "To Akulina Pétrovna Kourótchkin, Moscow, opposite the Aleksèy Monastery, in the house of the coppersmith Savélieff,

* Formerly in Russia the military only were allowed to wear moustaches.—Tr.

and you are humbly requested to forward this letter to
A. N. R."

Such of my readers as may not have lived in the
country, cannot imagine how captivating are these provincial young ladies. Brought up breathing the purest
air under the shade of their orchard trees, they only
draw their knowledge of life and of the world from
books. Solitude, freedom, and their love of reading,
develop in them early feelings and passions which are
unknown to our worldly beauties. The very sound of a
carriage-bell is an event to them; a sojourn in the neighbouring town is considered an epoch in their existence,
and the visit of a guest leaves behind it long, and occasionally everlasting reminiscences. Everybody is, of
course, at liberty to jeer at some of their peculiarities;
but the ridicule of a superficial observer cannot do
away with their existing good qualities, the chief of
which is independence of character, without which,
in Jean Paul's opinion, no human greatness exists.
Women may possibly receive better education in the
capitals, but intercourse with the world soon assimilates
characters and renders their souls as uniform as their
head-dresses. This is said neither in judgment nor in reproach; however, *nota nostra manet*, as has written an
old commentator.

It is easy to imagine the impression produced by
Aleksèy on our young ladies. It was he who first
appeared before them gloomy and disenchanted; who
first spoke to them of wasted joys, and of his withered
youth; he also wore a mourning ring with a death's

head. All this was something quite new in the province, and the girls were losing their senses.

But Lisa (or *Betsy*, as Grigory Ivánovitch generally called her), the daughter of my Anglomane, was more taken up with him than was anybody else. Their fathers did not visit, and she had not even seen Aleksèy when he had already become the subject of conversation of all her young neighbours. She was seventeen. Her black eyes lit up her dark and very agreeable face. She was an only, and consequently a spoilt, child. Her high spirits and her constant humour enraptured her father, and distracted her governess, Miss Jackson, a conceited spinster of forty, who painted her face and eyebrows, read "Pamela" twice a year, received the sum of two thousand roubles, and who felt bored to death in that barbarous Russia.

Lisa was waited upon by Nastia, who, though a little older, was quite as giddy as her mistress. Lisa was very fond of her, confiding to her all her secrets, and arranging with her all her little plans; in a word, Nastia was a much more important personage on the Anossoff estate than could be any one confidante in a French tragedy.

"May I go out to-day?" asked Nastia upon one occasion, whilst dressing her mistress.

"Certainly—where?"

"To Tugílevo, to the Beréstoffs. It is the Saint's-day of their cook's wife, and she came yesterday to invite us to dinner."

"Is that it?" said Lisa: "the masters are at enmity, and the servants entertain each other!"

"And what have the masters got to do with it?"
replied Nastia; "besides, I belong to you, and not to
your father, and you and young Beréstoff have not yet
managed to fall out: let the old people fight it out if it
pleases them."

"Do endeavour, Nastia, to see Aleksèy Beréstoff, and
tell me what he is like, and what kind of person he is."

Nastia promised; and Lisa spent the day impatiently
awaiting her return. In the evening, Nastia appeared.

"Well, Lisavéta Grigórievna," said she on entering
the room, "I saw young Beréstoff, and looked at him to
my heart's content; we were all day together."

"How was that?—tell me, tell me everything as it
occurred!"

"If you please, then; we went, I, Anisia, Egórovna,
Nénila, Dunka——"

"All right, I know; well, after that?"

"Allow me, I want to tell you everything as it occurred.
We arrived just in time for dinner. The room was full
of people. There were the Kolbiúsky, the Zaharévsky,
the clerk's wife with her daughters, the Krupiúsky——"

"Well! and Beréstoff?"

"Please to wait. So we sat down to dinner, the clerk's
wife at the post of honour, I next to her—the daughters
sulked; but much I care about them——"

"Dear me, Nastia, how tiresome thou always art with
thy endless particulars!"

"But you are so very impatient! Well, then, we got
up from table—and we had sat there three hours, and
the dinner was splendid; we had for sweets, blue, red,

and striped blancmange. On leaving the table, we went into the garden to have a game at catch-play, and there the young master joined us."

" Well! is it true that he is good-looking ?"

" Wonderfully good-looking—handsome, one may say. Erect, tall, with such a colour——"

" Really? and I always thought that he was pale. Well? what did he look like? Sad—pensive ?"

" Dear, no! I have never met with any one more lively than he is. He took it into his head to join in the game with us."

" To join in the game with you! Impossible !"

" Very possible. And what is more, he would catch and kiss us !"

" Say what thou wilt, Nastia, it is a story."

" Indeed, it is not. I could hardly get rid of him. He would spend the whole day with us."

" How is it, then, people say he is in love, and will look at no one ?"

" I do not know; as to myself he looked even too much at me, as also at Tánia, and the clerk's daughter, and at Pasha Kolbiúsky also; and, truth to say, he offended no one—he is so indulgent."

" Now you surprise me! And what do they say of him at home ?"

" They say he is a capital gentleman—so good, so cheerful. One thing only is amiss—he likes running after the girls too much. But, in my opinion, that is no great harm : he will sober down in time."

11

" How much I should like to see him!" said Lisa, with a sigh.

" Why, where is the difficulty ? Tugilevo is not far from us—three versts only : take a walk or a ride in that direction ; you are sure to meet him. He goes out daily, early in the morning, with his gun."

" No, that would not do. He might fancy that I am running after him. Besides, our fathers are not on good terms, so that anyhow I cannot make his acquaintance. But,— Nastia! shall I tell thee what ? I shall dress as a peasant girl !"

" Why, certainly : put on a coarse shirt, and a *sarafan*,* and go boldly to Tugilevo. I'll be bound Berestoff will not pass you by."

" And I can so well imitate the peasants, as they speak here. Oh, Nastia ! dear Nastia ! what a glorious idea !"

And Lisa laid herself down to sleep, fully intending to carry out her lively project. She set about to mature her plans, and the very next morning sent to the market for some coarse linen, blue nankeen, and brass buttons, cut out a shirt and *sarafan*, with the help of Nastia, and put all the female servants to work, so that everything was ready when evening came. Lisa tried on her new finery, and was obliged to confess before her looking-glass that she had never yet seen herself to such advantage. She rehearsed her part, bowed low when walking, and shook her head several times, in imitation of plaster-of-Paris cats, speaking the peasant dialect, and covering her face with her sleeve when laughing, all of which elicited

* The national female dress.—Tr.

Nastia's complete approbation. There was but one draw-back: she endeavoured to cross the yard barefooted, but the thorns pricked her tender feet, and the sand and stones she found unbearable. Nastia came to her aid here also: she measured Lisa's foot, and hurried off to the fields to the shepherd Trophim, to whom she gave an order for a pair of bark-shoes, according to the measure delivered. Day had dawned on the morrow, and Lisa was already awake. The whole house slept. Nastia was awaiting the shepherd at the gate. The horn sounded, and the village herds were driven past her master's house. Trophim, on seeing Nastia, gave her a pair of small parti-coloured bark-shoes, receiving in recompense a half rouble. Lisa quietly proceeded to attire herself as a peasant, and, having in a whisper given Nastia some directions respect-ing Miss Jackson, slipped through the back gate and ran across the kitchen-garden into the fields.

The sky was lighting up in the east, and the golden tiers of clouds appeared to await the sun as courtiers await their sovereign; the clear sky, the morning fresh-ness, the dew, the slight breeze, and the singing of birds, filled Lisa's heart with childish delight; the fear of encountering a familiar face seemed to give her wings. On reaching the limits of her father's property, she slackened her pace. It was here that she was to wait for Aleksèy. Her heart beat fast, she knew not why; but do not the very apprehensions which are associated with our youthful frolics constitute their principal charm? Lisa had now penetrated into the densest part of the wood. Its dull repeating murmur seemed to welcome the

11—2

young girl. Her mirth became less buoyant. She fell
little by little into a sweet reverie. She thought—but is
it possible to define accurately the thoughts of a young
lady of seventeen who is alone in a wood at five o'clock
on a spring morning? She walked thus pensively along
a road shadowed on both sides by tall trees, when she
was suddenly startled by the bark of a sportsman's
beautiful dog. Lisa screamed with alarm. A voice was
heard at the same moment, *Tout beau, Sbogar ici*——and a
young sportsman appeared from behind some bushes.

"Do not be afraid, my dear," said he to Lisa; "my
dog does not bite."

Lisa had already found time to recover from her fright,
and knew how to take advantage of such an opportunity.

"But, sir," said she, feigning to be partly shy and
partly frightened, "I am afraid; look, she is a wicked
one, she might fly again."

Aleksèy (my reader has already recognized him) was
in the meantime eying narrowly the young peasant girl.

"I shall escort thee, if thou art afraid," said he; "thou
wilt let me walk by thee, wilt thou not?"

"Who hinders thee?" answered Lisa; "freedom is for
the free, and the road is public."

"Where dost thou come from?"

"From Prilútchino; I am the daughter of Vasily, the
blacksmith, and I am going to gather mushrooms."

Lisa was carrying a bark-basket suspended by a cord.

"And thou, sir? thou art from Tugilévo, I suppose?"

"I am, indeed," said Aleksèy, "I am the young master's
valet."

Aleksèy wished to assimilate their positions. But Lisa looked at him and burst out in a laugh.

"Thou art telling a story," said she; "but it is not a fool thou hast got hold of. I can see that thou art the master himself."

" What makes thee think so ?"

" Everything."

" But—— ?"

" Well, how is it possible not to distinguish the servant from the master ? Thy dress is different, thou speakest differently, and thou even callest the dog in an outlandish way."

Aleksèy fancied Lisa more and more, and not being accustomed to stand upon ceremony with young country girls, he was about to embrace her, but Lisa jumped aside, and assumed suddenly such a severe and freezing look, that Aleksèy was amused; it kept him from any further attempts.

" If you wish that we should remain friends henceforth," said she, with importance, "you must, please, not forget yourself."

" Who taught thee so much wisdom ?" said Aleksèy, with a laugh. " Can it be my friend, Nástinka, your young mistress's maid ? Is that the way civilization travels ?"

Lisa felt that she had overdone her part, and corrected herself immediately.

" And what dost thou fancy ?" said she : " thinkest thou that I have never been in a gentleman's house ? No fear; I have seen and heard most things. However," she continued, "it is not in talking to thee that I shall find mushrooms. Thou, sir, must go one way, and I another. Fare thee well."

Lisa was about to withdraw.

Aleksèy seized her hand. "What is thy name, my soul?"

"Akulina!" answered Lisa, endeavouring to free her fingers from Aleksèy's grasp. "Let go, sir; it is time for me to be running home."

"Well, my friend Akulina, I shall certainly come and see thy father, Vasily the blacksmith."

"What next?" replied Lisa quickly: "for Heaven's sake do not come. It will go badly with me, if they find out at home that I have been taking a walk in the woods with a gentleman; my father, Vasily the blacksmith, will beat me to death."

"But I must see thee again, without fail."

"Well, then, may be I shall come again to gather mushrooms some day."

"When?"

"Well, say to-morrow."

"Dear Akulina, I would kiss thee, but dare not. To-morrow, then, about this time, eh?"

"Yes, yes."

"Thou wilt not deceive me?"

"I shall not."

"Swear that thou wilt not."

"Well then, by Holy Friday, I shall come."

The young people separated. Lisa went out of the wood, scampered across the fields, stole into the garden, and ran headlong towards the farm, where Nastia was awaiting her. There she changed her dress, gave disconnected answers to the questions of her impatient confidante, and proceeded to the drawing-room. The table was laid, breakfast ready, and Miss Jackson, already painted and laced in until her figure assumed the shape of a wine-glass, was cutting thin slices of bread and butter. Her father praised her for taking an early walk.

"There is nothing healthier," said he, "than to rise with the dawn." And he thereupon cited several instances of human longevity, taken from English journals, remarking that none of those who had lived over a century had been addicted to spirits, and that they all rose at daybreak in winter as in summer.

Lisa did not listen to him. She was mentally reviewing all the circumstances attending her morning meeting and the entire conversation of Akulina with the young sportsman, and her conscience began to smite her. It was in vain that she tried to persuade herself that the nature of their interview had not exceeded the bounds of propriety, that her frolic could have no consequences whatever,—her conscience spoke louder than her reason. The promise she had made for the next day tormented her more than anything, and she was all but determined not to keep to her solemn oath. But might not Aleksèy, after vainly expecting her, go into the village, and find Vasily the blacksmith's daughter, the real Akulina, a fat, pock-marked girl, and thus obtain a clue to her thought_ less artifice? This idea horrified Lisa, and she made up her mind to appear in the wood as Akulina, the next morning.

At to Aleksèy, he was enchanted; he spent the whole day thinking of his new acquaintance; the image of the dark beauty haunted his imagination even at night. It was barely dawn, and he was already dressed. He did not wait to load his gun, but went into the fields accompanied by his faithful Sbogar, and hurried to the trysting-place. Nearly half an hour was spent in insupportable expectation; at last he caught a glimpse of a blue *sarafan* in the bushes, and rushed to welcome his dear Akulina. She smiled at his enraptured show of gratitude; but Aleksèy at once noticed that her face bore traces of sadness and anxiety. He insisted upon knowing the cause.

Lisa avowed that she considered her conduct imprudent, that she repented, that she did not wish to fail in her promise this time, but that this meeting was to be their last, and she begged him to break off an acquaintance which could be productive of no good. All this was of course said in the provincial dialect, but the ideas and feelings, so uncommon in a simple country girl, struck Aleksèy with astonishment. He exhausted all his eloquence in endeavouring to deter Akulina from her decision; he assured her of the purity of his intentions, promised never to give her cause for repentance, to submit to her in all things, and implored her not to deprive him of the one joy—that of seeing her alone, were it but every other day, but twice a week. He spoke in the language of true passion, and was at that moment really in love.

Lisa listened in silence. "Promise me," said she at last, "that thou wilt never seek me in the village—never inquire after me. Promise me not to look for other meetings but those which I shall myself assign."

Aleksèy was about to swear by Holy Friday, but she stopped him with a smile. "I do not require oaths," said Lisa, "thy word is sufficient."

After that they walked about in the wood in friendly conversation, until Lisa said : "It is time." They parted, and Aleksèy, when left alone, could not understand how a simple country girl had contrived in two meetings to possess such influence over him. His intercourse with Akulina contained all the charms of novelty, and although the restrictions imposed by the strange maiden seemed burdensome, the idea of breaking his word never entered his head. The fact was, that in spite of his ominous ring, his mysterious correspondence, and his gloomy disenchantment, Aleksèy was a good and ardent youth, with a pure heart, capable of innocent enjoyments.

Were I to follow my inclinations, I would here certainly give a detailed account of how the young people met, of their growing attachment and confidence in each other, and of their occupations and discourse ; but I am aware that the greatest portion of my readers would not share this pleasure with me. As a rule these details are nauseating, and I shall therefore pass them over and remark briefly, that two months had scarcely gone by before my Aleksèy was hopelessly in love, and Lisa, though more reserved than he, not more indifferent. They were both happy in the present, and cared but little for the future.

The thought of inseparable ties had crossed their minds

more than once; but they had never hinted at it to each other. The reason is obvious: however much attached to his dear Akulina Aleksèy might have been, he could not forget the distance which separated him from a poor country girl. Lisa, on her part, knew of the enmity which existed between their fathers, and dared not hope for a mutual reconciliation. Besides, her vanity was secretly stimulated by the fanciful hope of at last seeing the owner of Tugilevo at the feet of the Prilútchina blacksmith's daughter.

An important event suddenly threatened to interrupt their mutual relations.

On a clear cold morning (one of those in which our Russian autumn abounds) Ivan Petróvitch Beréstoff went out for a ride, taking with him three couples of sporting dogs, a groom, and several stable boys, provided with rattles. Grigory Ivánovitch Múromsky, tempted by the brightness of the weather, ordered his short-tailed mare to be saddled, and at about the same hour rode out at a trot round his Anglicized domain. On nearing the wood he noticed his neighbour, who sat his horse proudly in an overcoat lined with fox-fur, on the look-out for a hare which the boys were hunting out of the thicket with their shouts and rattles. Had Grigory Ivánovitch been able to foresee this encounter, he would certainly have turned back; but he had come upon Beréstoff quite un-expectedly, and was now within pistol-shot of him. There was no help for it; Múromsky, like a well-bred European, rode up to his enemy, and politely addressed him. Beréstoff replied with something of the zeal a chained bear displays when ordered by his keeper to make his bow to the public. At that moment a hare leapt out of the thicket and ran off into the fields. Beréstoff and the groom shouted with all their might; they loosed the dogs, and followed· at full speed. Múromsky's horse, unaccustomed to the chase, started and ran away with him. Múromsky, who considered himself a good horseman, loosened the reins, and was secretly congratulating himself upon such an opportunity for freeing himself from an undesirable companion. But having gone as far as a ravine which it had not hitherto noticed, his horse suddenly swerved and unseated its rider. Having fallen rather heavily on the frozen ground, he lay cursing his short-tailed mare, which, as if coming to her senses, stopped so soon as she became aware of the removal of her burden. Ivan Petróvitch rode up to him, inquiring whether he were hurt. The groom, having in the meantime secured the peccant horse, led it by the bridle. He assisted Múromsky into his saddle, and Beréstoff invited him to his house. Múromsky could not refuse, feeling that he was under an obligation, and it was thus that Beréstoff returned home full of honours, having hunted down a hare, and leading his wounded adversary, almost like a prisoner of war.

The two neighbours breakfasted together, conversing in quite a friendly way. Múromsky asked Beréstoff for his *droshky*, acknowledging that he was unable to ride home after his fall. Beréstoff saw him himself over the threshold, and Múromsky would not take his leave until he had exacted the promise that he and Alekséy Ivánovitch would dine at Prilútchino the very next day. In this manner an old and deeply rooted enmity seemed about to be brought to an end through the shyness of a short-tailed mare.

Lisa rushed out to meet Grigory Ivánovitch. "What does this mean, papa?" asked she in surprise: "what makes you lame? Where is your horse, and whose *droshky* is this?"

"That is what thou wilt never guess, my dear," replied Grigory Ivánovitch, and he then related to her what had occurred. Lisa could not believe her ears. Grigory Ivánovitch, without giving her time to recover from her surprise, informed her that both the Beréstoffs were to dine with them on the morrow.

"What are you saying!" exclaimed she, turning pale: "the Beréstoffs, father and son, dine with us to-morrow! No, papa, you may please yourself, but nothing will make me show myself."

"Art thou out of thy senses?" replied her father. "How long is it since thou hast become so shy? or dost thou nurse an hereditary hatred like a heroine of romance? Come, don't be silly."

"No, papa, nothing on earth, no treasure in the world, will persuade me to appear before the Beréstoffs!"

Grigory Ivánovitch shrugged his shoulders, and knowing that nothing was to be gained by contradicting her, ceased the discussion, and retired to rest after his eventful ride.

Lisavéta Grigórievna went into her own room, and called Nastia. They conferred long together on the ap-

proaching visit. What would Alcksèy think were he to recognize his Akulina in a well-educated young lady? What
opinion would he form of her conduct, of her principles,
of her good sense? On the other hand, Lisa was anxious
to see what impression such an unexpected meeting
would produce. Suddenly a thought crossed her mind.
She hastened to communicate it to Nastia; both exulted
at the idea, and they made up their minds to carry out
the plan without fail.

Grigory Ivánovitch inquired of his daughter the following day at breakfast whether she still intended to
conceal herself from the Beréstoffs.

"Papa," answered Lisa, "I shall receive them if you
wish it, but upon one condition—that, whatever my
appearance, whatever I may do, you will not scold me,
nor show any sign of surprise or displeasure."

"Some new freak!" said Grigory Ivánovitch, laughing.
"Well, all right, I consent; do what thou wilt, my black-
eyed little rogue."

With these words he kissed her on the forehead, and
Lisa ran off to make ready.

At two o'clock precisely, a home-built coach, drawn by
six horses, drove up to the door, round the green lawn in
front of it. The old Beréstoff alighted with the aid of
two of Múromsky's liveried servants. His son had followed him on horseback, and together they entered the
dining-room, where the cloth was already laid. Múromsky
received his guests in the most friendly manner, and
having proposed a turn in the garden before dinner, and
a look at the park, led the way along the carefully swept

and gravelled walks. The old Beréstoff was mentally lamenting the labour and time lost on such unprofitable fancies, but considerately kept his thoughts to himself. His son did not participate either in the disapprobation of the practical landowner, or in the enthusiasm of the vain Anglomane; he was impatiently awaiting the appearance of his host's daughter, of whom he had heard much, and though his heart was, as we know, already full, youth and beauty still influenced his imagination.

Upon their return to the drawing-room, the three seated themselves; and while the old gentlemen revived reminiscences of the past days, and recapitulated anecdotes having reference to their services, Aleksèy was musing upon what part he had best enact in the presence of Lisa. He decided that cold indifference was under all circumstances the best suited. The door was opened; he turned his head with so much nonchalance, such cold carelessness, that the heart of the most inveterate coquette would have been set beating. But ill luck would have it that instead of Lisa there entered old Miss Jackson, who, painted and laced in, made a slight curtsey with lowered eyes, and Aleksèy's manly military bow was lost upon her. He had no time to prepare for a new effort, for the door was again opened, and this time Lisa walked in. All rose; her father was about to introduce his guests, when he suddenly checked himself, and bit his lip. Lisa, his dark Lisa, was painted to her eyebrows, and rouged to an extent which outdid Miss Jackson herself: false curls, much lighter than her own hair, were arranged after the model of a Louis XIV. wig; sleeves, *à l'imbecile* stuck out like Madame de Pompadour's hoops; her waist was contracted into the shape of the letter X, and those of her mother's diamonds which had escaped being pawned sparkled on her fingers, her neck, and in her ears. Aleksèy could not possibly have recognized his Akulina under this ridiculous and gorgeous disguise. His father kissed her hand, and he, though vexed, followed his example; he fancied that the small white fingers trembled as he touched them, and he at the same time noticed her small foot, which was coquettishly shoe-strung and designedly thrust out. This somewhat reconciled him to the rest of her attire. As to the white and rouge we must avow that in the innocency of his heart he at first did not notice, and never afterwards suspected such a thing. Grigory Ivánovitch recollected his promise, and endeavoured not to show even a symptom of astonishment; but his daughter's joke appeared so ludicrous, that he could scarcely refrain from laughing. It did not, however, excite the risible faculties of the prime Englishwoman. She conjectured that the paints were produced from her drawers, and a deep blush of vexation was visible through the artificial whiteness of her face. She cast angry glances at the young offender, who, putting off all explanations to a more suitable occasion, did as if she saw them not.

They sat down to dinner. Aleksèy continued absent and thoughtful. Lisa looked prim, spoke through her teeth in a drawling voice, and only in French. Her father was watching her incessantly, not comprehending her object, but finding it all very amusing. The Englishwoman was wrathful and silent. Ivan Petróvitch alone was thoroughly at his ease; he ate for two, drank profusely, enjoyed his own merriment, conversing more freely and laughing with more zest from hour to hour.

At last they rose; the guests took their leave, and Grigory Ivánovitch gave free vent to his laughter and to his questionings.

"What put it into thy head to make fools of them?" he inquired of Lisa. "But shall I tell thee what? White paint really suits thee. I do not wish to pry into the secrets of a lady's toilette, but were I in thy place I would always use paint—of course not immoderately, but just a little."

Lisa was delighted at the success of her scheme. She embraced her father, promised to consider his advice, and ran off to pacify the irritated Miss Jackson, whom she with difficulty prevailed upon to open the door, and to listen to her justification. Lisa was ashamed to appear with such a dark complexion before a stranger; she dared not ask — she felt sure that dear, kind Miss Jackson would forgive her, &c., &c. Miss Jackson, being satisfied that Lisa had not meant to ridicule her, was appeased, kissed her, and in token of reconciliation presented her with a small pot of English paint, which Lisa accepted with a show of sincere gratitude.

My reader will guess that Lisa was not slow in seeking the meeting-place in the wood on the following morning.

"Thou wentest to our master's last night, sir," said she to Alekséy immediately. "What dost thou think of our young mistress?"

Aleksèy replied that he had not taken notice of her.

" What a pity !" said Lisa.

" And why ?" was his question.

" Because I wanted to know whether what they say is true."

" And what do they say ?"

" Is what they say true, that I am like her ?"

" What nonsense ! Why, she is a perfect fright compared to thee."

" Oh, sir ! what a shame to talk like that ! Our young mistress is so fair, dresses so beautifully. How is it possible to compare me to her ?"

Aleksèy swore that she was prettier than all the fair ladies put together ; and, anxious to reassure her, he began to describe her mistress in such ridiculous colours that it made Lisa laugh heartily.

" But," said she, with a sigh, " however absurd our mistress may be, still I am an unlettered dunce compared to her."

" Oh !" said Aleksèy, " much there is to be unhappy about ! Why, if thou wishest it, I will teach thee to read."

" Why should I not indeed try ?" said Lisa.

" All right, my dear, let us begin at once."

They sat down. Aleksèy drew out his pocket-book and pencil, and Akulina learned the alphabet with surprising facility. Aleksèy could not sufficiently wonder at her aptness. The next morning she wished to learn to write. The pencil would not at first obey her, but in a few moments she formed her letters pretty fairly.

" What a wonder !" Aleksèy would say ; " why, we learn
more quickly than if we had followed Lancaster's system."
And in truth, at her third lesson, Lisa was able to spell .
" Natalia, the Boyar's daughter," intermixing with her
reading remarks which truly surprised Aleksèy, and she
filled a sheet of paper with extracts from the same story.

A week elapsed, and they began to correspond. A
hollow in an old oak served as their post-office. Nastia
was fulfilling the duties of postman on the sly. Aleksèy
used to deposit his half-text epistles, and find the hieroglyphics of his beloved one written on common blue
paper. Akulina was rapidly acquiring a more elegant
mode of expressing herself, and her mind was evidently
being developed and instructed.

The reconciliation between Ivan Petróvitch Beréstoff
and Grigory Ivánovitch Múromsky had in the meantime
progressed to intimacy, and at last ripened into friendship under the following circumstances : Múromsky often
mused on the fact that all Ivan Petróvitch's property
would at his death pass on to Aleksèy Ivánovitch, that
Aleksèy Ivánovitch would thus become one of the richest
landowners in the province, and such being the case there
could be no reason why he should not marry Lisa. The
old Beréstoff, on his part, although aware of his neighbour's peculiarities (or, as he termed them, English follies),
did not for all that ignore his many good qualities. For
instance : his rare abilities ; Grigory Ivánovitch was
nearly related to Count Pronsky, a well-known and in-
fluential man ; the count might be of service to Aleksèy ;
and Múromsky (so thought Ivan Petróvitch) would surely

be glad of the opportunity of having his daughter so comfortably settled. The old people thought over the project so frequently in their own minds, that they at last exchanged their views, embraced each other, promised to make matters straight, and set-to maturing their plans, each after his own fashion. Múromsky foresaw a difficulty; he would have to persuade his *Betsy* to become better acquainted with Aleksèy, whom she had not met since the memorable dinner. He fancied they did not much care for each other; at least Aleksèy had never again called at Prilúchino, and Lisa withdrew whenever Ivan Petróvitch would honour them with a visit. "Well," thought Grigory Ivánovitch, "if I could get Aleksèy to come here every day, Lisa must end by falling in love with him. That is in the course of nature. Time will do the rest."

Ivan Petróvitch was less uneasy about the success of his plans. He called his son into his study that same evening, lit his pipe, and after a pause, said, "Methinks it is a long time, Alyósha*, since thou hast last talked of entering the army. Or has the Hussar's uniform lost its attractions?"

"No, my father," answered Aleksèy reverently, "I see it is not your wish that I should join the Hussars; it is my duty to obey you."

"That's right," answered Ivan Petróvitch; "I see thou art an obedient son: that is a consolation. I on my part do not wish to stand in thy way: I do not wish to hurry

---

* Pet name for Aleksèy.—Tr.

12—2

thee to enter the Civil Service at once; in the meanwhile,
I should like thee to marry."

" Whom, my father?" inquired the astonished Aleksèy.

" Elisavéta Grigórievna Múromsky," answered Ivan
Petróvitch.   " What a bride! eh?"

" Father, I have not as yet thought of marriage."

" Thou hast not thought!—that is why I have thought
for thee."

" As you please, but I do not like Lisa Múromsky."

" Thou wilt like her by-and-by.   Habit will bring the
liking with it."

" But I feel incapable of making her happy."

" Her happiness need not trouble thee.   What! is this
the way thou respectest thy father's wishes?   Very
well."

" As you please, but I do not wish to marry, and I
shall not marry."

" Thou shalt marry, or I shall disinherit thee, and as to
the estates, by ——, I shall sell or squander them away,
and shall not leave thee the fraction of a kopeck.   I give
thee three days to think it over, and do not thou dare to
come to me in the meanwhile."

Aleksèy knew that when his father took a thing into
his head, not even a nail, as Tarás Skotinine* has it,
would drive it out; but Aleksèy took after his father,
and was quite as difficult to overcome.   He retired to his
room and meditated upon the limits to a parent's will,
upon Elisavéta Grigórievna, upon his father's solemn
threat to make a beggar of him, and finally he thought

* A character in Von-Visen's comedy "Nedorosl."—Tr.

of Akulina. He felt for the first time clearly that he was passionately in love with her : the romantic idea of marrying a country girl, and earning his own living, flashed across his mind, and the more he dwelt upon such a project, the more reasonable it appeared. The meetings in the wood had not been continued for some time in consequence of wet weather. He wrote a distracted letter to Akulina, in an easily legible hand, informing her of the evil which threatened them, and offering his hand. He at once deposited the letter in their post-office, and retired to rest perfectly at ease.

Firm in his decision, Aleksèy rode over to Múromsky's early on the following morning, to inform him frankly of his intentions. He hoped to excite his sympathy, and to gain him over.

" Is Grigory Ivánovitch at home ?" asked he, pulling up his horse at the gate of the house at Prilútchino.

" No, sir," replied the servant ; " Grigory Ivánovitch left quite early this morning."

" How provoking !" thought Aleksèy. " Is Elisavéta Grigórievna at home ?"

" Yes, sir."

And Aleksèy, jumping off his horse, gave the servant the bridle, and walked in, without being announced.

" All will be decided," said he to himself, as he approached the drawing-room. " I shall explain it all to herself."

He entered—and remained petrified ! Lisa—no, Akulina, dear dark-haired Akulina, not in her *sarafan*, but in a white morning-dress, sat by the window, reading his letter; she was so taken up with it that she did not hear him enter the room. Aleksèy was unable to suppress a joyful exclamation. Lisa started, looked up, uttered a cry, and was about to run out. He rushed to hold her back.

" Akulina, Akulina !"

Lisa struggled to free herself.

" Mais laissez moi donc, monsieur—mais êtes-vous fou ?" she kept repeating, and turning away from him.

" Akulina, my friend Akulina !" reiterated he, kissing her hands.

Miss Jackson, who was witnessing the scene, knew not what to think. At that moment the door opened, and Grigory Ivánovitch entered.

" Aha !" said Múromsky; " why you appear to have settled the matter already."

My reader will spare me the unnecessary task of describing the *dénouement.*

THE PISTOL-SHOT.

I.

WE were quartered at ——. The daily routine of an officer in the army is not unknown. Drills and the riding school in the morning; dinner at the commandant's quarters or in a Jewish eating-house, and cards and punch in the evening, constitute the day's work. There was no society at ——, nor were there any marriageable girls; we used to meet at each other's rooms, where only men in uniform were to be seen.

One civilian, however, was admitted within our circle. He might have reached the age of five-and-thirty, and we therefore looked upon him as being greatly our senior in years. His large experience secured to him a certain amount of deference, and his usual moroseness, his stern and sarcastic disposition, exercised a powerful influence over our youthful imaginations. His past career seemed shrouded in mystery. Though bearing a foreign name, he was apparently a Russian. He had served at one time in the Hussars, and had even been fortunate in professional advancement; none of us knew the reason why he had retired from the service and taken up his abode in this wretched neighbourhood, where he lived penuriously, and yet extravagantly; he invariably went out on foot, and he was always seen in a black surtout the worse for wear, but at the same time he kept open house for all the officers of our regiment. Truth to tell, two or three dishes, cooked by an old pensioner, constituted his dinner, but, on the other hand, champagne flowed at his table. His circumstances and his income were unknown, and none of us presumed to ask any questions about either. His only books were works connected with the military service, and some novels which he willingly lent, never asking to have them returned, but neither did he give back those which he had borrowed. His chief pastime consisted in pistol-practice. The walls of his apartment were well riddled and perforated like a honeycomb. A valuable collection of pistols formed the only luxury of his humble habitation. The degree of perfection he had attained in this art was inconceivable; and had he required to shoot at a pear on any one's head, not one of our fellows would have hesitated to offer himself. Our conversation often touched on the subject of duelling. Silvio (as I shall name him) never joined in it; and when asked whether he had ever had occasion to fight, would answer dryly that he had; but he entered upon no details, and it was evident that these and similar questions were distasteful to him. We concluded that the recollection of some unfortunate victim to this dreadful accomplishment troubled his conscience, the idea of cowardice never even suggesting itself. There are people whose exterior alone suffices to disarm such suspicions. An unexpected occurrence disconcerted us all.

Some ten of us were one day dining with Silvio. We drank as usual,—that is, excessively,—and after dinner we endeavoured to prevail upon our host to be the banker in a game of faro. For some time he persisted in declining, for he seldom played, but at length he ordered the cards to be brought, threw fifty ducats on the table, and commenced to deal. We all took our places and the game began. Silvio was wont to keep the strictest silence upon such occasions, never discussing or explaining anything. If the punter chanced to make a mistake, he either paid up the balance immediately, or noted the surplus. We were already aware of this, and therefore never interfered. But of our number there was a young officer who had lately joined. He took part in the game, and in a fit of absence bent down one corner too many. Silvio took up the chalk and rectified the score, as was his custom. The officer thinking he was mistaken, began to explain matters. Silvio continued dealing in silence. The officer losing patience, rubbed out what to him appeared unnecessary. Silvio taking up the chalk, again marked the score. The officer, excited with wine, and by the game and the laughter of his comrades, imagined himself cruelly offended, and in his passion he lifted a metal candlestick off the table, and threw it at Silvio. who had barely time to evade the blow. We felt confused. Silvio rose, and with fire in his eyes said : " Please to walk out, sir, and thank your stars that this has happened under my roof."

We did not doubt the consequences; and we looked upon our new comrade as a dead man. He walked out, declaring himself ready to answer for the affront in such manner as the banker might elect. The game was continued for a few moments longer, but feeling how little our host's thoughts were in it, we left, one by one, and repaired to our quarters, discussing the possibility of a speedy vacancy.

When we met in the riding school on the following day, we immediately inquired of each other if our poor ensign was still alive. When he himself appeared, we greeted him, putting the same question! He replied that he had heard nothing of Silvio as yet. This surprised us. We went to Silvio, and found him in the yard, sending bullet after bullet into an ace of cards, which he had fixed to the gate. He received us as usual, and did not allude to the event of the preceding evening. Three days elapsed, and the ensign still lived. We asked in astonishment: "Can it be possible that Silvio will not fight?" Silvio did not fight. A very slight explanation satisfied him, and peace was restored.

Such conduct might have injured him excessively in the estimation of youth. The want of pluck is what young men excuse least, for they generally consider it the highest of human virtues—one that covers a multitude of sins! However, little by little, all was forgotten, and Silvio regained his former influence.

I alone could not become reconciled to him. Being naturally of a romantic turn of mind, I had, more than anybody, attached myself to the man whose very existence

was an enigma, and who appeared to me to be the hero
of some mysterious event. He liked me, at least it was
with me alone that he laid aside his usual cutting, ill-
natured observations, and that he conversed upon various
subjects with perfect good nature and rare pleasantness.
But I could not, subsequently to that unfortunate evening, rid myself of the idea that his honour had been tar-
nished, and that it was his own doing that the stain had
not been removed. This thought prevented my feeling
towards him as I had hitherto done, and I felt ashamed
to look upon him. Silvio was far too clever and too
shrewd, not to notice this and not to divine the cause.
He appeared hurt, and I fancied that I had more than
once detected a wish on his part to come to an understanding with me; but I avoided each opportunity, and Silvio
withdrew. Thereafter, I only met him in the presence of
my comrades, and our former intimacy came to an end.

The busy inhabitants of a capital can have no concep-
tion of the many excitements so familiar to those who
live in small towns or in villages—for example, the looking out for the periodical post-day; on Tuesdays and
Fridays our Regimental Office was crowded with officers ;
some expecting remittances, some letters, and some news-
papers. Letters and parcels were opened on the spot,
news communicated, and the office presented the most
animated appearance. Silvio's letters were addressed
under cover to our regiment, and he was therefore usually
present. Upon one of these occasions a letter was handed
to him, the seal of which he broke with a look of the
greatest impatience. His eyes brightened up as he perused

it. The officers were themselves too much engaged to notice anything. "Gentlemen," said Silvio, "circumstances require me to leave without delay; I go this night, and hope you will not refuse to dine with me for the last time. I expect you, also," he continued, turning to me; "I expect you without fail." With these words he hastened out, and we shortly dispersed, having agreed to meet at Silvio's.

I arrived at the appointed hour, and found nearly the whole of my brother-officers. Silvio's movables were all packed, and little remained but the bare and battered walls. We sat down to dinner; our host was in high spirits, and his cheerfulness was soon participated in; the corks flew incessantly, our glasses frothed and sparkled unceasingly, and we wished the traveller with all possible sincerity God speed, and every blessing. It was already late when we rose. While the caps were being sorted Silvio, bidding every one "good-bye," took me by the hand and detained me, just as I was upon the point of leaving. "I must speak to you," said he, in a low voice, I remained.

The guests had left; being alone, we sat opposite to each other, and silently began to smoke our pipes. Silvio was careworn, and there were no longer any traces of his affected cheerfulness. The pallor of his sombre face, his sparkling eyes, and the dense smoke issuing from his mouth, gave him a truly demoniacal look. Several minutes passed away, and Silvio broke silence:—

"We may perhaps never meet again," said he; "I wish to have an explanation with you before we part. You must have noticed how little I value the opinion of the world, but I like you, and I feel that it would prey upon me were I to leave an unjust impression respecting myself on your mind."

He stopped and began to re-fill his emptied pipe; I remained silent with lowered eyes.

"You thought it strange," he continued, "that I did not demand satisfaction from that tipsy fool R——. You will doubtless own that the right to choose weapons being mine, his life was in my hands, my own being almost beyond the reach of danger. I might ascribe this forbearance to pure generosity, but I will not deceive you. Had it been in my power to punish R—— without risking my own life in the least degree, I would by no means have let him off."

I looked at Silvio in surprise, and was completely taken aback by such a confession. Silvio went on:—

"That's just it. I have no right to imperil my life. I received a box on the ear six years ago, and my enemy still lives."

My curiosity was thoroughly awakened. "You did not fight him?" asked I. "Circumstances probably parted you?"

"I did fight him," answered Silvio; "and here is the memorial of our duel."

Silvio rose and took out of a hat-box a red cap, ornamented with a gold tassel and braid (what the French would call *bonnet de police*); he put it on; it had a hole about an inch from its edge.

"You know," continued Silvio, "that I served in the

— Hussars. My disposition is known to you. I am accustomed to take the lead, but in my early days it was a passion. At that time practical jokes were in fashion, and I was the greatest scamp in the whole army. We prided ourselves upon our drinking powers : I outdid the famous B**, whom D** D** has sung.* Duels took place constantly in our regiment. I took a part in all of them, either as a witness or as a principal. My comrades idolized me, and the regimental commanders, who were constantly changing, looked upon me as an unavoidable evil.

" I was thus quietly (that is, turbulently) enjoying my popularity, when there joined us a wealthy youth, a member of a well-known family (I do not wish to mention names). Never in my life have I met such a favoured child of fortune ! Imagine to yourself, youth, talent, good looks, the most exuberant cheerfulness, the most undaunted courage, a high-sounding name, wealth to which he knew no bounds, and you will form some idea of the impression his presence produced among us. My pre-eminence received a check. Dazzled by my reputation, he would have sought my friendship, but I received him coldly, and he turned from me without any show of regret. I began to hate him. His success in our regiment and in the society of ladies threw me into complete despair. I sought opportunities for a quarrel, but my epigrams were answered by epigrams, which always seemed to me more unexpected and more stinging

---

* A cavalry officer whose drinking powers and bravery have been immortalized by the warrior poet, Denis Davidoff (temp. Alexander I.)—Tr.

than my own: they were of course immeasurably more
lively. He was facetious; I was vicious. At last, upon
the occasion of a ball given by a Polish gentleman, seeing
that he was the object of attention of all the ladies, and
especially of the hostess herself, who was an ally of mine,
I whispered to him some grossly rude remark. He
warmed up, and gave me a box on the ear. We flew to
our swords. The ladies fainted; we were separated, but
that same night we drove off to fight a duel.

"The day was breaking. I stood at the appointed
spot, attended by my three seconds. I awaited with inexpressible impatience the arrival of my opponent. The
sun had already risen, and its rays were gathering heat.
I observed him in the distance. He was on foot, in uniform, wearing his sword, and accompanied by one second.
We walked on to meet him. He approached, holding in
his hand his cap, which was full of cherries. Our seconds
proceeded to measure twelve paces. I was to have fired
first, but my rage was so great that I could not rely upon
the steadiness of my hand, and to gain time, I conceded
to him the first shot. My opponent would not consent
to this. It was decided that we should draw lots; he,
with his usual good luck, won the toss. He aimed, and
his ball went through my cap. It was now my turn.
His life was in my hands at last. I looked eagerly at
him, trying to detect even a shadow of uneasiness. He
stood covered by my pistol, selecting the ripest cherries
out of his cap, and spitting out the stones, which nearly
reached me as they fell. His coolness exasperated me.
What is the use, thought I, of depriving him of his life,

when he values it so little? A wicked thought flitted
across my mind. I dropped the pistol. 'You are not
thinking of death now,' said I; 'you prefer to enjoy your
breakfast; I do not wish to disturb you!' 'You do not
disturb me in the least,' replied he, ' please to fire away;—
but, by-the-way, that is just as you please; your fire remains with you; I am always ready and at your service!'
I turned to the seconds, declaring I did not intend to
proceed at present, and thus our meeting ended.

"I quitted the service, and retired to this place. But
not a day has since passed without a thought of vengeance. Now my time has come . . . . . ."

Silvio drew out of his pocket the letter he had that
morning received, and handed it to me. Somebody (probably the person entrusted with the care of his business
matters) wrote word to him from Moscow, that *a certain
individual* was soon about to be united in lawful wed-
lock to a young and beautiful girl.

"You guess," said Silvio, "who is meant by this *certain individual*. I go to Moscow. We shall see whether
he will meet death as coolly on the eve of his marriage
as he once awaited it at his meal of cherries!"

Silvio rose at these words, threw his cap upon the
floor, and paced the room to and fro like a tiger in his
cage. I had listened to him in silence; strange and con-
flicting feelings had taken possession of me.

The servant walked in, and reported the horses ready.
Silvio pressed my hand warmly; we embraced each other.
He took his place in the *telega**, wherein lay two boxes,

* Country cart.—Tr.

one containing his pistols, the other his necessaries. We
bade each other good-bye once more, and the horses were
off.

II.

SEVERAL years had elapsed, and my private affairs necessitated my settling in a poverty-stricken little village in
the district of N——. Though occupied with the duties
of landlord, I could not help silently sighing after my
former rackety and reckless existence. I found it so
difficult to get accustomed to spend the long dismal
spring and winter evenings in such complete seclusion.
By chatting with the mayor, or going over new buildings
in progress, I managed somehow to drag through the day,
up to the dinner hour; but I literally knew not what to
do with myself at dusk. I had read the limited number
of books which I had found on the bookshelves and in the
lumber-room until I knew them by heart. All the stories
which the housekeeper Kirilovna knew had been told me
over and over again. I grew weary of listening to the
peasant women's songs, and might have had recourse to
sweet liqueurs, but that they made my head ache; and I
confess that I feared I might become a drunkard from a
feeling of wretchedness, that is to say the most wretched
of drunkards, of which I saw a number of instances in
our district.

I had no near neighbours, if I except two or three of
these wretched fellows, whose conversation consisted
chiefly of hiccoughs and sighs. Solitude was more en-
durable. At last I decided upon going to bed as early as

13

possible, and upon dining as late as possible; in this way I contrived to shorten the evenings and add to the length of the days, which I spent in useful occupations.

Four versts from me lay a very valuable estate belonging to the Countess B——; it was occupied by the agent only; the countess had visited it but once, and that in the first year of her marriage, when she had not stayed over a month. During the second year of my seclusion, rumours were current that the countess and her husband were coming to spend the summer. They really did arrive at about the beginning of June.

The appearance of a well-to-do neighbour is an important event to rustics. Landlords and tenants speak of it for two months previously and for three years subsequently. I confess that, so far as I was concerned, the presence of a young and beautiful neighbour seemed a matter of considerable importance to me. I burned with impatience to see her, and betook myself therefore after dinner, the first Sunday subsequently to their arrival, to pay my respects to their excellencies, as their nearest neighbour and most devoted of servants.

A footman showed me into the count's library and went to announce me. The spacious apartment was furnished with the greatest possible luxury; the walls were lined with bookcases, each of which was surmounted by a bronze bust; over the marble chimney-piece was placed a large mirror; the floor was covered with green cloth and spread with carpets. Having lost all habits of luxury in my poor retreat, and having long since ceased to be familiar with the effects produced by the riches of others, I became timid, and awaited the count with a certain trepidation, like a provincial petitioner expecting the approach of a minister. The doors opened, and a handsome man of two-and-thirty came in. The count approached me with frankness and friendliness. I endeavoured to muster courage and to explain the object of my call; but he anticipated me. We sat down. His easy and agreeable conversation soon dispelled my awkward shyness; I had already resumed my usual manner, when suddenly the countess entered, and my perturbation became greater than before. She was beautiful indeed. The count introduced me; I wished to seem to be at my ease, but the more I tried the more awkward did I feel. My new acquaintances, wishing to give me time to recover, and to feel myself more at home, conversed together, dispensing with all etiquette, thus treating me like an old friend. I had risen from my seat in the meanwhile, and was pacing the room inspecting the books and pictures. I am no judge of paintings, but one there was which specially attracted my attention. It represented a landscape in Switzerland; but I was struck, not by the beauty of the artist's touch, but because it was perforated by two bullets, one hole being just above the other.

"This is a good shot," said I, turning to the count.

"Yes," said he; "a very remarkable shot. Do you shoot well?" he went on.

"Pretty well," I replied, overjoyed that the conversation had turned upon a subject of interest. "I mean I

13—2

could not miss a card at thirty paces; of course, when I know the pistols."

"Indeed," said the countess, with a look of great attention : "and you, my dear, could you hit a card at thirty paces ?"

"Some day," answered the count, "we shall try. I was not a bad shot in my time, but it is now four years since I held a pistol."

"Oh," remarked I, "that being the case, I do not mind betting that your excellency will not be able to hit a card at twenty paces even : pistol shooting requires daily practice. I know this by experience. I used to be considered one of the best shots in our regiment. It so happened once that I had not touched a pistol for a whole month : my own were undergoing repair, and will your excellency believe it, when I took to shooting again, I missed a bottle four successive times at twenty paces ? Our riding-master, a sharp, amusing fellow, happening to be present, cried out : ' I say, old boy, thou canst not lift thy hand against the bottle, eh ?' No, your excellency, it is a practice that ought not to be neglected, if one does not wish to become rusty at it. The best shot I ever happened to come across practised every day, and would fire at least three times before dinner. This was a rule with him, as was his glass of *vodka*."

The count and countess appeared pleased at my having become talkative.

"And what kind of a shot was he ?" asked the count.

"Of that sort, your excellency, that if he happened to see a fly on the wall . . . You are smiling, countess. But it is true, indeed. . . . When he chanced to see a fly, he would call out: 'Kooska, my pistols!' Kooska brings him a loaded pistol. Bang! and there is the fly, flattened to the wall!"

"That was wonderful," said the count. "What was his name?"

"Silvio, your excellency."

"Silvio!" exclaimed he, jumping up; "you knew Silvio?"

"Knew him? Of course, your excellency. We were friends; he was considered by the regiment as being quite one of ourselves; but it is now five years since I heard anything of him. Your excellency appears also to have known him?"

"I knew him—knew him very well. Did he ever relate a very strange occurrence to you?"

"Your excellency cannot possibly mean a box on the ear, which some young scamp gave him at a ball?"

"And did he name that scamp to you?"

"No, your excellency, he did not; but,—your excellency," continued I, the truth beginning to dawn upon me, —"I beg your pardon—I was not aware—can it be yourself?"

"I, myself," answered the count, with an exceedingly perturbed countenance, "and the perforated picture is the reminiscence of our last meeting."

"Oh! pray, dear," said the countess, "pray do not speak of it. I dread hearing the story."

"No," replied he, "I shall relate the whole of it. He

knows how I offended his friend, let him now also know how Silvio took his revenge."

The count bade me be seated, and I listened with the liveliest curiosity to the following recital:—

"I was married five years ago. The first month, the *honeymoon*, was spent in this village. It is to this house that I am indebted for the happiest, as also for one of the saddest moments of my life.

"We were out riding one evening; my wife's horse became unmanageable; she got frightened, gave me her bridle, and set out homewards on foot. I saw upon entering the stable-yard a travelling *telega*, and was informed that a gentleman, who had refused to give his name, and had simply said that he had some business to transact, was waiting for me in the library. I entered this room, and in the twilight saw a man covered with dust and wearing a long beard. He was standing by the fire-place. I approached him, trying to recall to mind his features. 'Thou dost not recognize me, count,' said he, with trembling voice. 'Silvio!' exclaimed I; and I confess I felt my hair stand on end! 'Yes, it is I,' he continued, 'the shot remains with me; I have come to discharge my pistol; art thou ready?' The pistol protruded out of his side pocket. I measured twelve paces, and stood there, in that corner, begging him to fire quickly, before my wife returned. He hesitated, he asked for lights. Candles were brought in. I shut the door, gave orders that no one should come in, and again begged him to fire. He took out his pistol, and proceeded to take aim . . . I was counting the seconds . . . I thought of her . . . One dreadful minute passed.

Silvio let his arm drop. 'I regret,' said he, 'that my pistol is not loaded with cherry stones ... The bullet is heavy. This appears to me not a duel, but murder : I am not accustomed to aim at an unarmed man : let us begin anew; let us draw lots who is to have the first fire.' My head swam ... I suppose I was not consenting ... At last another pistol was loaded; two bits of paper were rolled up; he placed them in the cap I had once shot through ; I again drew the winning number. 'Thou art devilish lucky, count,' said he, with an ironical smile I can never forget. I do not understand what possessed me, and by what means he forced me to it ... but I fired—and hit that picture there."

The count pointed to the perforated picture ; his face was crimson, the countess had become whiter than her handkerchief; I could not suppress an exclamation.

" I fired," the count went on : " and, thank God, missed. Then Silvio ... (he looked really dreadful at that moment) Silvio aimed at me. Suddenly the doors opened, Masha* rushed in, and with a scream threw herself on my neck. Her presence restored to me all my courage. 'Darling,' said I, 'don't you see that we are joking ? How frightened you are ! Go and take a glass of water and come back to us; I shall introduce an old friend and comrade to you.' Masha still doubted. 'Tell me, is what my husband says true ?' said she, turning to the sombre Silvio, 'is it true that you are both in fun ?' 'He is always in fun, countess,' replied Silvio. 'Once upon a time he gave me a box on the ear, in fun; in fun, he shot through this

* The pet name for Maria.—Tr.

cap; in fun, he just now missed me; now I have a fancy to be in fun also.' So saying, he was about to take aim ... before her! Masha threw herself at his feet. 'Get up, Masha, for shame!' I exclaimed, enraged; 'and you, sir, will you cease jeering at a poor woman? Are you, or are you not, going to fire?' 'I am not going to,' answered Silvio, 'I am content. I have seen your hesitation, your timidity. I made you fire at me. I am satisfied. You will remember me. I leave you to your conscience!' Here he was about to take his departure, but stopping in the doorway, he looked at the perforated picture, fired his pistol at it, almost without aiming, and disappeared. My wife had fainted; the servants dared not stop him, and looked at him with terror; he walked out, called the *yemstchik**‎ and drove off, before I had even time to recover myself."

The count concluded. Thus did I learn the ending of a story which had so interested me at its commencement. I did not again meet its hero. It was said that at the time of the revolt under Alexander Ypsilanti, Silvio commanded a detachment of the Heteræ, and was killed in the combat before Skulleni.

* A driver of post-horses.—Tr.

THE SNOW-STORM.

TOWARDS the end of the year 1811, an ever-memorable epoch for us, the kind-hearted Gavrilo Gavrílovitch R—— lived on his estate Nenarádovo. He was well known in the whole district for his hospitality and benevolence; neighbours from all quarters were continually dropping in upon him to partake of his good fare; some came, looking forward to a game of Boston at five kopeck stakes with his wife, Prascóvia Petróvna, others chiefly to get a glimpse of their daughter, Maria Gavrílovna, an elegant, pale-faced girl of seventeen, who, being considered a rich heiress, was destined by many of the men for themselves, whilst others would elect her for their sons.

The reading of French novels had perceptibly influenced Maria Gavrílovna's character. and consequently she was ever feeling that she must be in love. The chosen object of her affections was a poor ensign in the army, just then at home on leave of absence. It should be understood that the young man was inflamed with a like passion, and the parents of his beloved one, upon discovering these their mutual inclinations, forbade their daughter even to think of him, and the youth was r ceived by them with as little courtesy as they would have shown to a superannuated assessor.

Our lovers corresponded, and met daily, unobserved, either in the shade of the pine forest or by the old chapel. Here they exchanged vows of constant love, bewailed their cruel fate, and meditated upon means of deliverance. These letters and secret conferences led them (and very naturally so) to the following conclusions: that life would be a burden were they to be separated from each other, and as her hard-hearted parents chose to place obstacles in the way of their happiness, would it not be possible to forego their consent altogether? Of course it was the young man who first originated this happy idea, which very much pleased the romantic Maria Gavrílovna.

Winter setting in put an end to their meetings, but their correspondence became the more active. Vladimir Nikoláevitch besought Maria Gavrílovna in each of his letters to give herself up to him, urging her to a clandestine marriage, proposing that they should keep themselves concealed for a while, and that they should finally throw themselves in repentance at her parents' feet, who by that time would doubtless be touched by such unequalled constancy, and by the unhappiness of the lovers, and would be certain to receive them with the exclamation, "Children! come to our arms."

Maria Gavrílovna wavered long; one plan of flight was dismissed for another. At last she consented: it was arranged that she should, on the appointed day, retire to her room before supper, under the pretext of suffering from a headache; that accompanied by her maid, who would be privy to the arrangement, she should descend to the garden, and pass out at the back gate ; that a sledge should be in readiness, and that she should drive to the village of Jádrino, about five versts from Nenarádovo, and alight at the church, where Vladimir would be found awaiting her.

Maria Gavrílovna passed a sleepless night ; she packed up her things into a bundle, and wrote one long letter to a certain friend, a sentimental young lady, and another to her parents. She bade them farewell in the most pathetic terms, urging in extenuation of her conduct, the unsurmountable strength of her passion, and concluded with the assurance that she would consider it the happiest moment of her existence when she should be able to throw herself at their feet. Having sealed both the letters with a Toula seal, bearing the representation of two flaming hearts and an appropriate motto, she flung herself upon her bed just before daybreak and slumbered. But her rest was disturbed by horrible dreams. Now she saw her father arresting her just as she was on the point of driving off to be married ; she felt that he was dragging her with lightning speed over the cold snow, and hurling her into a dark unfathomable pit, and she was falling headlong, with an inexpressible sickness at heart. Then she saw Vladimir, stretched on the ground, pale and bloodstained. He was dying, and calling upon her in a piercing voice to become his bride—these and other equally shapeless, equally wild visions, passed before her. She rose at last, paler than usual, and this time with a real headache. Her father and mother noticed her indisposition; their tender solicitude and constant inquiry, "What ails thee, Masha?" went to her heart. She tried to reassure them, and endeavoured to assume her usual cheerfulness, but she could not succeed. Evening came on. The thought that she was now spending her last day in her old home seemed unendurable. She was scarcely conscious, and was mentally bidding a secret farewell to everybody, to every object which surrounded her. Supper was served. Her heart beat fast. Her voice faltered as she declared she did not require any supper, and bade her father and mother "good-night." They kissed and blessed her as was their wont; she strove hard to conceal her tears. But upon reaching her room and finding herself alone, she threw herself upon a couch and wept. Her maid entreated her to be calm and to take courage. All was ready. But one half-hour, and Masha was to quit for ever her parents' roof, her room, her peaceful maiden existence. A snowstorm was raging: the wind howled, the shutters creaked and shook; she looked upon all this in the light of a warning, of a sorrowful omen. At last the household was wrapped in silence and sleep. Masha drew a shawl around her shoulders, threw on a warm cloak, took her casket, and slipped through the back entrance. Her maid followed her, carrying two bundles. They entered the garden. The storm had not abated, the wind blew violently into their faces, as if desirous of arresting the young culprit. The garden gate was reached with some difficulty. The sledge was in readiness. The chilled horses refused to stand still, and Vladimir's coachman was trying to curb their restlessness. He assisted the young lady and her maid into the sledge, stowed away the casket and bundles, seized the reins, and they were off.

Having entrusted the lady to the care and management of Teréska, the coachman, let us return to the young lover.

Vladimir had been astir all day. In the morning he had called on the priest of Júdrino, whose scruples he with some difficulty overcame; he then went to invite witnesses amongst the neighbouring landowners. He first unburdened himself to Dravin, a retired cornet of about forty, who willingly consented. "This incident," he said, "reminded him of times long gone by, and of his regimental sprees!" He pressed Vladimir to stay and dine, having first convinced him that he would meet with no difficulty in the choice of the two other witnesses. And he was right, for scarcely was dinner over, when there appeared Schmidt, the land-surveyor, who wore a moustache and spurs; and a youth of sixteen, the son of the Captain of Police, who had quite recently joined the Uhlans. They not only accepted Vladimir's invitation, but went so far as to assure him of their readiness to lay down their lives in his cause. Vladimir embraced them with rapture, and started off to prepare.

Twilight was already setting it. Valdimir despatched his *troika** to Nenarádovo in charge of his trusty Teréshka, with strict and detailed instructions, and ordered the small one-horse sledge to be got ready for himself, and dispensing with a coachman, he left for

* Any vehicle drawn by three horses abreast.—Tr.

Jádrino, where Maria Gavrílovna would be in a couple of hours. He knew the road, and it was but a twenty minutes' drive.

Vladimir had scarcely cleared the paddock, and found himself in the open country, when the wind rose and a blinding snow-storm set in. In an instant the road became undiscernible: the country around had disappeared in a thick, yellowish mist, across which the white snow-flakes were chasing each other. The sky and the earth had melted into one; Vladimir found that he had strayed into the fields, and endeavoured, but in vain, to regain the road; his horse went at random and was now lifting him over the drifted snow, then sinking him in a ditch; the sledge was continually upsetting; his only care was not to swerve from the right direction. But he fancied that half an hour, and even longer, must have elapsed, and the Jádrino wood was not yet reached. Ten minutes passed away, and still no wood was to be seen. He was now driving across fields intersected by deep ditches. The snow-storm was not abating, and the sky did not look any clearer. Vladimir's horse was beginning to show signs of fatigue, and he himself was drenched in perspiration, notwithstanding his being continually up to his waist in snow.

Convinced at last that he had taken a wrong direction, he stopped and began to reflect and to consider his position, when he felt persuaded that he should have turned to the right. He now did so. His horse could scarcely move. But he had already been driving over an hour. Jádrino could not be far off. He pressed on and on, however, and the fields seemed never to end. Snowdrifts and ditches still intercepted his progress; the sledge was still being upset, and he was continually righting it. Time sped on, and Vladimir became seriously alarmed.

At last a dark spot loomed in the distance. He turned in its direction, and discovered it to be a wood. " Thank God," thought he, "it is all right now." Vladimir kept close by its hedge, hoping either to come upon the well-known tracks or to make the circuit of the forest: Jádrino lay just behind it. The track soon appeared, and he plunged into the gloom of the now leafless trees. Here he was sheltered from the wind; the road was easy, the horse stepped out, and Vladimir's anxiety abated.

But he still travelled on and on, and Jádrino was nowhere to be seen. The track seemed endless. Vladimir now discovered with horror that he had penetrated into a strange forest. Despair seized hold upon him. He struck the horse; the poor animal started off at a trot, but soon relaxed its pace, and in a quarter of an hour it toiled on step by step, and all the unhappy Vladimir's efforts to hurry it onwards were fruitless.

By degrees the trees thinned and the wood was cleared; no Jádrino. It must then have been close upon midnight; Tears started to his eyes; he drove recklessly. The storm in the meanwhile abated; the clouds dispersed; a broad plain, a white undulating carpet, stretched before him. The night had cleared up. He observed that a hamlet, consisting of four or five tenements, was not far off. He drove to it. Pulling up at the first cottage, he jumped out of the sledge and rapped at the window.

Shortly the wooden shutter was raised and an old man pushed his gray beard through.

"What dost thou want ?"

"Is Jádrino far from here ?"

"Is Jádrino far ?"

"Yes, yes, is it far ?"

"Not far, ten versts may be !"

On hearing this, Vladimir clutched his hair, and remained motionless, like a man condemned to death.

"And whence art thou ?" continued the old man.

Vladimir had not the heart to answer his question.

"I say, old man," said he, "canst thou let me have horses to take me to Jádrino ?"

"What dost thou talk to me of horses for ?" answered the *mujik.**

"May I not at least have a guide ? He shall have whatever he asks."

"Stay," said the old man, letting down the shutter; "I shall send thee my son, he will conduct thee."

Vladimir waited. One minute could barely have elapsed, before he knocked again. The shutter was raised and the beard peeped out.

"What dost thou want ?"

"Well, what about thy son ?"

"Coming directly, he is getting his boots on. Maybe thou art cold ; come in and warm thyself."

"No, thanks ; send thy son quickly."

The gates creaked ; a lad came out armed with a club and took the lead, now pointing to the road, now searching for it, where the snow had drifted.

* Peasant.—Tr.

"What o'clock is it ?". asked Vladimir.

"It will soon be day-break," answered the young *mujik*.

Vladimir uttered not another word.

The cocks were crowing and the day was dawning when they reached Jádrino. The church was closed. Vladimir rewarded his guide and drove into the priest's stable-yard. No *troika* was to be seen, and what were the news which here awaited him ?——

But let us return to the good people of Nenarádovo and see what is going on there.

Nothing.

The old people rose and proceeded into the drawing-room—Gavrilo Gavrílovitch in his nightcap and warm jacket, Prascóvia Petróvna in a wadded dressing-gown. The *samovar* was brought in, and Gavrilo Gavrílovitch despatched the maid to inquire after Maria Gavrílovna's health, how she felt, and how she had slept. The girl returned declaring that the young lady had not had a good night, but she now felt better, and would herself be down directly. The door opened and Maria Gavrílovna walked in, and bade her papa and mamma good-morning.

"How is the head, Masha ?" asked Gavrilo Gavrílovitch.

"Better, papa," answered Masha.

"Perhaps the fumes from the stove had given thee a headache," said Prascóvia Petróvna.

"Perhaps, mamma," answered Masha.

The day passed happily, but that night Masha was taken ill. A messenger was despatched into the town for the doctor. He arrived towards the following even-

14

ing and found her delirious. A violent fever set in, and
the poor patient lay for a fortnight between life and
death.

No suspicion was entertained of the planned flight.
The letter written on the eve had been burned. The
maid had disclosed nothing, fearing the displeasure of her
master and mistress. The priest, the retired cornet, the
moustached land surveyor, and the charming young
Uhlan were equally reserved, and not without reason.
Teréshka, the coachman, was not in the habit of ever
dropping an idle word, not even in his tipsy moments,
and thus more than half a dozen actors maintained the
secret of the plot.

But Maria Gavrílovna herself was ready to disclose all
in her ravings.   Nevertheless, her utterances were so
disconnected, that even her mother, who never quitted
her bedside, could only gather from them that her
daughter was desperately in love with Vladimir Nikoláevitch, and to this attachment was due the cause of her
illness.   She consulted her husband and some of her
neighbours, and they all unanimously arrived at the conclusion that one could not flee one's destiny; that poverty
was no sin, that one did not marry riches, but a husband,
and so on.   It is wonderful how consoling moral precepts
become when we know of no excuse in exculpation of
our conduct.

The young lady was in the meanwhile recovering.
Vladimir had long since discontinued his visits. The reception he usually met with scared him. It was now
resolved that he should be sent for and made acquainted

with the unexpected happiness in store for him—consent to their union. What must have been their surprise when the only answer this invitation elicited was received in the shape of a disconnected and raving letter, in which Vladimir informed them that he could never again put his foot into their house, and begged them at the same time to forget the hapless being whose only comfort henceforth was to be looked for in the grave? They heard a few days later that he had rejoined the army. This was in 1812.

It was a long time before the convalescent Masha could be told of it.

She never mentioned Vladimir now. Upon seeing his name on the list of the severely wounded at Borodino, a few months after the preceding events, she fainted away, and fears were entertained of a relapse. But fortunately the swoon was followed by no serious consequences.

Another trial awaited her. Gavrilo Gavrílovitch died, leaving her sole heiress to all he possessed. But this legacy did not console her. Prascóvia Petróvna's grief was most sincerely shared by her daughter, who protested that she would never leave her; they quitted Nenarádovo, so replete with sad reminiscences, and settled on one of their other estates.

Admirers flocked here also around the amiable and wealthy heiress, but she encouraged none of them. Her mother sometimes urged her to make a choice, but on such occasions Maria Gavrílovna would only shake her head and look pensive. Vladimir had ceased to exist: he died at Moscow on the eve of the entry of the French

Masha held his memory sacred: that is, she treasured up whatever would recall him to mind—the books he had once read, his drawings, the music and poetry which he had copied for her. These facts having come to the knowledge of the neighbours, they wondered at so much devotion, and with curiosity awaited the hero who would overcome the sorrowful constancy of this maiden Artemesia.

The war had in the meantime come to a glorious termination. Our troops were returning from abroad. The people hurried to meet them. Bands were sounding strains of conquest: *Vive Henri Quatre*, Tyrolese valses, and airs from Jocunda. The fields of battle had changed those who had set out for the campaign as mere striplings into men, and they were now returning decorated with crosses. Soldiers were seen conversing gaily, mixing here and there French and German words in their conversation.

Oh! the never-to-be-forgotten time! A time of glory and rapture! How fast did the Russian heart beat at the word Fatherland! How joyous were the tears at meeting! How unanimously did we then unite our feeling of national pride to our love for the sovereign! And for himself,——what a moment!

The women, the Russian women, were then incomparable. Their habitual indifference had disappeared. Their rapture was simply intoxicating, when they met the conquerors with shouts of Hurrah!—

*"And threw their caps into the air."**

---

* Griboyedov's Comedy, "Gōre āt oumà," act ii. sc. 5.—Tr.

Which of our officers then would have hesitated to admit that it was at the hands of our Russian women that he met his best, his most precious reward ?

Maria Gavrílovna and her mother remained quietly in the country during this brilliant epoch, and did not see how the two capitals entertained the returning army. But in the country and villages the general enthusiasm had been raised, were it possible, to a still higher pitch. The appearance of an officer in such a neighbourhood was a real triumph, and woe betide the suitor in plain clothes !

As we have already stated, Maria Gavrílovna, notwithstanding her indifference, was surrounded by admirers. But all had to withdraw, when there appeared on the field the wounded colonel of Hussars, Bourmin, wearing the order of St. George * in his button-hole, and looking *interestingly pale*, as the young ladies of the place described him. He was about six-and-twenty, and had returned on leave of absence to his estate, which adjoined that of Maria Gavrílovna. Maria Gavrílovna singled him out in a marked manner. His presence cheered her. One cannot say that she coqueted with him, but a poet observing her would have said—

"Se amor non è, che dunque."

Bourmin was in truth a charming young man. He had what always pleases a woman : a blending of good breeding and tact, a man with no pretensions, and yet withal slightly satirical in spite of himself. His deport-

---

* Decoration for valour.—Tr.

ment towards Maria Gavrílovna was open and frank, but do what she might, say what she would, his soul and his eyes pursued her. His manners were gentle and discreet, but rumour asserted that once upon a time he had been a sad scamp, a report which in no way affected him in the opinion of Maria Gavrílovna, who (like young ladies in general) was quite willing to forgive all follies characteristic of a dashing and high-spirited disposition.

But more than all—(more than his tenderness, more than his interesting paleness, more than his splintered arm),—more than all was it the young hussar's reserve that stimulated her curiosity and tortured her imagination. She could not help admitting that he was much prepossessed in her favour; no doubt he also, with his keenness and experience, must already have observed how much she noticed him; how was it then that she had not yet seen him at her feet, had not yet heard his avowal? What was it that kept him back? Was it timidity, ever inseparable from real love? Was it pride, or the toying of an astute hanger-on? She was puzzled. Having thought over the matter, she finally arrived at the conclusion that timidity must be the sole cause, and she resolved to encourage him by greater attentions, and should circumstances necessitate, even by tenderness. She was preparing a most unexpected *dénouement*, and impatiently awaited the moment for a romantic explanation. A secret, whatever its nature, always weighs heavily on a woman's heart. Maria Gavrílovna's tactics met with the desired success; at least Bourmin fell into a thoughtful mood, and his black eyes rested with so much passion on Maria Gavrílovna, that the decisive moment seemed near. Their marriage was talked of as a matter of course, and the good Prascóvia Petróvna rejoiced that her daughter had at last found a bridegroom worthy of her.

The old lady was sitting in the drawing-room, dealing cards at a game of fortune, when Bourmin entered and immediately inquired after Maria Gavrílovna.

"She is in the garden," was the reply; "go to her, I will remain and wait for you here."

The old lady crossed herself and thought, "Please God, the matter will be settled to-day."

Bourmin found Maria Gavrílovna by the lake under a willow, book in hand, and dressed in white—truly a heroine of romance. After the first interchange of words Maria Gavrílovna purposely let the conversation flag, increasing thereby their mutual embarrassment, from which perhaps only a sudden and decided explanation could now extricate them. And thus it was: Bourmin, feeling the awkwardness of his situation, declared that he had long sought an opportunity to lay open his heart and begged a few moments' attention. Maria Gavrílovna closed her book and drooped her eyes in token of consent.

"I love you," said Bourmin; "I love you passionately . . . ." (Maria Gavrílovna blushed and drooped her head still lower.) "I have acted imprudently in abandoning myself to the habit, the sweet habit of seeing you, of hearing you, daily . . . ." (Maria Gavrílovna called to mind St. Preux's first letter.) "It is now too late to rebel against one's destiny, and the remembrance of you, of

your dear incomparable image, must ever remain the joy
and torment of my existence; but a hard duty still
remains to be performed, the dreadful secret must be
disclosed, that secret which raises an insurmountable
barrier between us . . . ."

"That barrier has always existed," interrupted Maria
Gavrílovna with vivacity. "I never could have been
your wife . . . . "

"I know," answered he softly, "I know that you once
did love, but death, but three years of mourning . . . .
My dear, my good Maria Gavrílovna! do not seek to
deprive me of this last consolation, of the thought that
you would have consented to secure my happiness, were
it not that . . . . ."

"Leave off, for Heaven's sake, leave off! you torture
me . . . ."

"Oh yes! I know, I feel that you would have been
mine, but . . . . I am the most wretched of beings . . . .
I am married!"

Maria Gavrílovna looked up at him in astonishment.

"I am married," continued Bourmin; "I have been
married nearly four years, and I know not who my wife
is, where she is, and whether I shall ever see her again?"

"What is it you say?" exclaimed Maria Gavrílovna;
"how strange! go on, I will say something later . . .
pray do go on."

"Early in the year 1812," said Bourmin, "I was hastening to Wilna, where my regiment was quartered. Arriving
at a station late one evening I ordered horses to be got in
immediate readiness, when a dreadful snow-storm came

on, and the station-master and the drivers all urged my
waiting. I took their advice; but an unaccountable
uneasiness came over me, I felt strangely impelled to
push on. The fury of the storm remained unabated, but
I could wait no longer, and ordering the horses to be put
to a second time, I drove off, weather notwithstanding.
The driver bethought himself of a short cut across the
river, which would curtail our journey by three versts.
But the snow having drifted over the river bank we
missed the looked-for turning, and we thus found ourselves
in an unknown part of the country.

" The storm still raged; but I espied a light in the
distance, and we drove towards it. We entered a village;
in the little wooden church, the door of which stood open,
glimmered a light; several sledges stood outside the
paling and people loitered about the porch. 'This way,
this way!' exclaimed several voices. I ordered the man
to drive up. 'Dear me,' said one, 'what has delayed you?
The bride has fainted, the priest is at his wit's end, and
we have almost decided upon going home. But jump
out quickly !' I silently stepped out of the sledge and
entered the church, which was dimly lit up by two or
three candles. One young girl was sitting on a form in
a dark corner, another stood by chafing her temples.
'Thank God !' said the latter, 'here you are at last; you
have nearly been the death of my young lady.' The old
priest now approached me with the question, 'Do you
desire me to commence ?' ' Go on, go on, father,'
answered I absently. They raised the girl. I fancied
she was comely .... What incomprehensible, unpardon-

able wantonness ! . . . . I placed myself at her side before the reading desk ; the priest hurried on; three men and her maid supported the bride, and were occupied solely with her. We were married, and told to kiss each other. My wife turned her pale face towards me. I was about to kiss her . . . . She exclaimed, ' Oh, 'tis not he ! 'tis not he !' and fainted away. The witnesses raised their startled gaze at me. I turned, left the church without the slightest opposition, threw myself into the *kibitka*, and exclaimed, ' Go on !' "

" My God !" cried Maria Gavrílovna; "and you do not know what has become of your wife ?"

"I do not," answered Bourmin; "the name of the village is unknown to me ; I do not recollect the station which adjoined it, and I attached such little importance to my criminal frolic at that time that I fell asleep upon leaving the church, and did not awake until the next morning, when we were already nearing the third station. The servant who then accompanied me died on the march, so that I am bereft of even the hope of discovering her whom I so cruelly injured, and who is now so bitterly avenged."

" My God ! my God !" gasped Maria Gavrílovna, grasping his arm, "was it you ? and is it possible you do not know me ?"

A pallor overspread Bourmin's features . . . . and he threw himself at her feet. . . . .

THE UNDERTAKER.

THE last of the goods and chattels of the undertaker.
Adrian Próhoroff's were heaped into the hearse, and a
pair of lean horses dragged it along for the fourth time
from the Basmánaja to the Nikítskaja, for to the latter
street the undertaker was removing with all his household. Having closed his old shop, he nailed a notice to
the door, to the effect that the premises were to be sold
or let, and started off on foot to his new abode. He was
surprised to find on approaching the little yellow house,
which had so long taken his fancy, and which he had at
last bought for a considerable sum, that he did not feel in
good spirits. Having crossed the new threshold and
finding his new abode in great confusion, he sighed at the
recollection of the old hovel, where during eighteen years
everything had been conducted with the strictest regu-
larity, and he scolded his daughters and the maid-of-all-
work for their dilatoriness, and set to, assisting them
himself. Order was soon established; the sacred image-
case, the dresser with the crockery, the table, sofa, and
bed, occupied the corners assigned to them in the back
room; in the kitchen and the sitting-room was placed

the master's handiwork, which consisted of coffins of all
sizes and colours, and the cupboards were filled with
mourning cloaks and torches. Over the gate appeared a
sign-board, representing a corpulent Cupid holding a
reversed torch, with the inscription: HERE ARE SOLD AND
ORNAMENTED PLAIN AND PAINTED COFFINS; COFFINS ALSO
LET OUT ON HIRE, AND OLD ONES REPAIRED. The girls
retired to their room, and Adrian having inspected his
dwelling, sat down by the window, and ordered the
samovar to be got ready.

The enlightened reader is aware that both Shakespeare
and Walter Scott represented their grave-diggers as
cheerful and jocose persons, in order to strike our imagination more forcibly by the contrast. Out of regard to
truth, however, we cannot follow their example, and are
compelled to admit that the disposition of our undertaker
fully corresponded with his mournful calling. Adrian
Próhoroff was habitually sullen and thoughtful. His
silence might occasionally be broken for the sole purpose
of scolding his daughters when he chanced to find them
idle, gazing out of the window at the passers-by, or asking an exorbitant price for his goods, of those who had
the misfortune (and sometimes also the good fortune) to
require them. Thus it happened that Adrian, now sipping
his seventh cup of tea, was as usual sunk in melancholy
reflections. He thought of the pouring rain which fell at
the very outset of the retired Brigadier's funeral the
previous week. Many mourning cloaks had shrunk in
consequence, and many hats had been spoiled. He foresaw unavoidable expenditure, for his old stock of mourn-

ing attire had fallen into a pitiful condition. He hoped to charge a good round sum at the funeral of the merchant Truhin's old wife, who had now been nearly a year at death's door. But the old woman lay dying at Rasgoulaï, and Próhoroff feared lest her heirs, notwithstanding their promise, would neglect to send for him all that distance, and would come to terms with the nearest undertaker.

These meditations were unexpectedly disturbed by three freemason-like taps at the door.

" Who is there ?" asked Próhoroff.

The door opened, and a man in whom the German artisan was recognized at a glance, walked in, and cheerfully approached the undertaker.

"Pardon me, my dear neighbour," said he, in that Russian dialect which we cannot listen to without a smile. " Pardon my intruding upon you—I was anxious to make your acquaintance. I am a bootmaker, my name is Gottlieb Schulz, and I live across the street, in the little house facing your windows. To-morrow I celebrate. my silver wedding, and I came to ask you and your daughters to dine with us in a friendly way."

The invitation was accepted with good-will. The undertaker asked the bootmaker to sit down and take a cup of tea, and thanks to the cordial disposition of Gottlieb Schulz, their conversation soon became friendly.

"How does your trade prosper ?" asked Adrian.

" Ah—he—he !" answered Schulz, "so, so, I cannot complain, although my goods are of course different from yours : a live man can do without boots, but a dead man cannot do without a coffin."

"Very true," remarked Adrian; "however, if the live man has not got wherewith to pay for his boots, one cannot take it amiss in him if he goes barefooted, but a dead beggar has a coffin gratis."

In this manner they conversed for some time. At last the bootmaker rose, and taking leave of the undertaker, renewed his invitation.

The next day at twelve o'clock precisely, the undertaker and his daughters passed through the wicket of the newly bought house on their way to neighbour Schulz. I shall not describe either the Russian *caftan** of Adrian Próhoroff, or the European attire of Akoulina and Daria, departing in this respect from the now so prevalent custom among novelists. I do not, however, consider it superfluous to remark, that both young ladies wore yellow bonnets and red shoes; this they did only on grand occasions.

The small dwelling of the bootmaker was filled with guests, who chiefly consisted of German artisans, their wives, and their workmen; of Russian *employés* there was but one, the Esthonian, Yoorko the watchman, who had, in spite of his lowly calling, managed to secure the special good-will of his host. He had served in this capacity for five-and-twenty years, faithfully and honestly, like the postman† of Pogarelsky. The fire of 1812, which destroyed the chief capital, annihilated also his yellow watch-box. But as soon as the enemy was expelled, a new one appeared in its stead: it was gray,

---

* A long coat worn by the lower classes.—Tr.

† In "Grandmother's Cat."—Tr.

with small white Doric pillars, and Yoorko *in gray cloth armour and axe** was again seen pacing before it. Almost all the Germans who lived in the vicinity of the Nikitsky gates knew him, and some had even chanced to spend the night of Sunday to Monday morning under his roof. Adrian hastened to make his acquaintance as he would that of a man of whom he might stand in need, sooner or later, and when the guests took their seats at dinner, they sat next to each other. Monsieur and Madame Schulz and their daughter Lottchen, who had seen but seventeen summers, whilst dining with and entertaining their guests, assisted the cook to wait upon them. Beer flowed. Yoorko ate for four; Adrian did not cede to him; his daughters, however, stood on ceremony. The conversation kept up in the German language, was becoming louder and louder. Suddenly the host begged for a few moments' attention, and drawing the cork of a sealed bottle, exclaimed in a loud voice, in Russian: "The health of my good Louisa!" The so-called champagne sparkled. The host tenderly kissed the fresh face of his forty-year-old helpmate, and the guests drank noisily to the health of the good Louisa. "The health of my amiable guests!" exclaimed the host opening a second bottle. And his guests thanked him, and again drained their glasses. Here toast followed upon toast; the health of each guest was drunk separately; they toasted Moscow and an entire dozen of little German towns, all corporations in general, and each one in particular; they drank to masters, and they drank to foremen. Adrian drank sedulously, and

* Ismailoff's fables.—Tr.

was so elated that he himself proposed some jocular toast.
Suddenly, one of the guests, a fat baker, raised his glass,
and exclaimed: "To the health of those we work for—
unſerer Kunbleute!" This proposal, like all the others, was
joyously and unanimously applauded. The guests saluted
each other, the tailor bowed to the bootmaker, the bootmaker to the tailor, the baker to both; all to the baker,
and so on. Yoorko, in the midst of these mutual saluta-
tions, exclaimed, turning to his neighbour:

"What, now? drink, sir, to the health of thy dead
ones."

All laughed, but the undertaker considering himself
affronted, became sullen. Nobody noticed him; the party
continued its carouse, and the bells had already rung for
vespers when all rose from the table.

The guests dispersed at a late hour, and most of them
were elevated. The fat baker and the bookbinder, whose
face appeared as if bound in red morocco, led Yoorko
between them to his box, carrying out in this case the
Russian proverb: *A debt is rendered honourable by payment.* The undertaker returned home tipsy and wrathful. "Why, indeed," reasoned he aloud: "why is my
craft worse than any other? Is an undertaker, then,
brother to an executioner? What had the heathens to
laugh at? Is an undertaker a Christmas harlequin? I
meant to have asked them to a house-warming, to have
given them a feast; but let them wait till they get it.
And I shall now invite instead those for whom I work,
my orthodox dead."

"What, sir?" said the maid, who was pulling off his

boots, "what dost thou talk about ? Make the sign of the cross ! To ask the dead to a house-warming ! What horror !"

"By —— I shall ask them," continued Adrian; "I shall ask them at once, for to-morrow. Pray come, my benefactors, come to feast with me to-morrow evening; I shall entertain you with what God has given me." So saying, the undertaker tumbled into bed, and soon began to snore.

It was still dark when Adrian was roused. The merchant ‚Truhin's wife had died that very night, and a special messenger had been sent on horseback with this intelligence. The undertaker gave him a ten-copeck piece for a *vodka*,* dressed in haste, took a *droshky*, and drove to Rasgoulaï. The police were already stationed at the gates of the house where lay the defunct; tradespeople were going in and out, like ravens at their prey. The corpse lay on a table, yellow as wax, but not yet disfigured by decomposition. Relations, neighbours, and friends crowded around. All the windows stood open ; candles were burning ; priests were reading prayers. Adrian went up to Truhin's nephew, a young merchant in a fashionable coat, and assured him that the coffin, candles, pall, and other funeral furniture, would be delivered with all punctuality and without fail. The heir thanked him absently, saying that he would not bargain about the expense, but should trust implicitly to his conscience. The undertaker, as usual, swore that he

---

* A glass of spirits.—Tr.

15

would not overcharge; exchanged a significant glance
with his workmen, and started off to make the necessary
arrangements. The whole day was spent driving to and
fro between Rasgoulaï and the Nikitsky gates; towards
evening, all being arranged, he settled with his driver,
and returned homewards on foot. It was a moonlight
night. The undertaker had safely reached the Nikitsky
gates. At the Church of the Ascension, our friend
Yoorko hailed him, and on recognizing the undertaker
wished him good-night. It was getting late. The undertaker was approaching his house, when he suddenly
fancied he saw some one nearing it, open the wicket, pass
through, and disappear. "What can this mean?" thought
Adrian. "Who is it wants me again? Can it be a thief?
Do lovers perhaps visit my silly girls? It bodes evil!"
And the undertaker was on the point of calling his friend
Yoorko to come to his aid. Just then some other person
approached the wicket and was about to enter, but, on
becoming aware that Adrian was nearing hurriedly, this
person stopped, and raised his cocked hat; Adrian fancied
he knew the face, but was not, in his haste, able to
examine it closely. "You were coming to me," said
Adrian, breathlessly; "do me the favour to step in."

"No ceremonies, friend," said the stranger, in a hollow
voice; "walk on, show thy guests the way!"

There was no time to stand on ceremony. The wicket
stood open, Adrian went up the staircase, the person
following him. Adrian fancied that people were walking
about his rooms. "What devilry is this?" thought he,
and hurried in—but here his legs gave way. The room

was full of dead people. The moon shining through the windows, lit up their yellow and blue faces, sunken mouths, dull half-closed eyes, and thin protruding noses. Adrian recognized in them, with dread, people who had been buried with his aid; and in the guest whom he had preceded, the brigadier who had been interred during the pouring rain. All the women and men assembled, surrounded the undertaker, bowing, and greeting him; all except one poor fellow, who had quite recently been buried gratis, and who, shy and ashamed of his tatters, did not venture to come forward, but stood retiredly in a corner. The rest were respectably dressed : the women wore caps with ribbons; those men who had served the State, were in uniform, but their faces were unshaven; merchants wore their holiday *caftans.* "Seest thou, Próhoroff," said the brigadier, in the name of this select company, "how we have all risen at thy invitation. Those alone have remained at home who could not possibly come, who had quite crumbled to pieces, or who had no skin, but only their bare bones left; but even thus, one of them could not rest—so anxious was he to see thee !"

At that moment a small skeleton pushed his way through the crowd, and approached Adrian. His skull smiled affectionately at the undertaker. Bits of light green and red cloth, and of old linen, hung here and there about him, as upon a pole, whilst the bones of his feet rattled in his Hessian boots, like a pestle in a mortar. "Thou dost not recognize me, Próhoroff," said the skeleton. "Dost thou remember the retired sergeant of the

15—2

Guards, Piotr Petróvitch Kurilkin, the same for whom thou soldest thy first coffin, in the year 1799—and one of pine too, for one of oak!" So saying, the corpse extended his bony arms towards him; but Adrian, mustering all his strength, cried out, and pushed him from him. Piotr Petróvitch tottered, fell, and went to pieces.

A murmur of indignation was heard amongst the dead; they stood up for the honour of their fellow, threatening and upbraiding Adrian; and the poor host, deafened by their cries, and almost pressed to death, losing his presence of mind, fell across the bones of the retired sergeant of the Guards, and remained unconscious.

The sun-light had long been streaming across the bed on which the undertaker was sleeping. At last he opened his eyes, and saw before him the maid, blowing at the charcoal of the *samovar*. Adrian remembered with dread all the events of the preceding day: Truhin, the brigadier, and the sergeant appeared dimly before him. He was silently expecting the girl to begin the conversation, and to relate to him the results of the night's adventures.

"How thou hast overslept thyself, Adrian Próhoro-vitch, sir," said Aksinia, handing him his dressing-gown. "Thy neighbours, the tailor and the watchman, came to thee with the announcement that it was the Saint's-day of the Commissary of Police, but thou wast pleased to sleep, and we did not like to awake thee."

"And did they come to me from the late Madame Truhin?"

"Late? Is she then dead?"

"Fool that thou art! didst not thou thyself help me to arrange things for her funeral?"

"Hast thou lost thy senses, sir? or have the fumes of last night's drink not passed off yet? What funeral was there yesterday? Thou didst feast at the German's all day, and coming home tipsy, didst throw thyself on thy bed, and didst sleep until this very hour, when the bells have already rung for mass."

"Indeed!" said the rejoiced undertaker.

"Of course," answered Aksinia.

"Well, if that is the case, let us have the *samovar* quickly, and call my daughters."

THE STATION-MASTER.

Is there anybody who has not cursed the station-masters, who has not abused them? Is there anybody who has not demanded of them the fatal book in an angry moment, so as to enter therein the unavailing complaint against delays, incivility, and inexactitude? Is there anybody who does not look upon them as being the scum of the human race, like the late Government Clerks,* or at the least like the Mouromsky brigands?† Let us, however, be just; let us realize the position, and perhaps we shall judge them with some leniency. What is a station-master? The veritable martyr of the fourteenth class, whose rank serves only to save him from blows, and not so even at all times. (I appeal to the conscience of my readers.) What is the duty of these dictators, as Prince Viazemsky humorously styles them? Is it not in truth hard labour? No rest day or night. It is him the traveller assails irritated by the accumulated vexations of a tiresome journey. Is the weather atrocious; are the roads in a bad state; is the driver dogged; do the horses

* An allusion to the corrupt nature of those ill-paid employés.—Tr.

† *Murom*, a territory now included in the government of Vladimir, where robbers formerly infested the woods.—Tr.

refuse to go?—the fault is surely the station-master's. On entering his poor dwelling, the wayfarer looks upon him as he would a foe; the station-master may consider himself fortunate if he succeeds in ridding himself of his uninvited guest; but should there be no horses? Heavens! what abuse, what threats! He is about in the rain and sleet, and takes refuge in the lobby in storms, and during the Epiphanial frosts, to escape, were it but for a moment, the complaints and assaults of the irritated travellers. A general arrives: the trembling station-master gives his two last *troikas*, including the courier's. The general is off, without uttering so much as "Thank you." Five minutes later—bells!—and a state messenger throws his order for horses on the table! Let us examine these matters closely, and our hearts will commiserate rather than fill with indignation. A few words more. In the course of twenty years, I have travelled through Russia in all directions; I know almost all the post-roads, and I am acquainted with several generations of drivers; there are few station-masters unknown to me by sight, and few with whom I have not had some intercourse. I hope to publish at no distant period some interesting notes made during my travels; I shall here merely observe, that the station-masters as a class are most falsely represented. These much-calumniated station-masters are in a general way quiet people, naturally obliging, sociably inclined, unassuming, and not over money-loving. From their conversation (which travellers do wrong to scorn) one may learn much that is interesting and instructive. I must own, that so far as I myself am concerned, I much prefer it to the tall talk of some *employé* of the sixth class, travelling on the service of the Crown.

It will be easily guessed that I have some friends amongst this respectable class of men. Indeed, the memory of one of them is precious to me. Circumstances had once brought us together, and it is of him I now intend to speak to my kind readers.

In May, 1816, I happened to be travelling through the government of * * *, on a road which is now in disuse. My rank was insignificant; I changed carriages at every stage, paying post-rates for two horses. Consequently the station-masters did not treat me with any distinction, and I often had to obtain by force what should have been mine by right. Young and impetuous, I used to vent my indignation on the station-masters for their meanness and obsequiousness, when the *troika* to which I had a right was given up for the carriage of some person of high rank. Equally did it take me some time to get accustomed to being passed over by a discriminating serf at the governor's dinner-table. To-day, both these circumstances appear to me to be in the order of things. Indeed, what would become of us, if the one very convenient maxim, *Rank honours rank*, were superseded by this other, *Intellect honours intellect?* What differences of opinion would arise; and who would dependents wait upon first? But to return to my tale.

The day was hot. A few drops of rain fell at three versts from the station, but it soon began to pour, and I got wet through. On arrival, my first care was to change my clothes as quickly as possible, my second to order tea.

" Here, Dounia !" shouted the station-master ; " get the *samovar* ready, and run and fetch some cream."

At these words, a girl of about fourteen appeared from behind the partition, and ran into the lobby. I was struck by her beauty.

" Is that thy daughter ?" asked I of the station-master.

" Yes, it is," answered he, with an air of satisfied pride ; " she is so sensible and so quick, and quite takes after her poor mother."

Here he began to copy my order for horses, whilst I amused myself looking at the prints which ornamented the walls of his humble but neat chamber. They represented the story of the Prodigal Son : in the first, a venerable old man, in a night-cap and dressing-gown, parts with the restless youth, who hastily accepts his blessing and a bag of money. In the next, the dissipated conduct of the young man is portrayed in glaring colours : he is sitting at a table, surrounded by false friends and shameless women. Farther on, the ruined youth, in a tattered shirt and cocked hat, is seen feeding swine and sharing their meal ; his face expresses deep sorrow and repentance. His return to his father is last represented : the good old man, in the very same night-cap and dressing-gown, rushes to meet him ; the prodigal son is on his knees ; in the background, the cook is slaying the fatted calf, and the elder brother is inquiring of the servants the reason for so much rejoicing. Under each of these pictures, I read appropriate verses in German. All this has remained impressed on my memory, as have also the pots of balsam,

the bed with coloured curtains, and the other objects
which then surrounded me. I fancy I still see the host
himself, a fresh and good-natured looking man of about
fifty, wearing a long green coat, with three medals suspended by faded ribbons.

I had scarcely settled with my old driver, when Dounia
returned with the *samovar*. The little coquette had at a
second glance noticed the impression she had made on
me; she dropped her large blue eyes; I entered into conversation with her; she answered without the slightest
timidity, like a girl accustomed to the ways of the world.
I offered a glass of punch to her father, gave Dounia a cup
of tea, and we three conversed as if we had always known
each other.

The horses had long been ready, but I was unwilling
to part with the station-master and his little daughter.
At last I bade them "good-bye;" the father wished me
a prosperous journey, and the daughter accompanied me
to the carriage. I stopped in the lobby and asked leave
to kiss her: Dounia consented. I can remember having
given many kisses "since I first took to that occupation," but none have left such lasting, such pleasant
recollections.

Several years passed by, and circumstances led me to
the same places by the same roads. I remembered the old
station-master's daughter, and rejoiced at the prospect of
seeing her again. "But," thought I, "the old station-
master has perhaps been removed; Dounia is probably
married." The possibility of the death of the one or of the
other also crossed my mind, and I neared the station of

* * * with melancholy apprehensions. The horses stopped at the little post-house. On entering the room, I at once recognized the pictures representing the history of the Prodigal Son; the table and bed stood in their old places, but there were now no flowers on the sills, and everything showed symptoms of decay and neglect. The station-master was sleeping under his sheepskin coat; my arrival awoke him; he raised himself. It was Sampson Virin, indeed: but how he had aged! Whilst he was arranging the papers to copy my order for horses, I looked at his gray hairs, at the deep wrinkles on a long-unshaven face, on his bent form, and could not help wondering how it was possible that three or four years had changed him, hale as he used to be, into a feeble old man.

"Dost thou recognize me?" asked I; "we are old friends.

"Maybe," answered he, gruffly; "this is the high road, many travellers have halted here."

"Is thy Dounia well?" I continued.

The old man frowned. "God knows," answered he.

"Then she is married, I suppose," said I.

The old man feigned not to hear me, and continued reading my *padarojnaya** in a whisper. I ceased interrogating him, and asked for some tea. A feeling of curiosity disquieted me, and I was hoping that some punch would loosen the tongue of my old acquaintance.

I was not mistaken; the old man did not refuse the proffered glass. I observed that the rum was dispelling

---

* An official order for post-horses.—Tr.

his moroseness. He became talkative at the second glass, remembered, or pretended to remember me, and I learned from him the story, which at that time interested and touched me deeply.

"And so you knew my Dounia?" he began. "Who did not know her? Oh! Dounia, Dounia! what a girl she was. All who came here praised her; never a word of complaint. Ladies used to give her now a neckerchief, then a pair of earrings. Travellers would stop purposely, as it were, to dine or to sup; but, in truth, only to look at my Dounia a little longer. The gentlemen, however choleric, would calm down in her presence and talk kindly to me. Will you believe it, sir? courtiers, state messengers, used to converse with her for half an hour at a time. She kept the house; she cleaned up, she got things ready, she used to find time for everything. And I, old fool that I am, could not admire her sufficiently, could not appreciate her enough! Did not I love my Dounia? did not I pet my child? Was not her life happiness itself? But no, one cannot flee misfortunes; what is ordained must come to pass." Here he recounted his troubles in detail. Three years had passed since one winter evening, whilst the station-master was ruling out a new book, and his daughter was working at a new dress behind the partition, a *troika* pulled up, and a traveller, wearing a Circassian cap and military cloak, and wrapped in a shawl, entered the room, calling for horses. All the relays were out. At this piece of intelligence, the traveller was about to raise his voice and his stick, but Dounia, accustomed to such scenes, ran out, and softly addressing the stranger, asked him whether he would be pleased to take some refreshment! Dounia's appearance produced its usual effect. The traveller's anger passed off; he consented to wait for the horses, and ordered supper. Upon taking off his wet rough cap, undoing his shawl, and throwing off his cloak, the traveller turned out to be a slight young Hussar, with a small black moustache. He made himself at home, and conversed gaily with the station-master and his daughter. Supper was served. Horses had in the meanwhile returned, and the station-master ordered their being put to without being even baited; but on re-entering the room, he found the young man on a form, almost insensible: he had suddenly felt faint, his head ached, and he could not possibly proceed on his journey. What was to be done? The station-master gave up his bed to him, and it was decided that the doctor at S * * * should be sent for, should the patient not feel better in the morning.

The next day the Hussar was worse. His servant rode off to the town for the doctor. Dounia bound his head with a handkerchief steeped in vinegar, and sat down at her work by his bedside. In the station-master's presence, the patient groaned and scarcely spoke; but he managed nevertheless to empty two cups of coffee, and, still groaning, to order his dinner. Dounia never left him. He was constantly calling for something to drink, and Dounia would hold up a mug of lemonade, which she had herself prepared. The patient would wet his lips, and whenever he returned the mug, his feeble hand pressed Dounia's in token of gratitude. The doctor arrived towards noon. He felt the patient's pulse, had some conversation with him in German, and declared in Russian that all he required was rest, and that in a couple of days he would be able to resume his journey. The Hussar handed him twenty-five roubles as his fee, and invited him to dinner. The doctor accepted; they ate with good appetites, drank a bottle of wine, and parted perfectly satisfied with each other.

Another day passed, and the Hussar was quite himself again. He was exceedingly cheerful, joking incessantly, now with Dounia, then with the station-master, whistling all sorts of tunes, talking to the travellers, copying their orders for horses into the post-book, and he contrived to ingratiate himself so much with the good-natured station-master, that he felt sorry to part with his amiable host when the third morning arrived. It was a Sunday. Dounia was preparing for Mass. The Hussar's carriage drove up. He took leave of the station-master, having rewarded him liberally for his board and hospitality; he also bid Dounia good-bye, and offered to drive her as far as the church, which was situated at the very extreme of the village. Dounia looked perplexed—" What art thou afraid of?" said her father: "his excellency is not a wolf, and will not eat thee; take a drive as far as the church." Dounia took her seat in the carriage next to the Hussar, the servant jumped into the rumble, the driver whistled, and the horses were off.

The poor station-master was not able to understand how he, of his own accord, should have allowed Dounia to drive off with the Hussar; how he could have been blinded to such an extent, and what could have possessed him. Half an hour had not elapsed when his heart already ached, and he felt so much anxiety, that he could contain himself no longer, and accordingly strode off to the church. On reaching it, he saw that the people were already dispersing, but Dounia was neither within the enclosure nor yet at the porch. He hurriedly entered the church; the priest was emerging from behind the altar; the clerk was extinguishing the candles; two old women were still praying in a corner; but no Dounia was to be seen. The poor father could scarcely make up his mind to ask the clerk whether she had been at Mass. The clerk answered that she had not. The station-master returned home, neither dead nor alive. One hope remained. Dounia might possibly, young and thoughtless as she was, have taken it into her head to go on to the next station, where her godmother lived. He awaited in a desperate state of agitation the return of the *troika* which had carried them off. No driver returned. At last towards evening he appeared, but alone and tipsy, with the killing news that Dounia had gone off with the Hussar.

This disaster was too much for the old man; he immediately took to the bed where the young deceiver had lain but the day before. And he now conjectured, after pondering over all the late circumstances, that the illness had been feigned. The poor fellow was attacked by a serious fever; he was taken into the town of S * * *, and another station-master was temporarily appointed to replace him. The medical man who had seen the Hussar, attended him also. He assured him that the young man was in perfect health, and that he had, even when he visited him, a suspicion of his wicked intentions, but had observed silence for fear of his chastisement. Whether what the German said was true, or whether he only wished to make a boast of his foresight, he did not minister any consolation to the poor sufferer. Scarcely had he recovered from his illness than the station-master at once applied to the post-master at S * * * for two months' leave of absence, and without saying a word respecting his intentions, set out on foot, in search of his daughter. He knew by his papers, that the Cavalry Captain Minsky was going from Smolensk to St. Petersburgh. The man who had driven him had said, that though she appeared to go willingly, Dounia had cried the whole way. "It is just possible," thought the station-master, "that I may bring home my little lost sheep." He arrived at St. Petersburg with this idea, and stopping at the Ismailoffsky Barracks put up at the quarters of a retired sub-officer, an old comrade: and commenced his search. He soon learnt that Minsky was at St. Petersburg, staying at Demouth's Inn. The station-master decided upon going to him.

He appeared at his door early the following morning, and asked to be announced as an old soldier who wished to see his excellency. The military servant, who was cleaning a boot on a last, declared that his master was asleep, and that he saw no one before eleven o'clock. The station-master went away and returned at the appointed hour. Minsky himself came to him, in his dressing-gown and a red smoking cap. "What is it thou wantest, my friend ?" he asked. The old man's heart beat fast, tears gushed to his eyes, and he could only utter in a trembling voice: "Your excellency !—for God's sake do me the favour !"—Minsky threw a quick glance at him, bridled up, took him by the hand, led him into his study, and closed the door. " Your excellency !" the old man continued, " what is fallen is lost ; give me back my poor Dounia. You have trifled sufficiently with her; do not ruin her uselessly." " What is done cannot be undone," said the young man in extreme confusion. " I am guilty before thee and ready to ask thy forgiveness ; but do not imagine I can abandon Dounia ; she will be happy, I give thee my word for it. What dost thou want her for ? She loves me, she is no longer accustomed to her former mode of living. Neither of you will be able to forget the past." Here he slipped something into the old man's sleeve, opened the door, and the station-master found himself in the street, he scarcely knew how.

For a long time he stood motionless ; at last he noticed a roll of paper in the cuff of his sleeve ; he drew it out, and unrolled several bank-notes of the value of five and ten roubles. Tears came to his eyes again—tears of indignation ! He crushed the notes, threw them from him, trampled them under-foot, and walked away.—Having proceeded a few paces, he stopped, reflected,—and retraced his steps—but no bank-notes were there. A well-dressed young man on seeing him rushed up to a *droshky*, into which he hastily threw himself and shouted out: " Go on !" The station-master did not follow him. He

16

had made up his mind to return home, but he wished to
see his poor Dounia once again before leaving. With this
end in view he returned to Minsky two days later; but
the soldier-servant roughly told him that his master
received no one, and pushing him out of the hall, slammed
the door in his face. The station-master waited, and still
waited, and then went his way.

He was walking along the *Letéynaya* that same
evening, having listened to a *Te Deum* at the Church of
*Vsch Skarbiastchech.** A smart *droshky* suddenly dashed
past him, and he recognized Minsky. The *droshky*
stopped at the entrance of a three-storied house, and the
Hussar ran up the steps. A happy thought flashed across
the station-master. He turned back, and approaching
the coachman: "Whose horse is this, my friend?" asked
he; "not Minsky's?"—"Yes, Minsky's," answered the
coachman: "what dost thou want?"—"Why, this; thy
master ordered me to take a note to his Dounia, and I
have forgotten where his Dounia lives."—"It is here she
lives, on the second floor. Thou art too late with thy
note,' my friend: he is with her himself now."—"No
matter," said the station-master, with a violent beating
of the heart; "thanks for directing me; I shall know how
to manage my business." And with these words he
walked up the flight of stairs.

The doors were closed; he rang. For several seconds
he stood in uneasy expectation. The key rustled; the
doors were opened. "Does Avdotia Samsónovna live

* All the afflicted.—Tr.

here ?" asked he. "Yes," answered the young servant.
" What dost thou want her for ?" The station-master,
without saying a word, entered the ante-room. "You
cannot come in, you cannot come in," shouted the girl
after him—"Avdotia Samsónovna has visitors." But the
station-master walked on without heeding her. The first
two rooms were dark, there were lights in the third. He
approached the open door and stopped; Minsky was
seated thoughtfully in this richly furnished apartment.
Dounia, dressed in all the luxury of fashion, was sitting
on the arm of his easy-chair, like a horsewoman in her
English saddle, looking tenderly down upon Minsky, and
twisting his dark curls with her jewelled fingers. Poor
station-master! Never had he seen his daughter looking
so beautiful! He could not help admiring her. "Who
is there ?" asked she, without raising her head. He
remained silent. Not receiving any reply, Dounia looked
up—and uttering a cry, fell to the floor. The alarmed
Minsky rushed to raise her, but on becoming aware of
the old station-master's presence, he left Dounia and
approached him, quivering with rage : "What dost thou
want ?" said he, clenching his teeth. "Why dost thou
track me, as if I were a brigand ? Dost thou want to
murder me ? Be off!" And seizing the old man by the
collar, with a strong arm he pushed him down the stairs.

The old man returned to his rooms. His friend advised him to lodge a complaint; but the station-master
having reflected awhile, waved his hand, and decided
upon giving it up. Two days later he left St. Petersburg.
and returned direct to his station, where he resumed his

16—2

duties. "This is now the third year that I live without Dounia, and I have neither heard from her, nor have I seen her. God knows whether she is alive or dead. Anything may happen. She is neither the first nor the last who has been enticed away by a scampish wayfarer, and who has first been cared for, and then deserted. There are plenty of these young simpletons at St. Petersburg, who are to-day in satins and velvet, and to-morrow you see them sweeping the streets in degraded misery. When the thought crosses me that Dounia may be ruining herself in the same manner, one sins involuntarily, and wishes she were in the grave."

Such was the story of my friend the old station-master —a story more than once interrupted by tears, which he picturesquely wiped away with his coat-tails, like zealous Terentitch in Dmitrieff's beautiful ballad. Those tears were partly induced by the punch, of which he emptied five glasses during his recital; but be that as it may, they touched me deeply. Having taken my leave, it was long before I could forget the old station-master, and long did I think of poor Dounia.

Lately again, on passing through * * * I recollected my friend. I learned that the station which he had superintended had been abolished. To my inquiry, "Is the old station-master alive?" I could obtain no satisfactory answer. I made up my mind to visit the familiar locality, and, hiring a private conveyance, I left for the village of N.

It was autumn. Gray clouds obscured the sky; a cold wind swept over the reaped fields, carrying before it the red and yellow leaves that lay in its course. I entered the village at sunset and stopped before the little post-house. A fat old woman came into the lobby (where poor Dounia had once kissed me) and replied to my inquiries by saying that the old station-master had been dead about a year, that a brewer was settled in his house, and that she herself was the brewer's wife. I began to regret my useless drive and the seven roubles I had profitlessly expended.

"What did he die of?" I inquired of the brewer's wife.

"Drink, sir," answered she.

"And where is he buried?"

"Behind the enclosure, next to his late missus."

"Could anybody conduct me to the grave?"

"Why not? Here, Vanka! leave off pulling the cat about. Take this gentleman to the churchyard, and show him the station-master's grave."

At these words a ragged, red-haired lad, who was blind of one eye, ran up to me, and set out as my guide.

"Didst thou know the dead man?" I asked him by the way.

"How was I not to know him? He taught me how to make reed whistles. Many a time have we shouted after him when on his way from the public-house (God rest his soul!), 'Daddy, daddy, give us some nuts!' And he would then throw nuts at us. He always played with us."

"And do travellers ever talk of him?"

"There are few travellers now. The assessor may oc-

casionally turn in this way, but it is not the dead he cares
for! In the summer, a lady actually did drive by, and
she did ask after the station-master, and went to see his
grave."

"What lady?" asked I, with curiosity.

"A beautiful lady," answered the lad: "she drove a
coach and six horses, with three little gentlemen, a wet-
nurse, and a black pug dog, and when told that the old
station-master had died, she began to cry, and said to the
children, 'Sit you here quietly, whilst I go to the churchyard.' Well, I offered to show her the way. But the
lady said: 'I know the road myself,' and she gave me
five kopecks in silver—such a lady!"

We arrived at the cemetery, a bare place, with nothing
to mark its limits, strewn with wooden crosses, with not
a tree to shade it. Never in my life had I seen such a
melancholy grave-yard.

"This is the grave of the old station-master," said the
boy, jumping on a mound of earth, over which a black
cross with a copper image was placed.

"And the lady came here?" asked I.

"Yes," answered Vanka. "I looked at her from a distance. She threw herself down here, and so she lay a
long time. Then she went into the village, called the
priest, gave him some money, and drove away; and to
me she gave five kopecks in silver—a splendid lady!"

I also gave the lad five kopecks, and no longer regretted
my journey, or the seven roubles I had spent.

THE MOOR OF PETER THE GREAT.

CHAPTER I.

AMONGST the number of young men sent abroad by Peter the Great for the purpose of acquiring the knowledge so indispensable to an empire undergoing reformation, was his godson, the negro Ibrahim.* He had been educated at the Military Academy of Paris, which he quitted with the rank of a Captain of Artillery. He distinguished himself in the Spanish war, and returned to the French capital severely wounded. The emperor found time, in the midst of his extensive occupations, to inquire unceasingly after his favourite, and always received flattering reports of his conduct and progress. Peter was pleased with him above measure, and more than once invited him to return to Russia, but Ibrahim was in no haste. He found frequent cause for excuse; at one time it was his wound, at another a wish to perfect his studies, then a want of money; and Peter was indulgent, entreated him

* An ancestor of Poushkin, whose real name was Hannibal.—Tr.

to nurse his health, thanked him for his zeal in the pursuit of knowledge, and although extremely careful in his own expenditure, was not sparing in his supplies to him, and the ducats were accompanied by fatherly advice and instructions for his guidance.

Judging by all historical memoirs, nothing could be compared to the frivolity, folly, and luxury of the French at that period. No traces were left of the last years of the reign of Louis XIV., so marked by austere piety, gravity, and decorum at court. The Duke of Orleans, who to so many brilliant qualities united vice of every kind, was unfortunately free of every shadow of hypocrisy. The orgies of the Palais Royal were no secret; the example was contagious. At that time Law appeared, whose love of money was joined to a thirst after pleasures and enjoyment; fortunes were squandered, morality was on the wane; the French were merry and prodigal, and the empire was crumbling to the music of satirical *vaudevilles.*

Society in the meanwhile presented a most interesting picture. Civilization and a desire for amusements had made all classes akin. Riches, gallantry, fame, talents, peculiarities, even, everything that gave food to curiosity and promised diversion, was received with equal goodwill. Literature, learning, and philosophy quitted their retirement to appear within the circle of the great world, to gratify fashion and govern its opinions. The women reigned, but did not now clamour for adoration. A superficial politeness had replaced the profound respect which had formerly been paid to them. The follies of the Duke

de Richelieu, that Alcibiades of the modern Athens, belong
to history, and give an insight into the morals of those
times.

> *Temps fortuné, marqué par la licence,*
> *Où la folie, agitant son grelot,*
> *D'un pied léger parcourt toute la France,*
> *Où nul mortel ne daigne être dévot,*
> *Où l'on fait tout excepté pénitence.*

The appearance of Ibrahim, his exterior, his education,
and his natural talents attracted universal attention in
Paris.   All the ladies sought to receive *le Nègre du Czar*,
and caught at him from each other.   The regent invited
him more than once to his cheerful evening parties; he
was a guest at the suppers which were enlivened by the
youth of Arouet, the age of Cholier, and the conversation
of Montesquieu and Fontenelle.   He did not miss a single
ball, a single fête, a single first performance, and rushed
into the great whirlpool with all the impetuosity of his
years and of his temperament.   But it was not only the
idea of exchanging these brilliant entertainments for the
simplicity of the court of Petersburg that alarmed Ibrahim ; other and stronger ties bound him to Paris.

The Countess L——, no longer in the first bloom of
youth, was still famed for her beauty.   On leaving the
convent at the age of seventeen, she had been wedded to
a man to whom she had not had time to become attached,
and who did not afterwards try to gain her affections·
Rumour ascribed to her many lovers ; but owing to the
forbearing construction of society, she enjoyed an un-
sullied reputation, for no one had ever been able to lay at
her door any adventures in the least way ridiculous or

equivocal.   Her *salons* were among the most fashionable:
the *élite* of Parisian society assembled in them.   Ibrahim
had been introduced to her by young Merville, who was
generally supposed to have been her latest lover, a reputation he endeavoured to sustain by all possible means.

The countess received Ibrahim politely, but without
any marked attention: he was flattered.   The young
negro had got accustomed to being looked upon as a
wonder, to see himself surrounded and assailed by com-
pliments and questions; and this curiosity, hidden though
it was by a semblance of good-will, wounded his vanity.
The sweet attention of women, which we so strive by every
effort to win, far from causing him any pleasure, filled
him rather with bitterness and indignation.   He felt that
he was considered by them to be but a rare sort of animal,
of a different creation, who had accidentally dropped in
their midst, and who possessed nothing in common with
them.   He even envied those people who remained un-
noticed, and considered them fortunate in their insig-
nificance.

The feeling that nature had debarred him from in-
spiring any passion raised him above self-confidence and
ambitious pretensions, and invested his intercourse with
women with a rare charm.   His conversation was unaffected and dignified.   He pleased the Countess L——,
who had got weary of the refined jests and artful insinua-
tions of French wits.   Ibrahim, frequently visited her.
She gradually became accustomed to the young negro's
appearance, and ended by seeing something pleasant in
this curly head, the blackness of which stood out con-

spicuously among the powdered wigs in her reception-
rooms. (Ibrahim had been wounded in the head, and
wore a bandage in lieu of a wig.) His age was twenty-
seven, he was tall and well proportioned, and more than
one beauty had looked upon him with a sentiment far
more flattering than that of sheer cusiosity; but the prejudiced Ibrahim either was not aware of it, or considered
it mere coquetry. So soon, however, as his looks met
those of the countess, his mistrust vanished. There was
so much sweet kindliness in the expression of her eyes,
her deportment towards him was so frank, so unaffected,
that it was impossible to suspect in her the least shadow
of wantonness or mockery.

He never thought of love, but that he should see the
countess daily had become an absolute necessity. He
sought to meet her everywhere, and yet each meeting
seemed to him to be an unexpected favour from heaven.
The countess had guessed his feelings, before he himself
had done so, so certain is it that a hopeless, self-denying
love touches a woman's heart more surely than do all
the artifices of vice. When Ibrahim was present, the
countess followed all his movements, and cherished
every word he uttered; away from him she became pensive, and relapsed into her habitual absence of mind.
Merville was the first to notice this mutual inclination,
and congratulated Ibrahim. Nothing aids so much to
intensify love, as the approbation of a casual observer.
Love is blind, and afraid to trust itself; it clutches greedily
at any support.

Ibrahim's was roused by Merville's words. The possibility of possessing the woman he loved, had not hitherto crossed his mind ; hope burst suddenly into his very soul ; he loved desperately. It was in vain that the countess, alarmed at the demonstration of his passion, endeavoured to oppose it by friendly exhortations, and the counsels of reason ; she felt that she wavered . . . .

Nothing escapes the attention of an observing world. The countess's new attachment soon became universally known. Some ladies wondered at her choice ; many thought it a very natural one. Some jeered at it, whilst others called it an unpardonable imprudence. In their first rapture, Ibrahim and the countess remained insensible to what was passing ; but soon the ambiguous jokes of the men, and the caustic criticisms of the women, reached their ears. Ibrahim's dignified and cold demeanour had hitherto ensured him against such attacks. He bore them impatiently, and knew not how to avert them. Accustomed as she had been to the esteem of society, the countess could not bear with indifference to see herself becoming the object of scandal and ridicule. At one time she would complain with tears to Ibrahim ; at another, she would bitterly reproach him ; again, she would implore him not to take her part, so that she should not be entirely lost, through fruitless justifications . . . .

*　　*　　*　　*　　*　　*

Ibrahim loved passionately, and was also beloved ; but the countess was capricious and inconstant. It was not for the first time that she loved. Aversion, even hatred, would replace in her heart the most tender feelings.

Ibrahim already foresaw the moment when she would be lost to him. He had not hitherto known what jealousy was, but now felt a dread presentiment of it; he imagined that the pang at parting would be less terrible, and meditated the rending asunder of this unfortunate connection, by leaving Paris and returning to Russia, whither Peter, and a vague feeling of duty, had long been calling him.

CHAPTER II.

DAYS and months went by, and the enamoured Ibrahim could not make up his mind to quit the countess, whose attachment towards him grew with every hour. The busy tongue of scandal had ceased to work, and the lovers began to breathe more freely as they remembered in silence the storm which had passed over them, and endeavoured not to think of the future.

One day Ibrahim attended the Duke of Orleans' reception. The duke stopped as he passed him, handed to him a letter, and commanded that it should be read at his leisure. The letter was from Peter I. The emperor, guessing the real cause of Ibrahim's absence, wrote word to the duke that he had no intention of influencing Ibrahim's movements; that he left it to his free will whether to return to Russia or not; but in any case he would never forsake his foster son. This letter touched Ibrahim deeply. From that moment his resolution was taken. On the following day he informed the regent that it was his intention to proceed to Russia without delay. "Think

well over the step you are about to take," said the duke.
" Russia is not your country. I do not suppose that chance
will ever again lead you to see your burning native clime,
but your long sojourn in France has in an equal degree
estranged you from the climate and half savage mode of
life in Russia. You were not born a subject of Peter.
Hearken to my advice ; take advantage of his generous
permission, remain in France—a country for which you
have already shed your blood—and be assured that here
also your services and your talents will not go unrewarded."
Ibrahim thanked the duke warmly, but adhered firmly
to his resolution. "I regret it," said the regent; "but
you are right." He promised him his discharge from the
service, and communicated all that had taken place to the
Russian czar.

Ibrahim's preparations for his journey were soon got
over. On the eve of his departure, he spent the evening
as usual at the Countess L——'s. She was ignorant of
what was passing, Ibraham had not the courage to disclose
his plans to her. The countess was undisturbed and
cheerful. She called him several times to her side, and
teased him for looking so grave. After supper, her guests
left. The countess, her husband, and Ibrahim remained
in the drawing-room. The unhappy lover would have
given worlds to have been left alone with her ; but the
Count L—— had settled down so comfortably before the
fire, that there was no hope of getting rid of him. All
were silent. "*Bonne nuit,*" said the countess at last.
Ibrahim's heart failed him, and he suddenly felt all the
anguish of separation. He stood motionless. " *Bonne*

nuit, messieurs," repeated the countess. And still he remained immovable . . . . His eyes grew dim, his head swam: he was scarcely able to rush out of the room. Reaching home, he wrote in an almost unconscious state, the following letter :—

" I am going, dear Leonora; I leave thee for ever. I write, because I have not the strength to explain myself otherwise.

" My happiness could not have lasted; my destiny and nature were equally against me, and still, I was happy. Thou would'st have ceased to love me; the spell must have been broken. This thought has persecuted me, even at such moments when I fancied I had forgotten all; when at thy feet, my whole being was impressed by thy touching self-abnegation, thy unlimited tenderness . . . . The frivolous world persecutes mercilessly the facts, of which it admits the theory: its cold raillery would sooner or later have overcome thee, humbled thy proud soul . . . . and thou would'st at last have felt ashamed of thy passion . . . . What would then have become of me ? No, better to die, better to leave thee before that terrible moment . . . .

" Thy peace is dearer than all else to me; thou could'st not enjoy it, so long as the eyes of the world were fixed on us. Remember all thou hast suffered—thy wounded vanity, all the torments of apprehension . . . . Consider: am I justified in subjecting thee any longer to similar conflicts and perils ? Why should I struggle to unite the fate of such a tender, beautiful being, to the luckless destiny of a negro, a pitiful creature, barely worthy the name of man !

"Farewell, Leonora, farewell, my beloved, my only friend. I leave thee. I leave the first and last joy of my life. I have no fatherland, no kindred. I go to Russia, where my complete seclusion will become a consolation to me. Serious occupations, to which I devote myself from this hour, if they cannot smother, will at least divert the agonizing reminiscences of those days of rapture and delight. Farewell, Leonora, I tear myself from this letter, as I would from thy embrace. Farewell, be happy, and think now and then of the poor negro, of thy faithful

"IBRAHIM."

That same night he took his departure for Russia. He did not find the journey as insupportable as he had expected. His imagination triumphed over the reality. The farther he left Paris behind him, the more vividly, the nearer did he picture to himself the objects he was leaving for ever.

He found himself imperceptibly at the Russian frontier. Autumn was already setting in ; but the *yemstchicks*, notwithstanding the bad state of the roads, drove him with lightning speed—and he arrived on the seventeenth day of his journey at Krássnoye Seló, through which the post road at that time lay.

Petersburg was distant twenty-eight versts. Ibrahim entered the *yemstchick's* hut, while the horses were being changed. In the corner, leaning on the table, sat a tall man, dressed in a green *caftan* with a clay pipe in his mouth, reading the Hamburg paper. Hearing somebody enter, he raised his head. "Bah! Ibrahim!" he exclaimed, rising from the bench. "How art thou, godson?" Ibrahim recognized Peter, and was about to rush at him in his joy, but he respectfully checked himself. The emperor embraced him, and kissed him on the head. "I was apprised of thy approaching arrival," said Peter, "and I have come to meet thee. I have been waiting here for thee, since yesterday." Ibrahim could find no words to express his gratitude. "Order thy carriage to follow us," continued the emperor, "and sit with me."

The emperor's carriage drove up; they took their places, and galloped off. In an hour and a half, they reached Petersburg. Ibrahim looked with curiosity on the newborn capital rising out of a swamp, at the nod of the sovereign. Dams, canals without quays, wooden bridges, exhibited in every direction the recent triumph of human ingenuity over the oppositions of the elements. Houses had been hastily erected; there was nothing magnificent about the whole town with the exception of the Neva, which, though not yet adorned by its granite frame, was already covered with ships of war and merchant vessels. The imperial carriage stopped at the palace, that is to say at the Tzaritzin Gardens. Peter was met at the door by a woman of about five-and-thirty, beautiful, and dressed after the latest Paris fashions. Peter kissed her, and taking Ibrahim by the hand, said: "Hast thou recognized my godson, Kátinka? Pray love him as you have done before." Catherine fixed her sharp black eyes on him, and graciously held out her hand. Two youthful

17

beauties, tall, elegant, and blooming like two roses, stood behind her, and approached Peter respectfully. "Lisa," said he to one of them, "dost thou remember the little negro who used to steal for thee my apples at Oranienbaum? Here he is, let me introduce him." The grand duchess laughed and blushed. They proceeded to the dining-room. The emperor had been expected and the table was laid. Peter sat down to dinner with all his family, and Ibrahim whom he had invited. During dinner the emperor conversed with him upon various subjects, made inquiries about the Spanish war, asked about the internal state of affairs in France, after the regent, of whom he was fond, though he perceived much to blame in him. Ibrahim was endowed with a quick and observing mind. Peter was well pleased with his replies. He called to mind several incidents of Ibrahim's infancy, and related them with so much good nature and cheerfulness, that none could have suspected in the affable and entertaining host, the hero of Pultawa, the mighty, stern regenerator of Russia.

After dinner the emperor retired to rest, as is the custom in Russia. Ibrahim remained with the empress and the grand duchesses. He endeavoured to satisfy their curiosity, described the Parisian mode of life, the fêtes, the capricious fashions. Soon a few persons attached to the emperor's court, assembled in the palace. Ibrahim recognized the pompous Prince Menshikoff, who, upon seeing a negro conversing with Catherine, proudly surveyed him; also the Prince Yakoff Dolgorouky, Peter's harsh counsellor; the learned Bruce, who had acquired the appellation of the Russian Faust; young Ragouzinsky, his former companion—and others, who were the bearers of reports to the emperor, and awaited his orders.

In a couple of hours the emperor re-appeared.

"Let us see," said he to Ibrahim, "whether thou rememberest thy former duties. Take a slate and follow me."

Peter shut himself up in his workshop, and became engrossed in affairs of state. He worked in turns with Bruce, with Prince Dolgorouky, with General Devier, head of the police, and dictated several ukases and edicts to Ibrahim. Ibrahim was amazed at the quickness of his comprehension, the pliability of his powers of application, and the wide range of his sphere of action. At the completion of his labours, Peter drew forth his pocket-book to assure himself that the whole of the day's task had been performed. On leaving the workshop, he said to Ibrahim:—

"It is late; thou art probably tired; sleep here as thou used to in old times; to-morrow, I shall awake thee."

Left to himself, Ibrahim was unable to collect his thoughts. He was at Petersburg. He again saw the great man at whose side, ignorant of his worth, he had spent his childhood. He confessed to himself, almost repentantly, that for the first time since their separation, the countess had not been his only care throughout the day. He felt that the prospect of a new mode of life, activity, and constant occupation, might reanimate him, wearied as he was with passion, idleness, and secret grief

17—2

The idea—of becoming the auxiliary of that great man, to influence unitedly with him, the destiny of a great people —awakened in him for the first time the noble feeling of ambition. In this state of mind he laid himself down on the camp bed prepared for him—and was borne away in his dreams to distant Paris, to the arms of his beloved countess.

CHAPTER III.

THE following morning Peter, according to his promise, awoke Ibrahim, and congratulated him upon his promotion to the rank of Captain-lieutenant of the Bombardier Company of the Preobrajensky Regiment, of which he himself was captain. The courtiers surrounded Ibrahim, each trying in his own way to make the most of the new favourite. The haughty Prince Menshikoff shook him affably by the hand; Sheremetieff inquired after his Parisian friends, and Golovin invited him to dinner. This last example was followed by the rest, so that Ibrahim received invitations for at least a whole month.

Ibrahim spent his days monotonously but actively,— he did not consequently feel dull. His attachment to the emperor increased daily, as he comprehended his lofty soul the better. To observe the thoughts of a great man, is a most interesting study. Ibrahim beheld Peter in the

Senate, debating with Boutourline and Dolgorouky on important points of law; at the Admiralty College founding the greatness of Russia by sea; he saw him during his leisure hours with Feofan, Gavriel, Boujinsky, and Kopiebitch, looking over translations from foreign publications, or visiting manufactories, the artificer's bench, and the learned man's study. Russia appeared to Ibrahim to be an extensive workshop, a vast machine in motion, where each workman was employed, subordinate to an established order. He considered it to be equally his own duty to work at his lathe, and sought to regret the amusements of Paris as little as possible. He found it more difficult to obliterate that other beloved reminiscence; he often thought of the Countess L., pictured to himself her just indignation, her tears and grief . . . . But occasionally a fearful apprehension oppressed his bosom; the attractions of society, new ties, another favourite—he shuddered; jealousy made his African blood boil—and hot tears were ready to course down his sable face.

He was one morning sitting at work in his study, when he suddenly heard himself loudly addressed in French. Ibrahim turned round sharply—and young K., whom he had left at Paris in the whirlpool of the gay capital, embraced him with exclamations of joy.

"I have only just arrived," said K., "and have come straight to thee. All our friends at Paris desire to be remembered to thee, and regret thy absence. The Countess L. has bid me summon thee back, without fail; here is a letter from her."

Ibraham clutched it nervously, and gazed at the well-known handwriting on the address, not daring to believe his eyes.

"How glad I am," continued K., "that thou hast not yet died of *ennui*, in this barbarous Petersburg! What art thou doing here? How dost thou spend thy time? Who is thy tailor? Has the opera been introduced here?"

Ibrahim replied absently that the emperor was probably at work on the shipping wharf. K. burst out laughing.

"I see," said he, "that I am in the way just now; we shall chat to our heart's content by-and-by. I am going to present myself to the emperor."

With these words, he turned on his heel, and rushed out of the room.

Ibrahim opened the letter, as soon as he was alone. The countess complained, in gentle terms, and reproached him for his dissimulation and mistrust. "Thou sayest," she wrote, "that my peace is dearer than all else to thee. Ibrahim! if that were true, would'st thou have subjected me to the state into which I was thrown by the unexpected intelligence of thy departure? Thou wast afraid lest I might have detained thee. Be assured that in spite of my love, I should have known how to sacrifice it to thy happiness, and to what thou conceivest. to be thy duty." The countess concluded her letter with passionate avowals of affection, and implored him to write, were it even from time to time, if there should be no hope of their ever meeting again.

Ibrahim read the letter twenty times over, and covered

the precious lines with kisses of delight. He longed to hear more of the countess, and made up his mind to proceed to the Admiralty, where he hoped to find K——, when the door opened, and K—— himself again walked in. He had returned from his interview with the emperor, and seemed, as was his wont, very well satisfied with himself. "*Entre nous*," said he to Ibrahim, "the emperor is a very odd fellow; just fancy, I found him in a sort of linen blouse, at the top of the mast of a new ship, whither I was obliged to scramble with my despatches. I stood on a rope-ladder, without room enough to perform a decent bow, and I quite lost myself, a thing which has never yet happened to me. However, the emperor, after having read the papers, looked at me from head to foot, and was probably favourably impressed by the taste and elegance in my attire; at least he smiled, and invited me to this evening's assembly: but I am quite a stranger at Petersburg; during my six years' absence I have quite forgotten its usages; pray be my mentor, call for me, and introduce me." Ibrahim consented, and hastened to turn the conversation to a subject that interested him the most. "Well, what about the Countess L—— ?" "The countess? She was of course very much distressed at first, at thy departure; however, she naturally became consoled by degrees, and chose a new lover. Dost thou guess who he is? The long Marquis R——. Why dost thou strain thy negro eyes so? Is it possible that thou art surprised? Dost thou not know that a lasting sorrow is not in human nature, especially in women? Think it over while I go to rest after my journey, and do not forget to call for me."

What were the feelings that filled Ibrahim's soul? Jealousy? Rage? Despair? No; but deep dejection. He repeated to himself: "I had foreseen this; it could not have been otherwise." He re-opened the countess's letter, read it over again, bowed his head, and wept bitterly, He wept long. Those tears lightened his heart. On looking at his watch, he saw that it was time to go. Ibrahim would fain have stayed at home, but the assembly was a matter of duty, and the emperor rigidly required the attendance of his suite. He dressed, and repaired to K——'s room.

K—— sat in his dressing-gown, reading a French book. "So early?" he exclaimed, on seeing Ibrahim.

"Early! Why it is already half-past five; we shall be late; dress quickly, and let us go." K—— got flurried, and rang with all his might. Servants rushed in; he dressed in a hurry. A French valet handed to him his red-heeled shoes, blue velvet breeches, and a pink coat, embroidered with spangles; his wig, which had been hastily powdered in the ante-room, was also brought to him. K—— slipped his closely cut head into it, called for his sword and gloves, turned himself round at least ten times before the mirror, and declared to Ibrahim that he was ready. Menials assisted them to put on their bear-skin pelisses, and they drove to the Winter Palace.

K—— assailed Ibrahim with a multitude of questions. "Who was the greatest beauty in Petersburg? Who had the reputation of being the best dancer? What dance was

most in vogue ?" Ibrahim satisfied his curiosity, although
not disposed to converse, and in this way they reached
the palace. A great number of long sledges, old *kaly-
magas,** and gilt carriages were already standing in the
meadow. The entrance was crowded with moustachioed
and liveried coachmen ; runners in sparkling tinsel and
feathers, bearing maces ; hussars, pages, uncouth menials,
encumbered with the pelisses and muffs of their masters
and mistresses—the indispensable retinue of the Boyar of
those days. A murmur ran through the crowd, at the
sight of Ibrahim. "The negro, the negro, the czar's
negro !" He hurried K. on through this motley assembly ;
the court lacquey opened the door, and they entered the
ball-room. K—— stood petrified . . . . In a large room
lit up with tallow candles, which burned dimly amidst
the clouds of tobacco smoke, moved in a mass, to and fro,
to the sound of incessant music, great men, having blue
ribbons across their breasts, ambassadors, foreign merchants, officers of the Guards, in their green uniforms, and
ship-masters, in short jackets and striped trowsers. The
ladies sat round the room, the younger dressed in all the
luxury of fashion, their robes covered with gold and silver,
and their small waists rising like a flower-stalk out of
their extensive hoops ; precious stones glistened in their
ears, in their long curls, and around their necks. They
looked about them with smiling faces, in expectation of
partners, and the commencement of the first dance. The
elderly ladies cunningly contrived to combine the new

* *Kalymaga,* an old-fashioned vehicle.—Tr.

style of dress with that of the days which were passing
away; their caps resembled in shape the sable head-
dress of the Empress Natalia Kirilovna,* and their gowns
and mantles reminded one forcibly of the *sarafan* and the
doushegreyku. It seemed as if they assisted at these
newly introduced entertainments with more astonishment
than pleasure, and looked with vexation upon the wives
and daughters of the Dutch skippers, who, attired in
their dimity skirts and red jackets, knitted their stock-
ings, laughing and conversing among themselves, as if
they were at home. A servant, on noticing the new
arrivals, approached them with beer and tumblers. K——
could not get over his bewilderment. "*Que diable est
tout cela?*" asked he of Ibrahim in a whisper. Ibrahim
tried to suppress a smile. The empress and the grand
duchesses, distinguishable by their personal beauty and
elegance of attire, circulated among the rows of guests,
with whom they conversed affably. The emperor was
in the adjoining room. K——, who wished to present
himself, had some difficulty in squeezing his way into it,
through the continually moving crowd. It was filled
chiefly with foreigners, who smoked their clay pipes, and
emptied their clay mugs with much solemnity. The
tables were furnished with bottles of beer and wine,
leathern tobacco-bags, punch-bowls and chess-boards.
Peter sat at one of them playing at draughts with an
English skipper. They assiduously saluted each other
with puffs of tobacco smoke. The emperor was so taken

* Natalia Kirilovna Narishkin was the wife of Alexey Michailo-
vitch, and mother of Peter the Great.—Tr.

aback by an unexpected move of his adversary, that he did not notice K——, who was fidgeting about him. At that moment a fat man, whose breast was adorned with an enormous nosegay, burst into the room, announced in a loud voice that dancing was about to commence, and immediately disappeared. Many of the guests followed, among whom was K——.

He was puzzled at the strange spectacle that presented itself before him.

Ladies and gentlemen stood drawn up in two rows the length of the room, facing each other, to the sound of the most doleful music; the gentlemen bowed low; the ladies curtsied lower, first to their front, then to the right, then to the left; again to the front, to the right, and to the left as before. K. stared at this peculiar pastime, and bit his lip. This bowing and curtseying continued for about half an hour; at last it ceased, and the fat man with the nosegay proclaimed that the ceremonial dance was over, and ordered the musicians to strike up the minuet. K. felt delighted, and was preparing to show off. Among the young ladies there was one who had particularly taken his fancy. Her age was about sixteen; she was richly and tastefully dressed, and sat by the side of an elderly man who looked grave and stern. K. hurried up to her and begged that she would do him the honour to dance with him. The youthful beauty looked at him with confusion, apparently not knowing what to say. The gentleman who sat next to her frowned. K. awaited her decision; but the man with the nosegay approached him, led him to the centre of the ball-room, and said gravely:

" Sir, thou hast committed thyself; in the first place, by going up to that young person without making the three obeisances due to her, and in the next, by appropriating to thyself the right of selecting her, when in the minuet that right belongs to the lady and not to the gentleman; thou must therefore be severely punished— namely, thou art to drain the *Goblet of the Great Eagle.*"

K.'s wonderment went on increasing. In less than a minute he was surrounded by the guests, who noisily demanded the instant fulfilment of the law. Peter, on hearing the noise and laughter, emerged from the next room, for he was fond of assisting personally at similar punishments. The crowd made a way for him, and he entered the circle, wherein stood the culprit, and in front of him the marshal of the assembly, holding an enormous goblet, filled with malmsey. He was vainly trying to persuade the offender to submit of his own free will to the exigencies of the law.

" Aha!" said Peter, on seeing K., "thou art in for it, my boy. Deign to drink, *monssié*, and without wincing."

There was no refusing. The poor dandy drained the goblet at a pull, and returned it to the marshal.

" Listen to me, K.," said Peter; " the breeches thou hast on are of velvet, such as I myself do not wear, and I am a great deal richer than thou art. This is extravagance; look to it, that I do not quarrel with thee."

Having been thus reproved, K. was about to move out of the circle, when he staggered and all but fell, to the indescribable amusement of the emperor and all the gay company. This event, far from disturbing the equanimity of the guests, or their enjoyment, served rather to enhance the pleasures of the evening. The gentlemen recommenced scraping and bowing, the ladies curtseying and striking their heels with great animation, this time quite regardless of keeping time to the music. K. was unfit to take a part in the general merriment. The lady he had chosen, obeying her father, Gavrilo Aphanasitch R., approached Ibrahim, and, lowering her blue eyes, timidly held out her hand to him. Ibrahim danced the minuet with her, and conducted her back to her former seat; he then went in search of K., and leading him out of the ball-room, put him into his carriage, and drove him home. On the way, K. muttered, unintelligibly,

" D——d assembly ! . . . . . . Goblet of the Great Eagle ! . . . . . ."

But he soon fell into a deep sleep, and, without knowing how he got home, how he was undressed and put to bed, he awoke the following morning with a headache, with a vague recollection of the scraping and curtseying, the tobacco-smoke, the man with a nosegay, and the Goblet of the Great Eagle.

CHAPTER IV.

I MUST now introduce the indulgent reader to Gavrilo Aphanasitch R.* He was descended from an ancient line of Boyars, owned enormous property, was hospitable,

* R.—*R'jevsky*, an ancestor of Poushkin.—Tr.

fond of hawking, and had a numerous retinue; in a word, he was a genuine Russian *barin,** could not, as he expressed himself, bear German innovations, and did his best, so far as concerned himself, to maintain the customs of the good old times which he loved. His daughter was in her seventeenth year. She had lost her mother in her infancy, and was brought up in the old fashion; that is to say, she was surrounded by old women, nurses, lady-friends, and maid-servants, she did gold embroidery, and could neither read nor write. Notwithstanding her father's dislike to everything that came from beyond the seas, he could not resist her desire to learn the German dances of a Swedish officer, who was a prisoner, and lived in their house. This worthy dancing-master was fifty years old, his right leg had been shot through at Naron, and was, therefore, not very agile at minuets and courants; but, to make up for it, the left performed with the greatest aptitude and agility the most difficult steps. His pupil was a credit to him. Natalia Gavrilovna was noted for being the best dancer, and this partly accounted for K.'s blunder at the assembly. K. called on Gavrilo Aphanasitch the following day, to offer an apology, but the gay and smart young swell found no favour with the proud nobleman, who wittily termed him—a French ape.

It was a feast-day. Gavrilo Aphanasitch had invited some of his relatives and friends. A long table was laid in the old fashioned dining-hall. The guests assembled with their wives and daughters, who were at last freed from domestic imprisonment by the ukase of the

* Gentleman.—Tr.

emperor, who himself set them the first example Natalia Gavrilovna approached each with a silver tray, bearing small golden cups, and every guest drained one, at the same time regretting that the kiss, which used to be bestowed in olden times on such occasions, had gone out of fashion. Dinner was served. The seat of honour, next to the host, was occupied by his own father-in-law, Prince Boris Alekseyevitch Likoff, a septuagenarian; the other guests took their places according to family precedence, thus reminding one of the happy times when the ancient consideration for seniority was observed. The men occupied one side of the table, the women the other; the *barskaya barinya,** in an old-fashioned bodice; a dwarfish and prim little woman of thirty, very wrinkled; and the captive dancing-master, in his faded blue uniform, took their habitual places at the bottom of the table, which groaned under the weight of numberless dishes, and was attended by a great many domestics, amongst whom was the butler, conspicuous by his gravity, his corpulence, and pompous immobility. During the early part of the dinner the attention of the guests was entirely engrossed in the productions of our ancient culinary art; the clinking of plates and the jingling of spoons alone interrupted the general silence. At last the host bethought himself that the time had come for amusing his guests, and said aloud.

"Where is Yekímovna? Let her be called in!"

Servants were about to execute the order, when there suddenly entered, dancing and skipping about, an old

* A lady pensioner.—Tr.

woman, having her face gaudily painted, and herself
adorned with flowers and tinsel; she wore a silk robe,
and was bared at the neck and breast. Her appearance
was greeted with evident signs of satisfaction.

"Good-day, Yekímovna," said Prince Likoff. "How
dost thou fare!"

"Prosperously and healthily, *koum:* singing and
dancing, and on the look-out for lovers."

"Where hast thou been, thou fool?" inquired the host.

"Dressing up, *koum,* in the German fashion for our
esteemed guests, for this God's holy day, by order of the
czar, by my master's command, to be the laughing stock
of the whole world."

These words caused great merriment, and the fool took
her place behind her master's chair.

"The fool lies and lies, and yet in her lies she sometimes says the truth," said Tatiana Aphanasievna, the
host's elder sister, for whom he had great regard; "truly,
the present fashions are ridiculous. But whenever you,
my good sirs, have been obliged to shave off your beards
and don a short-tailed *caftan,* it is of course of little use
my alluding to female finery; and yet one does regret the
sarafan, the maiden's riband, and the *pavoïnik !** Look
at our young ladies now—it is laughable and yet sad: their
hair is frizzled until it looks like tow, soiled and sprinkled
all over with French flour; their waists are so straitened
that they are all but cut in two; their skirts are extended
with hoops; they have to get into a carriage sideways,
and to stoop when they enter a door; they can neither

* National head dress.—Tr.

stand, nor sit, nor breathe freely—they are real martyrs, the little dears!"

"Oh! my little mother, Tatiana Aphanasievna," said Kirila Petrovitch T——, an ex-voïevode of Riazan, where he had secured to himself 3000 souls and a young wife, neither the one nor the other quite honestly, "so far as I am concerned, a wife may dress exactly as she pleases; she may wear a wrapper or a baldachin if she prefers it, so long as she does not order a new dress every month, and throw the last one away quite new. In times gone by, the grandmother's *sarafan* formed part of the grand- daughter's dowry; look at the dresses now; to-day they are worn by the mistress, to-morrow by her maid. What is to be done? It is the ruin of the Russian nobility! A real misfortune!"

Having said so much, he sighed and glanced at Maria Ilyinitchna, who was not at all pleased, either at his commendation of the past, or his censure of the present customs. The other ladies shared in her displeasure, but were silent, for reserve was at that time considered indispensable in a young woman.

"And whose fault is it?" said Gavrilo Aphanasitch, filling a tankard with frothing *kisby stchi ;** "is it not our own? The young women make themselves ridiculous, and we encourage them."

"But what are we to do, when we have no choice in the matter?" reiterated Kirila Petrovitch; "some of us would be glad to shut up our wives in the women's apartments, but they are required at the beat of the drum

* A beverage similar to *koass.*—Tr.

18

to appear at the assembly! The husband is ready to handle the whip—and the wife adorns herself! Oh! these assemblies! They are God's punishment for our sins."

Maria Kymitchna sat as if on pins and needles, longing to speak; at last, unable to contain herself any longer, she turned towards her husband, and asked him with a forced smile, what harm he saw at the assemblies.

"This is the harm I see in them," replied the irate spouse; "since they have been introduced, the husbands cannot any longer control their wives; the wives have forgotten the words of the apostle: *and the wife see that she reverence her husband;* they do not look to their house-keeping, only to their finery; neither do they care how they please their husbands, only how to captivate the giddy officers. And is it becoming, I ask, madam, that a Russian *Bayarina* or *Bayarishna** should associate with German tobacconists and their workmen? Is it a heard-of thing, that one should dance late into the night and chat with young men! Good, if they were relatives; but when they are strangers, people they are not acquainted with!"

"I would also have said something, but that the wolf is not far off," said Gavrilo Aphanasitch, looking cross. "I admit that neither do I care for the assemblies; one runs up against a drunken man before one can look about him, or is even oneself made drunk for the amusement of the company. One has to look out lest some scamp takes

* *Bayarina,* wife, *Bayarishna* unmarried daughter of a Boyar.—Tr.

liberties with one's daughter; the young men of the day are so forward that they exceed all bounds. For instance, at the last assembly, the son of the late Yeograf Sergheitch, K., played such a trick with Natasha that it brought the colour to my cheeks. The next morning I saw somebody drive right into my yard, and I wondered who it was that God sent to me—it was perhaps the Prince Alexander Danilitch? But no; it was Ivan Yeografovitch! He could not stop at the gate and walk to the house, not he! In he rushed, bowed, scraped, and chatted, and enough I had of it! The fool Yekimovna imitates him in a most laughable manner; by-the-way, fool that thou art, perform the part of the ape from beyond the seas."

The fool Yekimovna seized a dish-cover, placed it under her arm as if it were a hat, and commenced cutting capers, scraping and bowing on all sides, muttering: *Monssié . . . Mamzelle . . . Assemblée . . . pardon;* the merriment that ensued was evidence of universal approbation.

"K. to a T. . . ." said old Prince Likoff, wiping away the tears excited by laughter. "We need not hide it from ourselves, he is not the first nor will he be the last to return to holy Russia from those Germans transformed to a perfect buffoon. What are our children to learn among them? To bow and scrape, to chat goodness knows in what sort of a tongue; to pay no respect to their elders, and to dance attendance upon other men's wives. Of all the young men educated in foreign parts (God forgive

18—2

me!) the czar's negro looks more like a man than any of them."

"Good gracious, prince!" said Tatiana Aphanasievna; "I have seen him, I have seen him close too; what a dreadful jowl he has got! And how he frightened poor, simple me!"

"He is certainly a steady, well-behaved man," observed Gavrilo Aphanastich, "and not to be compared to the others. . . . But who is that driving through the gate into the courtyard? Can it again be that ape from beyond the seas? What are you gaping at, beasts that you are?" he continued, turning to the servants, "run and say I cannot receive him, and that he is not in future . . ."

"Old beard, art thou raving?" interrupted the fool Yekimovna, "or art thou blind; it is the emperor's sledge; the czar has come."

Gavrilo Aphanasitch rose hastily; all rushed to the windows, and saw that it was indeed the emperor, who was walking up the steps, leaning on his soldier servant. Great confusion ensued. The host hastened to meet Peter; the domestics hurried about in a state of excitement; the guests, taken aback, were thinking, some of them, how to get away. Suddenly the loud voice of Peter resounded in the hall; in the midst of perfect silence the czar walked in accompanied by the master of the house, who was beside himself with joy. "Good-day, gentlemen!" said Peter, cheerfully. All bent low. The czar's quick sight had at a glance sought out the host's youthful daughter; he called her to him. Natalia Gavrilovna approached him bravely enough, though blushing to her shoulders. " Thou art becoming more beautiful every hour," said the emperor, kissing her on the head, as was his wont. Then, turning to the guests : "How now? I have disturbed you. You were at dinner; pray be seated again ; as for myself, Gavrilo Aphanasitch, give me some aniseed *vodka.*" The host flew at the majestic butler, seized the tray out of his hands, filled a small gold cup, and presented it to the emperor with a suitable inclination. Peter emptied it, took a cracknel, and for the second time invited the visitors to continue their meal. They all resumed their places, with the exceptions of the dwarf and the *barskaja-barinya,* who did not dare to remain at a table honoured by the czar's presence. Peter sat next to the host, and asked for a plate of *stchi.* The emperor's servant handed to him a wooden spoon, set in ivory, and a knife and fork with bone handles painted green, for Peter never used any others but his own. The dinner-party which a few minutes previously had been so animated and jovial, was now silent and under restraint. So happy and deferential was the host, that he ate nothing; the guests followed his example, and listened with reverential awe to the emperor's conversation in German with the Swedish prisoner, on the subject of the campaign of 1701. The fool Yekimovna, whom the emperor had several times addressed, replied with studied timidity, which by-the-way went far to disprove any notions of her innate stupidity.

At last the dinner ended. The emperor rose, the invited doing the same. " Gavrilo Aphanasitch !" said he to his host; " I must speak to thee alone." And taking his arm, he led him into the drawing-room, closing the door behind him. The company remained in the dining-room, and discussed in whispers the cause for this unexpected visit, and fearing that they might be in the way, they dispersed one by one, without waiting to thank their entertainer for his hospitality.

CHAPTER V.

AFTER the lapse of half an hour the door opened, and Peter walked in. A dignified inclination of the head was his sole acknowledgement of the triple bow of the Prince Likoff, Tatiana Aphanasievna, and Natasha, on his way to the hall. The master of the house helped him on with his red *touloup*, accompanied him to his sledge, and again thanked him for the honour done to him.

Peter drove off.

On his return to the dining-room, Gavrilo Aphanasitch looked very much troubled; he angrily ordered the servants to clear away the table as quickly as possible, dismissed Natasha to her own room, and announcing to his sister and father-in-law that he had something to say to them, led them to the bed-chamber where he usually rested after dinner. The old prince threw himself on the oak four-poster; Tatiana Aphanasievna sank into an old-fashioned silk arm-chair, having provided herself with a foot-stool. Gavrilo Aphanasitch closed the door, took his seat on the bed at the feet of Prince Likoff, and in a low voice commenced the following conversation.

"The emperor did not come to me for nothing ; guess what his communication was about ?"

"How can we know, brother?" said Tatiana Aphanasievna.

"Has the czar perhaps appointed thee a voïevode ?" said his father-in-law : "it is quite time it should be so; or has he entrusted to thee an embassage ? What then ? Are Secretaries of State only to be thus employed, and may not men of birth also be sent to foreign sovereigns ?"

"No," answered the other, knitting his brows: "I am one of the old-fashioned ones; our services are not required nowadays, although, perchance, an orthodox Russian nobleman is worth all the modern upstarts, bakers and heathens. But this is quite another subject."

" What was it, then, brother?" said Tatiana Aphanasievna, "that kept him talking to thee so long ? No evil threatens thee, I trust. God keep and guard us !"

"It is not an evil exactly, but I confess that I am troubled."

" But what is it, brother ?   What is it about ?"

"It concerns Natasha : the czar came to ask her in marriage."

" Thank God !" said Tatiana Aphanisievna, crossing herself. "The girl is marriageable, and such as is the suitor, so must be the bridegroom. May God bless us with love and good counsel; the honour is great. But to whom does the czar want to marry her ?"

"Hm!" grunted Gavrilo Aphanasitch; "To whom? that's it. To whom?"

"Who can it be?" repeated Prince Likoff, who had already begun to doze.

"Guess," said Gavrilo Aphanasitch.

"Goodness me, brother," replied the old lady: "how can we guess? As if there are not enough eligible bridegrooms at court; every one of them would be glad to wed thy Natasha. Is it Dolgorouky perhaps?"

"No, not Dolgorouky."

"Well, he's no loss, he is too haughty. Is it Shéïn? Troyekouroff?"

"Neither the one nor the other."

"Well, I do not care about them either; they are too wild, and are too much imbued with German notions. Well, then—Miloslavsky?"

"No, it is not he."

"Then we pass him over: he is rich, but stupid. Who, then? Yeletsky? L'voff? Can it be Ragonzinsky? I can think of no one else. For whom is it, then, that the czar wants Natasha?"

"For the Moor, Ibrahim."

The old lady threw up her hands with an exclamation. Prince Likoff raised his head off the pillow in astonishment, and repeated: "For the Moor, Ibrahim!"

"Brother!" said the old lady in a suffocating voice: "do not ruin thy own dear child, do not deliver Natashinka into the claws of that black demon."

"But what am I to do?" reiterated Gavrilo Aphanasitch. "Can I refuse the emperor, who, in return, promises to be gracious to me and to all my house."

"How!" exclaimed the old prince, who was quite awake now: "to marry my grandchild, Natasha, to a bought Moor?"

"He is not of mean extraction," said Gavrilo Aphanasitch; "he is the son of the Moorish Sultan. The heathens captured and sold him at Constantinople, and it was our ambassador who redeemed and made a present of him to the czar. The Moor's eldest brother came to Russia with a handsome ransom, and——"

"We know the story of Bova Karalievitch and Yerooslan Lázarevitch!"*

"My little father, Gavrilo Aphanasitch," interrupted the old lady: "let us rather know what answer thou gavest to the emperor?"

"I told him that we were in his power, and that our duty as serfs was to obey him in all things."

At that moment a noise was heard behind the door. Gavrilo Aphanasitch essayed to open it, but met with some resistance. He pushed violently—it gave way, and they beheld Natasha stretched on the floor bleeding and swooning.

Her heart had misgiven her when she saw the emperor closeted with her father. She had a sort of presentiment that their business concerned herself, and when Gavrilo Aphanasitch had dismissed her with the announcement that he had to confer with her aunt and

---

* Characters in a popular tale.—Tr.

grandfather, she could not resist the impulse of female curiosity, so, creeping noiselessly through the inner apartments to the bedroom door, she had not let a single word of the fearful conversation escape her; but on hearing her father's last words, the poor girl lost all consciousness, and fell, striking (in her fall) her head against the edge of the iron-bound box which served as the receptacle for her dowry.

The servants assembled; Natasha was lifted and carried to her own room and laid on the bed. After a few minutes she opened her eyes, but did not recognize either her father or her aunt. A violent fever declared itself; she raved continually about the czar's negro, and of a wedding, and would suddenly cry out, in a plaintive and piercing voice: "Valerian, dear Valerian! my life! save me: here they come! they come! . . . ."

Tatiana Aphanasievna looked anxiously at her brother, who, turning pale, left the room in silence. He returned to the old prince, who had remained below, unable to ascend the stairs.

"How is Natasha?" asked he. "Very ill," answered the grieved father; "worse than I imagined. She is unconscious, and raves about Valerian."

"What Valerian?" asked the old gentleman, in alarm. "Can it be possible that it is the orphan, the son of the Strelitz whom thou had'st educated?"

"Himself, unhappily for me," replied Gavrilo Aphanasitch. "His father had saved my life during the insurrection, and it was the devil who induced me to take into my house the rascally little wolf. When I, at his entreaty, got him into the regiment two years ago, Natasha cried bitterly at parting with him, and he himself stood as if petrified. It struck me then as suspicious, and I spoke of it to my sister. But Natasha has never named him since, and he has given no signs of life. I therefore concluded that she had forgotten him; but she has not. However, it is settled; she is to marry the Moor."

Prince Likoff said nothing in opposition; it would have been useless; he went home. Tatiana Aphanasievna remained by Natasha's bedside. Gavrilo Aphanasitch, having sent for a medical man, shut himself up in his room, and the house became still and gloomy.

The unexpected proposition had astonished Ibrahim fully as much as it had Gavrilo Aphanasitch. It happened thus. Whilst at his work with Ibrahim, Peter said to him, "I have noticed my boy, that thou art out of spirits; say, what is it thou wishest for?"

Ibrahim assured the emperor that he was perfectly contented, and could desire nothing.

"Very good," said the emperor, "if thou mopest without cause, then I know how to cheer thee up."

When the work was over, Peter asked Ibrahim, "Does the girl thou didst dance the minuet with at the last assembly please thee?"

"She is very charming, sire, and appears to be a modest, good girl."

"Then I shall contrive that you should know each other better. What sayest thou to marrying her?"

"I, sire?"

"Just listen to me, Ibrahim; thou art a lonely man, of no birth or parentage, a stranger to all but me. Were I to die to-morrow, what would become of thee, my poor Moor? Thou must make thyself a home, whilst there is yet time; thou must find support in new ties, by entering into union with the Russian Boyars."

"Sire, I am happy under your protection, and in the favour of your majesty; God grant that I may not outlive my czar and benefactor. I wish for no more; but were I even to entertain the idea of marrying, would the young girl and her relations consent? My exterior——"

"Thy exterior? What nonsense! What is there wrong about thee? A young girl must submit to the will of her parents; and we shall see what old Gavrilo Aphanasitch has to say when I myself shall appear to him as thy suitor."

So saying, the emperor ordered the sledge and left Ibrahim plunged in thought.

"Marry!" thought the African, "and why not? Can it be that I am to spend my life in solitude; that I am not destined to know the noblest joys and the holiest duties of man, simply because I was born under a burning zone? I cannot hope to be loved: childish argument! For can one believe in love? Does it exist in the frivolous heart of woman? Having for ever renounced such fascinating delusions, I had devoted myself to other and more real pursuits. The emperor is right; I must think of the future. By marrying this young girl I shall become connected with the proud Russian nobility, and shall thus cease to be an intruder in my new fatherland. I shall not exact any love from my wife; I shall remain satisfied with her fidelity; I shall secure her friendship by unremitting devotion, trust, and tenderness."

Ibrahim was about to return to his occupations, but his imagination had been too much excited. He dropped the papers, and walked out on the quay of the Neva. He suddenly heard Peter's voice, and turning round saw the emperor, who, having dismissed the sledge, walked towards him with gaiety in his air.

"It is all over," said Peter, taking his arm; "I have made the proposal for thee. To-morrow thou must go to thy father-in-law, but be mindful that thou flatterest his Boyar vanity. Leave thy sledge at the gate, and walk up to the house on foot; talk to him about his merits, and his high name, and he will be delighted with thee. Now," he continued, swinging his cane, "accompany me to that rogue Danilitch with whom I have to settle for his last break out."

Ibrahim having thanked Peter warmly for his fatherly solicitude, attended him as far as Prince Menshikoff's magnificent mansion, and then returned home.

CHAPTER VI.

THE lamp was dimly burning before the glass *kivott*,* in which glittered the gold and silver mountings of the

* A glass case made to contain images, and thus becoming a shrine.—Tr.

family heirlooms, the Holy Images. The flickering light feebly illuminated the curtained bed and small table, on which stood the medicine bottles with their long slip labels.

A serving-woman was sitting by the stove at a spinning-wheel, and the gentle sound of her spindle alone broke the deep stillness of the room.

" Who is there ?" uttered a faint voice.

The woman instantly rose, approached the bed, and softly raised the curtain.

" Will it soon be day ?" asked Natasha.

" It is already noon," replied the servant.

" Oh ! dear me ; but why is it so dark ?"

" The shutters are closed, miss."

" Help me to dress at once."

" No, miss ; it is against the doctor's orders."

" Am I ill, then ?   How long have I been ill ?"

" Two weeks already."

" Is it possible ?   To me it seems that I lay down only yesterday."

Natasha relapsed into silence ; she endeavoured to collect her scattered thoughts ; something had happened to her, but what it actually was she could not remember. The servant awaited her orders.   Just then dull sounds were heard proceeding from below.

" What is that ?" asked the patient.

" The masters have dined, they rise from table.   Tatiana Aphanasievna will be here directly."

Natasha looked pleased.   She waved her feeble hand.

The servant dropped the curtain and again sat at her spinning-wheel.

A few minutes later, a head in a large white cap with dark ribbons peeped in at the door, and asked in a whisper, " How is Natasha ?"

" Good-day, aunty," said the patient in a debilitated voice, and Tatiana Aphanasievna hurried to her.

" Miss is conscious," said the servant, gently pushing an arm-chair towards her. The old lady, with tears in her eyes, kissed the pale worn face of her niece, and sat by her side. She was followed by a German doctor in a black *caftan* and a sage-looking wig, who felt Natasha's pulse, and announced in Latin, then in Russian, that all danger was over. He called for paper and ink, wrote out a new prescription, and took his leave; the old lady again kissed Natasha and hastened downstairs to Gavrilo Aphanasitch with the pleasing intelligence.

The czar's Moor, in uniform and sword, hat in hand, sat in the drawing-room in respectful conversation with Gavrilo Aphanasitch. K., lounging on the luxurious sofa, an inattentive listener, was teasing an old harrier; having tired of this occupation, he approached the mirror, the usual resort of idlers, and in it saw reflected Tatiana Aphanasievna looking in at the door, and making signs to her brother, which however he did not notice.

" You are wanted, Gavrilo Aphanasitch," said K., turning to him and interrupting Ibrahim.

Gavrilo Aphanasitch instantly joined his sister, and closed the door after him.

" I admire thy patience," said K. to Ibrahim ; " to have

to listen for hours to such rantings on the antiquity of the race of the Likoffs and R'jevskys, and even to have to add thy instructive observations! In thy place, *j'aurais planté là* the old liar and all his breed, Natasha Gavrilovna included, so full of affectation and feigning to be ill —*une petite santé.* Tell me frankly, is it possible that thou art in love with that little *mijaurée?*"

"No," said Ibrahim, "I certainly do not marry from love, but as a speculation, and this only in the event of of her not entertaining a decided dislike to me."

"Now see here, Ibrahim," observed K., "take my advice this once only; really I am a much more sensible fellow than I appear to be. Give up this silly idea; do not marry. Methinks thy intended has no particular liking for thee. Do not odd things take place in this world? For instance, I am certainly not a bad-looking fellow, and yet it has so happened that I have deceived husbands, who, by Jove, were no worse than I. Take thy own case; dost thou remember our Parisian friend, Count L.? One cannot rely upon woman's fidelity; happy he who can take such things coolly. But then? Is it for thee, with thy excitable, melancholy, and suspicious disposition, with thy flattened nose and thick lips, with that woolly head,—is it for thee to plunge into all the hazards of married life?"

"I thank thee for thy friendly advice," interrupted Ibrahim coldly; "dost thou know the proverb: *it is not thy charge to rock strangers' children to sleep.*"

"Beware, Ibrahim," replied K., mirthfully, "lest thou should'st have to realize that proverb in its literal sense."

In the meantime the conversation in the adjoining room was waxing warm.

"Thou wilt kill her," the old lady was saying; "she will not survive the sight of him."

"But judge for thyself," retorted the obstinate brother; "he has been calling at the house for the last fortnight as an accepted suitor, and has not seen his intended yet. He might come to the conclusion that her illness is a mere sham, and that we only seek to gain time so as to get rid of him somehow. What will the czar say? As it is, he has already sent three times to inquire after Natasha's health. Please thyself, but I do not mean to quarrel with him."

"My God!" said Tatiana Aphanasievna, "what will become of her, poor thing? Allow me, at least, to prepare her for such a visit."

Gavrilo Aphanasitch assented, and returned to the drawing-room.

"God be praised!" said he to Ibrahim; "all danger is over; Natasha is much better. I am unwilling to leave my esteemed visitor, Ivan Yeografitch, alone, or I would have conducted thee upstairs to have a look at thy bride elect."

K—— congratulated Gavrilo Aphanasitch, begged that he would not mind him, assured him that he was obliged to leave just then, and ran out into the ante-room without permitting his host to accompany him.

Tatiana Aphanasievna had hurried to prepare the patient for the reception of the strange visitor. She entered the room, and sitting down out of breath by the

19

fireside, took Natasha's hand, but before she had time to
utter a single word, the door was opened.

Natasha inquired, " Who has come ?"

The old lady started. Gavrilo Aphanasitch drew aside
the curtain, looked frigidly at the patient, and asked her
how she felt. The sick girl made an effort to smile; she
was struck by her father's stern manner, and was oppressed with anxiety. She now fancied she saw some
person standing at the head of the bed. Raising her head
with an exertion, she recognized the czar's Moor. Then
it was that she recollected all, the frightful prospect of
the future presented itself vividly before her. But exhausted nature received no visible shock. Natasha let
her head drop on the pillow, and closed her eyes . . . her
heart beat feverishly. Tatiana Aphanasievna motioned
to her brother that the patient wanted to sleep, and all
left the room noiselessly with the exception of the servant, who returned to her spinning-wheel.

The unhappy beauty opened her eyes, and finding that
she was alone, despatched the maid for her nurse. At
the same moment a rotund little mite of a woman rolled
like a ball towards the bed. Lástotchka (it was the nurse's
nickname) had followed Gavrilo Aphanasitch and Ibrahim upstairs as fast as her short legs could carry her, and
had concealed herself behind the door, faithful to the
innate curiosity of the fair sex. On perceiving her,
Natasha dismissed the maid, and the nurse took her seat
on a footstool. Never had so much energy of mind dwelt
in so small a body. She mixed herself up in everything,
knew everything, fidgeted about everything. She had

succeeded, by her cunning and insinuating ways, in securing the love of her masters and the hatred of the whole household, over which she ruled absolutely. Gavrilo Aphanasitch hearkened to her reports, complaints, and petty solicitations; Tatiana Aphanasievna was continually inviting her opinion, and suffered herself to be guided by her advice; and Natasha, whose attachment to her was unlimited, confided to her all her thoughts, all the sensations of her youthful heart.

"Dost thou know, Lástotchka," said she, "my father weds me to the Moor ?"

The nurse heaved a deep sigh, and her wrinkled face became still more wrinkled.

"Is there no hope ?" continued Natasha; "will my father have no pity on me ?"

The nurse shook her capped head.

"Will not my grandfather or aunty intercede for me ?"

"No, miss; the Moor has bewitched everybody during thy illness. The master's head is turned; the prince raves about him, and Tatiana Aphanasievna says, 'What a pity it is that he is a negro, for it would be a sin to wish for a better bridegroom.' ".

"My God! my God!" groaned poor Natasha.

"Do not grieve, my pretty one," said the nurse, kissing her emaciated hand. "Even if thou art fated to wed the Moor, yet thou shalt be free. It is not now as in olden times; husbands do not lock up their wives. The negro, I hear, is rich; your house will be like a full cup—you will live merrily."

"Poor Valerian!" said Natasha, but in so low a voice that the nurse could only guess and not hear the words.

"That's just it, miss," she whispered, mysteriously; "if thou hadst thought less of the orphan of the Strelitz, thou wouldst not have raved about him in thy illness, and thy father would not have been angry."

"What!" said the frightened Natasha; "I raved about Valerian? My father heard it? My father was angry?"

"That's just the misfortune," replied the nurse. "If thou wert to beseech him now not to give thee to the Moor, he would only think that Valerian was the cause. There is nothing to be done; try to submit to thy parent's will, for what is to be, must be."

Natasha made no reply. The idea that her secret was known to her father acted powerfully on her imagination. One hope still remained : to die before the fulfilment of this hateful marriage. This reflection consoled her. She resigned herself to her lot, dejected and sorrow-stricken.

CHAPTER VII.

THERE was in the house of Gavrilo Aphanasitch, to the right of the lobby, a small one-windowed room. A common bed, covered with a flannel blanket, stood in it ; before the bed was a little table, on which burned a tallow candle, and lay an open music-book. An old dark blue uniform coat and a cocked-hat, its contemporary, hung on the wall; above the latter was attached, with

three nails, a coarse engraving representing Charles XII.
on horseback. The sounds of a flute filled this humble
abode ; its lonely occupier the captive dancing-master, in
his dressing-gown and night-cap, was whiling away the
dull winter evening by playing old Swedish marches.
Having devoted two whole hours to this pastime, the
Swede took his flute to pieces, put it into its case, and
proceeded to undress.

*   *   *   *   *   *

THE END.

BILLING, PRINTER, GUILDFORD, SURREY.